Memories
for a Lifetime

by

Jane Drager

Memories for a Lifetime

Cover Art by *Kristian Norris*

The Wild Rose Press, Inc.
PO Box 708
Adams Basin, NY 14410-0708
Visit us at www.thewildrosepress.com

Publishing History
First Crimson Rose Edition, 2020
Print ISBN 978-1-5092-3035-8
Digital ISBN 978-1-5092-3036-5

Published in the United States of America

Oh, God, help me. She was about to meet her fiancé, a man from her past and one who might provide answers. Would she recognize him? Even worse, would she *like* him? Above everything, she should refrain from comparing him to Lance and give the guy a chance. Just because Lance became her knight in shining armor and the man who saved her from disaster didn't mean her fiancé wouldn't do the same. *So, remember. Don't compare.*

Lance chuckled.

The deep tone sent a flush of heat straight to her core. Yep, so much for not comparing. She glared at the floor buttons above the door. Why wasn't the elevator stopping at every floor? What were they in, some kind of express?

"Relax, Dana. He's not your execution squad."

She increased her pacing. "I'm so scared."

"Of course, you are. You're confronting the unknown. But look on the bright side. He could snap your memories to the forefront, and all your troubles will be over."

The elevator jerked to a stop. *Oh, joy. We're here.* Fists tight, she plastered her back to the wall.

He patted her shoulder. "Take a deep breath."

Deep breath? She sucked in the entire volume in the elevator and half-expected Lance to drop from lack of oxygen.

The doors opened. *A now-or-never time.* Glancing at Lance for one last ounce of encouragement, she stepped out.

Praise for Jane Drager

"*ASK NOTHING IN RETURN* is a fantastic story with plenty of twists. Was so good, I couldn't set it down and read it in eight hours. Wish I had a man like Sam to come home to every night!"

~*AnnMarie D.*

~*~

"*SECRETS AND ASSUMPTIONS* was such a great book, I couldn't put it down. Nothing pleases me more than a woman who takes charge of her own destiny."

~*Elizabeth J.*

~*~

"*THE RIDDLE KEY* was, by far, the best romantic suspense novel Jane Drager has written. The characters were complex and fascinating, never boring. You always wondered what would happen next in their developing relationship. The reveal at the end will surprise you."

~*Toni C.*

~*~

"I loved every chapter of *INFINITE CHOICES*. When Carisa and Mitch collided on someone's front lawn, they started their story off with a bang. The suspense grew from that point on. I've read it twice already and will probably read it again."

~*Joy H.*

Dedication

To my husband,
who is a constant source of encouragement

Chapter One

Hobbling through the precinct doors, Detective Lance Barnes tugged on his leather gloves before gripping the cold, metal handrail by the steps. A blustery wind blew the February air straight through to his underwear and shriveled his privates, despite the length of his heavy wool overcoat. If he had half a brain in his head, he'd wrap his neck scarf around his face like everyone else in this blessed city. Maybe then, his nose would stop dripping like a faucet.

Oh, hell. Who was he kidding? Cold weather never bothered him, not in New York and not here in Baltimore. Normally, he enjoyed winter, but these past few months had been brutal. One storm after another blanketed the city in white fluff and created massive tie-ups on the Beltway. The beauty of a fresh snowfall lasted all of two hours before city traffic blackened the snow to make sidewalks and streets ugly as mud. With a city ordinance to keep sidewalks clear, store and home owners shoveled relentlessly while dump trucks carted mountains of dirty crud to the Chesapeake Bay…until environmentalists screamed bloody murder about polluting the water. Left with no other choice, the trucks dumped the filth onto vacant lots, which, of course, meant the snow would eventually melt and flow into the Chesapeake anyway. Even now, the overhead clouds threatened to unleash another layer of inconvenience just to piss off the city residents. Not a bad time of year to be out on medical leave.

Sighing, he descended the few steps with support of the handrail on one side and the use of his wooden cane on the other. During his last homicide investigation, some punk suspect with more murder on his mind pulled a gun and fired. If that thirty-eight slug had hit his thigh and ripped a major artery... Inwardly shuddering, he didn't want to think about where he'd be. By a sheer miracle, the bullet struck his right calf but damn near tore his muscle in half. He hated how messed up his calf looked, but at least, he still had his leg. Over the weeks, the pain had lessened and no longer felt like a softball in the middle of his muscle. With the help of his cane, he hobbled along the sidewalk.

Midway down the street, a police cruiser slid into one of the open slots alongside the Homicide Division building. Recognizing the two uniformed officers alighting, he stopped and leaned on his cane like a hoofer on center stage, even though he couldn't dance worth a damn.

The older officer, Jenkins, broke into a smile. "Yo, Detective, how's the leg?"

Lance glanced at his leg like all the world could see his injury through his pant leg. Never one to admit weakness, he shrugged in the male fashion of 'no big deal' and chatted with the two men he'd known from the days when he wore a uniform and patrolled inner city streets. Whatever they wanted to talk about suited him just fine. Nothing waited for him home except mind-boggling boredom.

Over the past three weeks, he'd read every book

and magazine thrown his way, groaned at the latest male fashions that fit only skinny men, learned how a woman measured a bra size, and discovered how jock itch and breast chafing were related. When cross-eyed with reading, he cleaned out his clothes drawers, called his sister—who fainted on the spot—and sat through his fair share of talk shows. If he watched one more celebrity hyping a movie, he might go stark-raving mad.

Convalescing was hell.

Since his calf threatened to cramp from the cold, he said goodbye to the officers, who hurried through the side door and into the warm precinct. Maybe he'd stop at Mae's Deli for a late lunch and call the meal dinner. A large cheese steak with a load of fried onions sounded perfect, along with a chef salad on the side. Top the meal off with a beer and—

"Aaggh!"

What the hell… Whirling her arms like a windmill in a hurricane, a ragamuffin darted from two parked cars and plowed into him. She struck his chest in rapid succession—bam-bam-bam. Beating with a frenzy, her small fists hardly penetrated his thick overcoat. Since he'd rather not extend his medical leave, he used his free right hand to grab onto her small wrist, yanked her arm behind her back, and slammed her face-first into the concrete wall of the precinct.

"Ouch!"

He smirked. "Yeah, well, you're lucky I didn't waffle you with my cane." She struggled, but he held her easily against the wall. Hell, she probably weighed all of a hundred pounds, and he could bench-press two hundred. "You attacked a police officer."

"Y-yes, I know. I h-heard those cops call you detective."

Her words were slurred, but the voice had a certain depth of maturity. The realization rattled him. All right, so she wasn't a child but, sure as hell, wasn't an adult either. He sniffed for the odor of liquor but, instead, smelled the odoriferous stench of garbage and jerked backward. "If I release you, can I expect another physical assault?"

"Y-yes. I'll keep s-swinging until you toss me in jail."

Another homeless street urchin, no doubt. Anyone who preferred a criminal record for a few hours of warmth in a jail cell had some screws loose in the brain compartment.

She squirmed under his grip. "These b-bricks are cold."

"I should think so. The thermometer is hovering at the forty-degree mark." Anything above freezing helped melt some of the ice only to refreeze again at night, making for slick spots every morning. He shifted his grip. "Do you promise not to swing your arms or legs?"

"Will y-you arrest me?"

"If that's what you want."

She shivered beneath his hand. The tremor in combination with her slurred speech indicated hypothermia. He cast a quick downward glance at her smudged clothes. She wore a lightweight sweatshirt, blue jeans, and sneakers—indoor attire, as if she just stepped out the door—but not every street person had an adequate wardrobe.

Shoulders slumping, she stopped struggling. "All rright, deal."

"Word of honor?"

"Yes."

He wasn't born yesterday. She'd turn on him the second he dropped his grip. But he hadn't the patience to stand here and debate the decision. With a practiced swiftness, he released her wrist and rotated her to face him while holding her shoulder at arm's length against the wall. He expected her knee to swing and crack his nuts, but she complied with his request and kept knees and arms stationary.

Breath catching, he felt sucker punched, and every muscle in his body tightened. A pair of beautiful green eyes stared back, red-rimmed and wide. Swallowing a wave of irritation, he narrowed his gaze. "What's your name?"

"I d-don't know."

His skill at estimating a person's age abandoned him. She stood perhaps five foot five with a young face smeared with dirt. Her blue jeans hugged small hips, and she wore a dark green sweatshirt two sizes too large. The rich green color emphasized her extraordinary eyes, but every part of her clothes had a stain of some sort. No socks covered her feet and, of course, no coat blocked the cold. Her blue lips shivered, and a fresh red scrape covered her right cheekbone where he'd slammed her into the wall. At the sight of the abrasion, he cringed, but he couldn't drop his guard. The stench of someone's leftovers reminded him of who and what she was.

He dropped his hand to his side. "Why do you want to get arrested?"

"I'm f-freezing." She wrapped her arms around her

small torso to control a violent shiver.

He snorted. "I'm not surprised. We have homeless people dressed better than you. Tell me your name."

Her gaze flitted, and she bit her lip. "I d-don't know my name, sir. I woke this m-morning in an alley with a knot on my head and a h-headache. I don't know who I am or w-where I'm from." Tears glistened in her eyes.

Uh-oh. The old sympathy tactic. Did he have 'sap' stenciled on his forehead? Or maybe she figured his cane symbolized weakness and, therefore, an easy target. He clenched his jaw. "Let me see the knot." And hopefully, creepy-crawly lice wouldn't hop all over his hand.

With a dirty finger, she pointed to the left side of her head.

He lifted a lock of her dark hair to find a blood trail behind her left ear. The trail led upward to a whopper of a lump on the side of her scalp. *All right, so she's hurt.* What about the rest of her story? He released her hair. "Why didn't you go to the hospital or one of our urgent care centers?"

"I w-walked for blocks and didn't see one." Shivering, she clamped her hands under her armpits. "I knew I was in Maryland from the license p-plates but only discovered the city when I read the precinct sign above the door."

She exhibited intelligence. Now, if he could determine her age. Eighteen? Nineteen? Either a high schooler or a first-year college student. More likely, she was another teenage runaway who had her possessions stolen. *And now, she comes crying for help.* Sighing, he snapped up his coat collar to cover his neck. "So, you attacked me, hoping I'd throw you in jail. Not a bad move." Not a brilliant one either, but her pained stare spoke volumes. She hung from the end of her rope. She needed shelter—and soon. He studied her. "Why me? Why not one of our uniformed officers?"

A smile played on the edge of her mouth. "You have a kind f-face."

The story of his life. No poster-boy look for Lance Barnes. Just once, he'd like a woman to go gaga over him. Nothing embarrassing. Maybe a brief fussing to boost his ego.

"I didn't hurt you, did I?"

At her shy tone, he almost laughed. "Hardly."

Something bothered him. Yes, she sounded intoxicated, but hell, her lips were blue, and her shivers hadn't eased. If she was assaulted, she needed help. Thumping his cane on the sidewalk, he gave a curt nod. "Come with me. I'll take you to the urgent care center around the block. A doctor should look at your head."

With her gaze darting toward the precinct entrance, she pointed. "I'd rather go in there."

Of course, she would, idiot. She probably felt no safer with him than being stuck in a cage with a rabid dog. He pursed his lips. "You're right. Follow me." Retracing his steps toward the main entrance, he ascended the steps. Holding open the door, he waved her inside.

The sergeant at the reception desk glanced up with a cocked brow. "Trouble, Barnes?" Grimacing, he waved a hand in front of his nose. "Not her again. We just cleared the air from her last visit."

Now that the girl stood out of the wind, the full intensity of her garbage stench overpowered the reception area and wafted through the room faster than cheap perfume.

Several people waiting on chairs crinkled their nose.

Lance shot his gaze from the girl to the veteran cop. "You turned her away?"

"Had to, Barnes. No ID. I directed her to the homeless shelter downtown."

He clenched his jaw. "And how do you suppose she'd get *downtown*? She's half-frozen and has a head injury."

Lips tight, the officer pointed his pen at Lance. "You know damn well how many times a day a homeless person steps through our doors for the chance to thaw. Yeah, they're battered and bruised, but the city built care centers for the sole purpose of handling cases like her. Besides, she said nothing about a head injury."

His little companion compressed her blue lips and hunched her shoulders. "He didn't give me a chance."

An overall weighty feeling tightened Lance's shoulders. While he sympathized with her plight, he also understood the sergeant's response. The police department had no obligation to help the homeless. The job fell mainly to case workers who referred the unfortunate to shelters. After a silent curse for a situation branching beyond his control, Lance faced the little woman and offered his best reassuring smile, which wasn't much considering the awkwardness clouding his mind. "We'll start with your photo and do a DMV data search. Follow me."

He avoided the elevator. Putting her into a confined box could cause him to lose what remained of his breakfast. Besides, stairs were good exercise for his injured leg. Shrugging off his gloves and stuffing them into his coat pocket, he led the way down one flight. The step depth pulled his sore calf muscle, and he grimaced.

She tugged on his coat sleeve. "Can I use a bathroom first?"

"You're in luck." He pointed to the left. She hurried into the Ladies Room and, a few minutes later, emerged with a clean face.

Aside from the scrape on her cheek, her skin appeared absolutely flawless. A plus in her favor. He didn't know too many street people with perfect complexions.

A whisper of a smile touched her lips. "I looked pretty bad."

And still pale. She also attempted to tame her wild, shoulder-length hair, but the strands had a mind of their own. "Let's go." He turned right and approached another officer shuffling through photographs on his desk, pen in hand.

Raising his head, the officer locked his gaze onto the girl and crinkled his nose. "Let me guess. Another homeless person with no ID."

At such a careless remark, Lance scowled. "Run her photo through the database, will you, man? Maybe I'll get lucky."

"You know those people are off the grid, Barnes."

"Do your job, Hansell."

Throwing his pen onto the desk, the officer stood while suppressing a sneer. "I'll take the photo, but I can't run the info through the database. The system's off-line until morning for upgrade, and I've four unknowns ahead of her." He crooked a finger at the girl. "Over here, please."

She shot a quick glance at Lance, stumbling slightly on nothing in particular, then took a position before a white screen.

The photo session complete, Lance led her upstairs to the main entrance. She tripped on a few steps, but he resisted the urge to reach out. With his luck, she'd cry cop abuse and create a shit-load of trouble. "We're heading for the urgent care center." Without waiting for a reply, he stepped outside into the cold air with her closely behind.

Maybe a strong gust of wind would come along and blow her away. Better yet, she'd collapse into a frozen heap. Then, he'd notify EMS and let them handle her. Of course, he had no inkling why he bothered. The smart course would be to activate child services—although, he still had doubts about her age. Regardless, he'd drop her at the care center and say adios. Nothing more.

As she followed along the crowded sidewalk, she wrapped her arms tight around her body and shuddered.

Despite the brief reprieve inside the precinct, she still had blue lips, and he suspected she fought like mad to contain the shivers. If she spoke the truth and awoke in an alley, she should be near frozen. As with the case for most street people, someone bopped her on the head to steal her worldly possessions. Sad to say, the homeless lived in a survival-of-the-fittest world.

"Oops!" She slipped on a patch of ice.

Lance extended a hand to catch her, but her footing held.

Street person or not, she was freezing, and he had a mother who raised him to be a gentleman. Pausing, he removed his overcoat and wrapped the garment around her.

She gasped and side-stepped. "I can't w-wear this. I stink."

Even with the protest, she clutched the coat's collar close to her neck. Eyes closing, she released a soft moan.

The sound had the depth of a good sexual encounter, and his insides flipped. She might be older than he guessed, but he shook away the notion. Obviously, three weeks of convalescence turned his brain into mush. He twisted his mouth to the side. "Your temp is too low, little lady. I don't see any warm breath coming from your nose or mouth."

Her green eyes searched his face. Something stirred within his chest. He wasn't sure what. Curiosity, maybe? He cocked his head. "Only to the care center. Let's hurry before I turn as blue as you."

****

The heat of his body had saturated the overcoat, and she relished the warmth like a lifeline to the living. She had been cold for so long, she'd forgotten how heat felt. Even the scent of his spicy aftershave helped mask the stench of her own clothes. Falling in step alongside the big man, she slipped both arms through the sleeves and tugged the coat tighter to her body.

How had she gotten into this mess? She was lost in a city with no memory, had a dull, unrelenting headache, and her limbs shook from both fear and cold. She took a chance going after this man, but uncontrollable shivering robbed her inhibitions. A warm jail cell would be a hell of a lot more attractive than freezing to death. A stupid alternative, but numb limbs had a way of increasing desperation.

When her gaze caught sight of the Baltimore Police sign over the doors, she felt hope for the first time in hours. Ever since daybreak, she wandered among derelicts and abandoned houses until the neighborhood changed to better-kept homes with parked cars that weren't burned-out shells. But everyone she encountered diverted their gazes and ignored her pleas for help. Not like she blamed them. One glance at herself in the restroom mirror confirmed her sewer-rat look. Given similar circumstances, she'd back away, too.

After spotting the police station, she ran across four lanes of traffic and straight through the double doors only to be stopped by the cop at the desk. Once outside again, she paced near the parked cars then spotted this big man in a black overcoat. His size made her pause, but not for long. Somewhere in her frozen brain, she concocted a ludicrous plan to attack him. He had an unexplainable openness that calmed her frazzled nerves. When he stopped to talk to the officers, she inched closer and waited between two cars. The deep resonance of his voice convinced her she *had* to take a chance.

She glanced at the detective. Without the overcoat, he had a physique worthy of any woman's attention. Broad shoulders hid under a black sweatshirt and tapered to slim hips. Despite the hobble, he had powerful leg muscles bulging through blue jeans. A grimace covered his face which coincided with every step on uneven pavement. Because of his limited mobility, she easily kept to his pace and, truthfully, couldn't walk any faster. Her feet felt like two blocks of ice, and with every step, she struggled not to stumble.

His offer to escort her to the urgent care center shocked her as much as the loan of the coat. He could have left her at the station. Was she another homeless person, lost and forgotten, her possessions stolen, and with no one who cared? What if her memories vanished forever? What could she do? *No, think positive. Get warm first.* Scanning the length of this tall man beside her, she cleared her throat. "Your name is Barnes?"

"That's right. Lance Barnes." He shot her a quick glance. "I'll make sure you're settled at the care center before I head home."

Her heart sank for reasons she had no clue why.

Chapter Two

A short walk later, Lance ushered his little companion through the automatic doors of the University of Maryland Medical Center's satellite care facility. Doctor Cynthia Doyle stood at the front counter, writing a prescription for a woman holding a baby. Relief flooded him to see that familiar long mane of curly blonde hair. He'd known Cynthia for years, and her physician skills were the best. She'd provide some necessary answers.

Cynthia glanced his way, cocked a brow, and with a finger, gestured for him to wait.

After bidding farewell to the woman and tickling the baby, Cynthia approached Lance with a smile. "I haven't seen you in a while." Then her gaze shifted to the young woman by his side. "What's going on?" Not missing a beat, Cynthia lifted the woman's blood-stained hair. "You have quite a lump. Let's take an X-ray of your head before we go any further."

The young woman turned a pair of tired green eyes onto him. "Thank you for letting me wear this." She slipped his overcoat off her shoulders. "You might want to clean the inside."

The word *sterilized* entered his mind. He took the coat and then gave Cynthia a brief rundown of their encounter.

An inner voice nagged at his gut. Why, he wasn't

sure, but his cop instincts shot into high-alert territory. Something about her bothered him. What, though? Not able to put his finger on anything specific, he draped his coat over his arm and headed toward the exit. "She's all yours, Cynthia." He accomplished his good deed for the day.

"Hey, you're not staying?"

He glanced over his shoulder. "Nope. Call headquarters to tell them she's here. Maybe you'll get lucky, and the DMV search will give you her name." Provided the computers came back online. In either case, the young woman wasn't his problem.

"All right then. Take care, Lance." She ushered her patient toward the curtained bays.

Well, what the hell had Cynthia expected? He was on medical leave with his own problems. Like the cold cramping his leg. He should be home soothing the muscle with a heating pad, not wandering the streets rescuing strays.

Walking through the automatic doors, he held the coat at arm's length to catch the breeze. The people passing on the sidewalk peered like he waved a flag in front of a bull. *Yeah, so what*? He'd give the coat another minute to air then head home. The woman's garbage stench killed his appetite, but he sure craved a cold beer. Maybe a quick stop at the bar…

Oh, who the hell was he kidding? He couldn't squelch the unending curiosity about this girl. Who was she, and what happened? Was she really assaulted and left unconscious in an alley? Yes, multiple stains covered her clothes, but her garments weren't ratty. Street people had a tendency to pick discarded clothing from the trash, whether the material contained holes or not. Her jeans and sweatshirt looked new, and her sneakers had a designer label on the side. Definitely not cheap. Her fingernails…

Yes, those damn fingernails. Her unpainted nails hadn't the imbedded crud so common for people living on the street, and they looked manicured. Another point, her ears appeared clean with no wax buildup popping from the canal. The homeless were notoriously unkempt. Silently cursing his cop's curiosity, he turned on his heel and re-entered the facility. After a quick word with the desk receptionist to notify Doctor Doyle, he found a seat in the crowded waiting room.

According to the constant moaning and groaning from some patients, the world would end before a nurse called their name. One guy claimed to have the bubonic plague and hacked the phlegm into a tissue to show everyone nearby. Another man complained of a bellyache and swore to the heavens above he'd caught a parasite from yesterday's meal. After one bronchitic cough too many, Lance took a standing position by the restroom doors until one man's dump permeated the entire waiting area and sent several patrons into an asthma attack. After that, all hell broke loose as nurses scrambled to treat the asthmatics.

Why am I torturing myself? A normal man would high-tail out the door faster than a supersonic jet. The young woman wasn't his concern any more than the little boy vomiting into the wastebasket. Then again, her assault created a break in his humdrum routine of doing nothing day after day. The extent of his outdoor excursions included trips to physical therapy, psychology sessions, and like today, a brief visit to the precinct to make sure the station hadn't packed and moved in his absence. Being February, snow and ice put a damper on daily walks.

In all honesty, he valued Cynthia's expertise. She'd determine the validity of the little woman's amnesia. He'd hate like hell to discover he'd been had by a damn good actress. He had no question about her assault—unless her injury resulted from a drunken fall.

"Lance?"

Cynthia waved him toward a set of double doors. She hadn't changed much over the years, still with her beautiful curves and full lips. Their wild sexual romps flashed through his mind. She was a lot of fun. He hobbled over.

Brown gaze twinkling, she smiled. "I knew you wouldn't leave. You're too much of a cop."

Yeah, nothing worse than a bored cop.

Cynthia led him through a wide hall to a cubicle where her patient slept under a bundle of blankets. Something slammed his chest at the sight. She looked so small and vulnerable, like a child lost in a big city. He prayed she wasn't another teenage runaway.

Leaning close, Cynthia nodded toward the bed. "She sustained a head injury. Someone struck with a side blow to her left temporal lobe." She placed a finger on the side of her own head to indicate the injury site. "She has a small linear crack with a scalp laceration of about one inch in length. Congealed blood already sealed the skin so I reinforced the area with liquid adhesive. The CT scan showed negative for internal bleeding, but she has a whale of a contusion. Her system's negative for drugs or alcohol."

His gut tightened. "Then, her assault is real."

"Without question. If the person hit any harder,

she'd be in the morgue. Aside from minor bruises, she sustained no other injuries." Sighing, she stuffed her hands into her lab coat pockets. "Because of her memory loss, I consulted neurology. He's already seen her but went to answer a page. He's—oh, good, here he comes."

A stout, elderly man joined them.

Cynthia took Lance by the arm and urged both men away from the cubicles. She stopped by the staff lunch room.

Even before introductions, Lance noted the dominance of the man's straight nose, high bridge, and skin that never saw the sun. He was probably Russian, one of many foreign physicians who practiced in the United States. Unfortunately, the man walked like his shoes were too tight.

"This is Doctor Anton Klavoff," Cynthia said. "He's our neurologist on call today."

The elderly man thrust out a hand to shake Lance's. "A remarkable woman you brought in, Detective. She recognized my accent and, without hesitation, spoke in my native tongue. Her Russian was absolutely perfect, and we conversed at length."

Woman? Maybe the old guy needed eyeglasses.

Dropping his hand, the doctor beamed. "On a lark, I switched to Finnish and interspersed with German. She raised an eyebrow but never hesitated. She spoke all three languages fluently. Yet—" He held up a crooked finger. "I believe she is American, and if I'm not mistaken, I detect a Pennsylvania accent."

Lance cocked a brow. "That's helpful, Doctor. We can narrow her identity search."

"I thought as such." With brows creasing together,

he fixed his gaze on Lance. "She is suffering from a retrograde amnesia, which is the inability to recall certain memories—in this case, who she is and where she lives. Damage to the temporal lobe is the likely cause. The syndrome is usually temporary and improves over time. Recovery can take a few days or a few months." He shrugged. "We don't know for sure. However, her recall of three foreign languages is extraordinary." Removing a pad and pen from his breast pocket, he scribbled a few notes then turned to Doctor Doyle. "She'll be transferred to the hospital's psych ward for further evaluation. They will keep her for the standard twenty-four hours before transfer to the state hospital." Replacing the pad and pen to his pocket, he rotated to Lance. "The overnight stay should allow you sufficient time to uncover her identity and notify her family. If not, you know where the state hospital is."

His stomach churned. He knew enough about Maryland's state facility for the mentally incompetent and the patients who frequented the halls. Most were deranged or suffered severe retardation. Some others were so heavily medicated, they slept throughout their meager existence. Lance cleared his throat. "What about her cracked skull? Isn't her injury enough to send her to a general floor?"

Lips twisting to the side, Cynthia cocked her head. "Only if complications develop. A bad headache, for example. She told me she had one for the better part of the morning, but the pain turned into a dull ache. Rest is her best option."

Doctor Klavoff clamped onto Cynthia's hand and shook. "Thank you, Doctor Doyle, for consulting me on this most interesting case. You can be assured I will follow her closely." He hurried off.

Heart like a rock in his chest, Lance stared after him. "I feel as if I condemned her to prison."

"You brought her in, Lance. That's enough." She patted his shoulder. "She'll be admitted under Jane Doe. If she's lucky, she'll remember her name before transfer." Sighing, she crossed both arms over her chest.

Cynthia Doyle always had nice breasts. She made a great bed partner, too, but after eight months, he'd had one date too many. She asked *him* to move in with *her*, and nothing made his skin itch like commitment.

"Eyes up, Lance."

He jerked his gaze to her face. "Sorry. My memories are intact." He grinned.

"Uh-huh." She rolled her eyes. "Are you filing a police report?"

Frowning, he slipped on his overcoat. After the brief airing, the odor eased somewhat. Instead of garbage truck, the smell was more garbage can and tolerable. "No avoiding the inevitable. You confirmed the assault." Shifting on his cane, he stared in the direction of the young woman's cubicle. "How long before she leaves here?"

Cynthia followed Lance's gaze. "Several hours. Her temp on arrival registered only ninety-three degrees. I've applied a warming pad. Luckily, we caught the frostbite on her toes in time. When her temp reaches ninety-seven, she'll be released to our main facility." Facing Lance, she shifted on her feet. "While she walked, she was smart enough to hug the buildings and kept from collapsing into critical hypothermia."

He cocked his brow. "She told you that?"

"In the course of her memory evaluation, I kept her talking. She said she recalled how buildings held their heat."

He rubbed the back of his neck. "Remarkable."

Cynthia uncrossed her arms and pointed to his cane. "How's the leg?"

Grimacing, he tapped the cane on the linoleum floor. "My leg's fine. My attitude isn't, but I go on desk duty next week."

"Poor baby. I imagine you're bored to death." A laugh rumbled in her throat. "This case might be perfect for your psyche while convalescing. She's cute."

Yeah, sure—if a man enjoyed a woman smelling like leftover table scraps and hair resembling a post-cyclone hit. But knowing Cynthia, she had something up her sleeve. "Just because you think she's cute doesn't mean a hill of beans."

"Oh, come on, Lance. Have you seen her eyes? My God, they're gorgeous." Grabbing an alcohol wipe from a nearby med cart, she opened the packet and cleaned the bell portion on the stethoscope around her neck. "You need to stop being so cynical. She's no ordinary street person." She tossed the used wipe into the trash bin. "When was the last time you saw a homeless person with pink painted toenails and clean feet?"

Well, okay. He was right. Homeless people had horrible feet since foot care stayed at the bottom of their priorities. "Don't women paint all their nails and not just their toes?"

"Most of the time. A nice sheen of clear polish coats her fingernails."

"Oh." What the hell would he know? When his

sister was younger, she painted all her nails a different color. Drove their parents nuts. But after catching a quick glimpse at Cynthia's sparkling gaze, he knew for certain she connived a little scheme to ruin his remaining medical leave. He eyed her through narrowed lids. "Why should I care if she's cute?"

"Because you work too much. You weren't ready for a serious relationship when we were together. I'm hoping this bullet hole in your leg gave you time to re-evaluate your lifestyle."

"Not really." He hadn't a damn complaint about his lifestyle. Granted, his boring medical leave threatened to drive him to drink, but the situation was temporary. "You put too many bad words in one paragraph, Cynthia."

"You mean like work and relationship?" She shook her head. "You haven't the foggiest idea how you'll feel to go home to someone you love."

In his profession, love was severely overrated. Love didn't mean bludgeoning your partner or poisoning them to death. Hell, he'd spoken to people who were afraid to close their eyes at night. For Lance Barnes, living alone had its advantages. He came and went as he pleased, ate at all hours, and even strolled around naked. For eight months, he and Cynthia enjoyed their time together simply because she proved so damn good in bed. But he wasn't about to spoil his living arrangement by having any woman move in permanently.

"Your condo has a second bedroom."

Lord, deliver me from women and their hair-brained ideas. He clenched his jaw. "Are you suggesting I play nursemaid to a teenager? Are you out of your mind?" He shuddered.

"Your *teenager*, dear, is close to thirty, or maybe more. I checked her teeth. She's had excellent dental care."

Thirty? "You can't be serious!" He'd noted the breasts beneath the sweatshirt, but even his thirteen-year-old niece had breasts. Glancing toward the cubicle, he frowned. "I don't have time for such nonsense."

"Considering your convalescing, you have plenty of time."

"She's not my type." He shouldn't stand here and argue. No woman would be welcomed in his home. Period.

"And who's your type?"

Leaning close, he met her gaze. "You."

She rolled her eyes. "If that were true, we'd still be together."

Well, all right, she hadn't fallen for a typical male line. Their affair followed a nice steady path—until the subject of living together surfaced. Leave it to a woman to spoil everything.

Chuckling, Cynthia patted his arm. "One of these days, a woman will crack your cynical attitude and drag you to the altar." Grabbing his hand, she squeezed. "Nice to see you, Lance. Take care of yourself." She ambled toward the central nursing station and disappeared into one of the curtained cubicles.

Lance stared at the floor. Cynthia had a screw loose for suggesting he take the little woman home. How could he, a thirty-six-year-old bachelor, possibly consider the idea? What if she had a criminal record or a jealous husband waiting at home? A half dozen scenarios popped into his mind with the top one being her supposed age of thirty. *Get real, Doctor Doyle.*

****

Lowering her blankets away from her face, she peeked at Lance Barnes pacing in front of her cubicle, his frown so deep, the creases distorted his handsome face. He debated something profound. About her? Why hadn't he left? She had supervised medical care and, hopefully, wasn't on her way to an imminent demise.

At least, the shivering subsided. The warming pad helped, and she relished the warmth seeping into her cold bones. The nurse had fussed with her feet until the numbness eased. At the moment, her toes tingled, as did the ointment the nurse rubbed over the scrape on her cheek. Overall, she felt almost human again. *But, why can't I remember anything?* Doctor Klavoff explained her injury in detail and the disruption to her neural pathways. Yet somehow, her brain remembered three difficult languages. *Go figure.*

She stole another glance in Lance's direction, but he either stopped pacing or left. Throat tight, she craned her neck to see better, but he disappeared…as he should. For some reason, a sense of abandonment swept through her. She fought the urge to jump from the stretcher and run after him. What would be the point? He'd done more than enough and, rightfully, left her to fend for herself. She had no name and no identity. Within a few short hours, she'd be heading to a psych ward. Even with blocked memories, she grasped the inevitable danger of what such a place meant. With moisture accumulating behind her eyes, she closed her lids to hold in the tears.

Her bed rail rattled. Startled, she opened her eyes to see Lance standing alongside. Even in her tired state, the sight of him created a few dancing hormones low in her belly. His trimmed jet-black hair emphasized the pale blue of his eyes, like two Robin's eggs sitting in a nest. Clean-shaven with a strong jaw, she couldn't tear away her gaze if she tried. But what thrilled her even more, he returned, and her heart skipped a few beats.

He thumped his cane. "They're sending you to the psych ward at the University of Maryland Medical Center."

Blinking to break the spell of his gorgeous eyes, she straightened to take in his full form. "Yes, I know."

"Any opinions on the matter?"

The question surprised her. "I haven't a choice—unless my memory miraculously returns."

He narrowed his gaze. "Now that your words aren't slurred, you sound more mature than you look. You impressed Doctor Klavoff by being multi-lingual. So, I'm guessing you're highly educated." He twisted his lips to the side. "I'm also guessing by the way you're dressed, you hadn't planned on being outdoors for any length of time. You were either assaulted inside then carried out or attacked after stepping outside for a breath of fresh air." He waved a hand. "My words are supposition, of course. I'm telling you what I see."

The detective at work. She smiled. "All right. I can't dispute your words, but they sound plausible."

She locked gazes a little too long, and heat rose from her core. If she had an IV line, she'd blame the nurse for shooting her with something to cause the flush. But no IV, so maybe the heating pad chose this precise moment to go bonkers. Breaking the eye lock, she fussed with her sheets.

"Yeah, well—" With a finger, he pulled his

sweatshirt collar from his neck. "If your identity is not uncovered in the next twenty-four hours, they'll transport you to the state hospital, and you don't belong in such a hellhole. You're coming home with me."

Her fingers froze on the bed sheets. Mouth dropping to her chest, she stared. Was he out of his mind?

With a smile touching his lips, he leaned on the bed rail. "I can see I surprised you. Quite frankly, I surprised myself, but I'm a cop who can help you and maybe discover who hit you and why." His gaze scanned her hospital gown then the sheets. Jaw twitching, he stepped away from the stretcher.

What should she do? Go to the mental ward at a state hospital where she wouldn't know a soul, or take a chance with Lance Barnes? The latter had more appeal, but could she trust him?

He tugged on his overcoat. "Look. Doctor Doyle said you need rest. You can accomplish rest at my place while I investigate your case. FYI, I'm single and have been with the Baltimore police department for nine years."

Confusion clouded her brain. If she only had some idea who she was. On the other hand... She shot him a one-eyed stare. "Why inconvenience yourself?"

His mouth twisted into a half-smile that nearly bowled her over. In two seconds flat, he changed from handsome to downright sexy. If she hadn't already been on a gurney, she'd be stretched out on the floor in a swoon.

"Tell you what." He stuffed his free hand into his coat pocket. "Think about my offer. To help ease your mind, Doctor Doyle can give a character reference. I'll find her and send her in."

Feeling totally flabbergasted, she followed his movements until he disappeared from her view. To hell with trusting him. Could she trust herself? Despite a head injury, she recognized attraction, and this man had hunk written all over him. But she had a bigger question rolling around in her brain. How many chances should she take in one day?

Chapter Three

With age came wisdom. Lance accepted the old adage because he lived through experiences and learned valuable lessons, both personal and professional. With luck, he passed the knowledge onto anyone who'd listen—which, for him, was no one these days. He'd like to think he acted sensibly with this little woman, but for the life of him, he couldn't figure out why he volunteered to shelter her. What force in nature possessed him to consider Cynthia's suggestion? *I'm out of my ever-loving mind.*

For sure, he threw caution into the wind. So many alternatives were at his disposal—like shelters or half-way houses. Why hadn't he dragged her sorry ass into the precinct and locked her in a jail cell? Plain and simple, she assaulted him. All right, he sustained no injury, and he shuddered at the idea of the paperwork involved, but swinging at an officer of the law fetched an automatic booking at the jailhouse hotel. The trouble being, she had an ineffective punch, which he somehow suspected was on purpose. She no more wanted to hurt him than he wanted to lock her away. From experience, he recognized a non-violent person, and she fit the bill. So instead, he took her for medical care, and now, she followed him home like a puppy on a leash.

He stole a quick glance at the woman walking two steps behind him. Cynthia had hit the mark on one important fact. Despite hair looking like a rat's nest, the little woman had an intriguing attractiveness. Something about her differed from a lot of woman. He couldn't quite put his finger on anything in particular. Earlier, she had a spark in her green eyes that showed spunk, a survivor, and one willing to beat the odds. After her brief reprieve in the care center, her gaze had dulled, and she looked plumb exhausted. He had serious doubts whether she'd make the next three blocks to his condo. He stopped to let her step alongside, but she collided into his broad back.

Eyes wide, she retreated a step. "Sorry."

She had the weight of a beach ball being thrown full force at his body. Like her punches, he felt nothing. "You realize, of course, I need to give you a temporary name." He continued walking.

"You can call me anything you want."

He glanced back to see her sidestep a patch of ice. "How about Pixie?"

Her mouth gaped. "Pixie? You're using the word in reference to my size, aren't you?" She huffed. "I'm not small."

He resisted the urge to laugh. "The name suits you, and compared to me, yes, you're small."

The cop and the teenybopper. That's how she appeared beside him. The nurse wrapped her in a blanket for their walk home. She clutched the ends tight to her body, unwilling to let through the slightest breeze. The gesture was a futile exercise since hospital blankets were of the summer/winter variety with large weave patterns. But the protection should trap in some heat for their short walk to his condo.

After the respite in the hospital, her age became

more evident. Fatigue emphasized fine lines around her eyes and mouth. Her lips were no longer blue, and they transformed into a pale pink with a tempting softness to her lower lip. Her green eyes, though clouded with exhaustion, had the color of a lush summer lawn, a pleasure to see after months of winter gray.

The stench of fresh asphalt reached his nose and grew stronger as he neared the corner. Two men from the road department worked shovels of the aggregate mixture into a large pothole. A little boy stood at the curb fascinated with the process while his mother shifted through her cellphone's screen. Any second now, the boy would hop the curb into the soft tar and ruin his snow boots. *Yep, there he goes.* The men yelled, the mother dropped her phone, and the boy laughed with glee. Lance chuckled.

His companion lifted her gaze and met his. "If Doctor Doyle hadn't vouched for your integrity, I wouldn't be here, but I'm still scared." She tugged on her blanket.

"You have every right to be scared. You're facing a lot of unknowns." Taking hold of her elbow, he urged her across the street.

She glanced right and left before following. "Doctor Doyle mentioned something about your cynicism. Is she right?"

After stepping onto the pavement, he snorted. "I trust my partner explicitly and also my family. Otherwise, people have to earn my trust." Gaze stern, he held up his index finger. "You're staying one night, Pixie. I'm making my offer perfectly clear."

"Noted." One side of her mouth curled upward. "I'd rather take a chance with you than head to a mental ward." She used the blanket to rub her nose. "I got the impression you and Doctor Doyle were an item."

Frowning, he avoided eye contact. "Very perceptive, with the emphasis on *were*. She's married to a great guy who I swear I'll beat to a pulp if he hurts her." With a two-finger pinch on her blanket, he guided her around a store owner chopping ice from the pavement.

"Why'd you break up?"

He sniffed. "She wanted a commitment, and I couldn't give her one." A lame-o excuse, but Cynthia walked out and never looked back. He had no regrets either, and every woman afterward received his famous speech of a job consuming all his time.

With another finger pinch on her blanket, he stopped her. "Hold on, Pixie. I'm dropping my overcoat at the dry cleaners. My condo is right around the corner. Wait here." Tugging off his gloves and stuffing them into his jeans rear pocket, he entered Lin's Dry Cleaning shop and greeted Mrs. Lin behind the counter. Keeping his conversation short, he exited and found Pixie standing in the vestibule while watching traffic. She turned, and he motioned with his head toward the store. "She knows me and will have the coat cleaned by morning. Let's go before I freeze to death."

While waiting for her discharge, he had debated hailing a cab, but hell, he lived a total of five blocks from the precinct and only three from the care center. By the time the cab followed the flow of traffic up, down, and around the block, she'd be warm inside his condo. Even more important, he hadn't a pocketful of gold to pay for the exorbitant cab fare, especially for a stranger.

"Here we are." Holding open a glass door, he waved her into the condo building and toward the single elevator. He got lucky when a developer renovated this old office building so close to the precinct. With five floors containing two condos per level, the price was perfect for his budget. Once in the elevator, he hit the button for the fourth floor then faced her, his face stern. "For tonight, you'll be comfortable. Tomorrow, we'll head to the precinct. If your identity is not uncovered by then, off to a safe house you go."

"All right."

The elevator stopped, and he led Pixie down the hall. As she walked the short distance to his door, she tripped.

She frowned at the hall rug.

"You're dragging your feet, Pixie." She was too damn tired and caught her foot on the thin carpet. Unless she was a total klutz since she already tripped on the precinct stairs and collided into his back. He'd reserve judgment and call it fatigue. Approaching his door, he stopped, half expecting her to smack into his back.

Her footsteps faltered.

Glancing over his shoulder, he caught the strange look on her face. Given the right incentive, she'd bolt faster than a cockroach in daylight. "You can always return to the hospital."

"I'm apprehensive." Her gaze darted to the door on the opposite side of the hall. "My coming to your home might not be the smartest course of action."

He did his best to give her a reassuring smile, but she wasn't the only one to feel apprehension. "I'm your answer for tonight, Pixie. You can trust me." But could he trust *her*? He was about to take the biggest gamble of his career. His simple act of kindness could screw him big time.

After inserting his key into the lock, he opened the door and waved her in, dropped his cane into the umbrella holder by the door, and then hobbled across the living room to switch on both lamps by the sofa. "Doctor Doyle relayed specific instructions. A hot shower and hot food. The shower's first. Follow me." He led her to his spare bedroom located at the far end of the hall past the master suite. "Let me give you some light." Turning to the dresser inside the door, he flicked on the small lamp. Just to make her feel better, he approached the bed to click on the night table lamp. "The room isn't much, but you'll find everything clean. You'll use the bath in the hall. I have my own."

She peeked around the doorway as if searching for lurking monsters.

Suppressing a chuckle, he held up a finger. "Wait here. I'll get you a pair of pajamas." He hadn't slept in pj's since high school, but his sister claimed they were an essential part of a wardrobe should he fall ill and find himself in a hospital. Well, his leg kept him in a hospital bed for a week, and throughout, he wore shorts and T-shirt because his roommate kept the heat too damn high.

Grabbing a pair from the array his sister sent every Christmas, Lance returned to the spare bedroom. He should tell Angela he had enough pj's to clothe a hospital ward, but she'd buy some other necessity…like sweaters. Every woman in creation bought a man sweaters. Ugh. "Here you go."

Pixie stared out the room's one window but turned

at his words. "Why are you helping me?"

He handed her the pj's. "I'm a cop. We help people." A shit-ass excuse, but he couldn't kid himself. He hated cases with more questions than answers, and this case was a doozy. He crooked his finger for her to follow to the hall bathroom. Wrapping an arm inside the doorframe, he flipped on the light. "Leave your clothes outside the door, and I'll throw them and the blanket into the wash. Then, we'll eat."

After a quick peek into the bathroom, she faced him. "Thank you, Mr. Barnes."

"You're welcome. I'll check my phone messages." If he had any. Better than standing outside the bathroom door waiting for her clothes. He hobbled toward the living room.

No messages. Naturally. Nobody bothered a detective on leave.

A few minutes later, he grabbed her clothes, sneakers, and blanket and headed to the laundry room. His condo might not look like much with its hodgepodge assortment of furniture, but the place had everything to suit his needs, maybe more than he needed as a bachelor, but hey, he caught the mortgage at a great rate.

By habit, he checked pockets before tossing the garments into the machine. He'd washed his fair share of money, packs of gum, and the worst, tissues. Her jeans rear pocket stopped him. Eyes widening, he extracted a flash drive and plastic hotel door key. No hotel name front or back. For sure, a tangible piece of the puzzle.

He rotated the flash drive in his hand. The device appeared new and not something she picked up off the street. Squelching his curiosity, he threw the clothes into the washer, dumped in a sufficient amount of detergent, and then started the cycle. Returning to the kitchen, he placed the two items from her pocket on the table.

Now, for food. He considered himself a decent cook, but a proper meal would take too much time. She'd fall asleep in her plate. Soup made a good choice for a cold winter evening. Reaching into the top cabinet, he surveyed the selection then grabbed two cans of the hearty variety, pouring both into a saucepan.

Twenty minutes later with his stomach rumbling for sustenance, Lance peered down the hall to see the bathroom door ajar. She hadn't come into the living room nor could he hear any movement. He limped to her open bedroom door.

Bundled in blankets, she was fast asleep.

How bloody rude. He could be starving to death.

Unsure whether to wake her, Lance hobbled to her bedside and stared at the woman all curled under the covers like an exhausted child. The nearby table lamp provided illumination, and the glow highlighted a hint of red in her dark hair. The strands were cut to a mid-neck length and appeared in a fly-away pattern, and all this time, he thought her hair needed a good combing.

She looked peaceful with her breathing deep and regular. The fine lines around her mouth and eyes had disappeared, as had the garbage smell. Long lashes covered her extraordinary eyes, and her skin had the creaminess of good genes. Even with the salve, the scrape on her cheek looked a little raw, and her nose had a cute upturned curve that complemented her face. With a start, he finally understood why he took her home. The dirt had hidden so much of her delicate features, and watching her sleep, he agreed with Cynthia's assessment of her age. Pixie was definitely not a child. What's more, she was absolutely beautiful.

To prevent her suffocating to death, he adjusted the blanket away from her face, and that quick, his body reacted, as if he snapped his fingers and said "get ready." *I'd better hurry the hell out of this room.* God forbid, she should wake and see the bulge straining his zipper.

He switched off the lamp by her bed but kept on the small lamp sitting on the dresser by the door. His pj bottoms rested on the dresser, refolded. He hadn't considered their length. The top alone should fit like an oversized nightshirt on her small frame. In case she called for him, he left the door ajar...provided he heard anything at all. Lately, he slept like a bear in hibernation.

Pausing in the doorway, he stared at the sleeping bundle. Something in his chest stirred. She trusted him enough to sleep with the door open. Her simple action caused a slew of emotions to run through him, none of which he understood. Maybe someday, he'd analyze the feelings, but for now, he'd fulfill his promise to help her. "Good night, Pixie." Whatever mystery surrounded her must wait until morning.

Chapter Four

A thud jarred him awake. Heart racing, Lance yanked open the nightstand drawer and wrapped his fingers around the cold metal of his thirty-eight special. Ears straining, he stared into the darkness while shaking the sleep from his vision. Uncertain of the direction of the noise or if the sound happened inside his condo, he slipped from the bed with the gun in his right hand and a small flashlight in the left.

Gun barrel upright, he plastered his body against the wall while stealing peeks around the doorframe. The faint light from her bedroom allowed a clear view of the end of the hall, but nothing illuminated the living room. Flashlight on, he approached the front door and found the deadbolt secure. Next, he inspected the kitchen and laundry room. Not like anyone had the ability to climb the outside wall on a four-story building to sneak in a window. Hobbling toward her bedroom, he stole a quick glance around the doorframe. She wasn't in the bed. Panic choked his airway. Where was she? With the front door secure, where would she go?

A soft whimper to his right drew his gaze downward.

Pixie sat crouched in the far corner of the room, her arms wrapped around her knees with head bent and body shaking.

The sight gripped his heart in a way never before

experienced, like a child frightened by the shadows in the room. He slipped his gun into his boxer shorts' rear elastic waistband, which promptly dropped the material to expose his butt. *Too heavy, idiot.* Left with little alternative, he placed the gun and flashlight on the dresser and bent over her. "What happened?"

She lifted her head and met his gaze. Tears clouded her eyes.

Her face had the sheen of a white sheet. He felt the unmistakable urge to wrap her in his arms and ease her fears, but hell, the gesture could frighten her more.

Blinking away the moisture, she half-laughed and coughed at the same time. "Nightmare. I fell out of bed, but when I opened my eyes, I couldn't remember where I was."

The tightness in his chest eased, and he straightened. "You remember now?"

Forcing a smile, she nodded. "I'm sorry I woke you." Using her rolled-up shirt sleeves, she wiped the tears from her cheeks. "What's the time?"

"A little after three." He held out a hand. "Come on. Back to bed."

With her gaze averted, she slid her small hand into his, and a strange surge of…something shot up his arm. *Holy crap*!

Had she felt the same surge? Judging from her wide-eyed look, maybe she did. A spark? No, more like blood pumping through his veins with tidal-wave force. He coughed. "Static electricity." What a crock of shit. He stood in bare feet, and no way could skin generate an arc, even with his cheap-ass carpet. He helped her to her feet.

Wearing only his pajama top, she appeared lost in

the material. Even rolled-up, the sleeves fell below her hands, and thankfully, the hem on the body material covered her feminine parts. He had caught a glimpse of her round butt, though, and shapely legs enticed his eyes. They tapered to a pair of small feet and her pink-painted toenails.

Looking at her, clean and awake—if somewhat groggy—he still pondered her supposed age of thirty. Twenty something, maybe, but not thirty. Everything about her screamed teenager. She could easily pass for a high schooler.

With a grimace, Pixie eased onto the corner of the bed. While one shaky hand brushed hair from her forehead, the other tugged the hem of her top. She showed no fear of his close proximity, but a flush crept into her cheeks. The color increased her attractiveness tenfold.

After clearing her throat, she met his gaze. "Can I eat something?"

"I have leftover soup from dinner." Lucky for her. He almost ate the entire two cans. Heading for the door, he retrieved his gun and flashlight. "Meet me in the kitchen."

"Detective?"

"Call me Lance." Glancing over his shoulder, he paused in the doorway.

A curl twisted one corner of her mouth. "I like your boxer shorts."

Oh, hell. His erection shot up like a bullet, and without blue jeans to contain the rise, he hurried from her room. No wonder she blushed and averted her gaze. With chest bare and nothing more than shorts to cover his privates, he stood practically naked in front of her.

After replacing his gun and flashlight into the nightstand drawer, he yanked his robe from behind his bedroom door and slipped his arms through the sleeves. While tying the sash, he headed for the kitchen.

A minute later, she entered wearing the pajama bottoms, clutching the waistband.

He silently thanked her for slipping them on and waved her toward the table. With the soup hot from the microwave, he placed the bowl and crackers on the place mat then took a standing position by the table. Hell, he looked like he was on guard in case she bolted for the front door. He relaxed his stance and leaned against the counter.

"You have a nice place, Mister—er…Lance."

"I like it." He crossed both arms and legs. "Tell me about your dream."

She blew on a spoonful of soup. "Nothing to tell. I woke in an alley with a rat in my face. Not a pretty sight." She tasted the soup and then grabbed a cracker.

She relayed a post-injury flashback. He needed to jog memories prior to her assault in order to help. "Did you see anyone?"

"No. The area was dark and cold. Someone covered me with trash bags and loose papers. I guess that's why I didn't freeze to death."

Whoever assaulted her either believed her dead and covered her to hide her body, or the assailant purposely protected her, which made no sense at all. The first scenario fits the common practice for a city murder—discard and conceal. "Do you think you can find the alley again?"

"I'm not sure." She slurped more soup. "I wandered for hours and struggled to stay warm." While staring at the wall, she crunched on a cracker. "As daylight approached, I met a line of homeless people waiting for a soup kitchen to open. No one answered any of my questions. They probably thought I was crazy." She shot him a quick glance. "I wandered in a poor neighborhood. A lot of the homes had boards covering doors and windows. Quite a few appeared gutted by fire." She slurped several more spoonfuls of soup. "Once the area changed to better homes, I spotted your police station and ran in. You know the rest of the story." Her voice cracked.

Gut lurching, he scrubbed one hand over his face. The system failed yet another person, and anger surfaced at the fellow officer who ignored her desperate plea for help. How often were the homeless shunned because they smelled bad? He shook his head. "I'm surprised your brain functioned with your body temp so low. What about the flash drive and plastic card?" He pointed to the two items on the table. "Do they trigger any memories?"

Finished with the soup, she nudged the bowl to the side and then fingered the flash drive. "No." She met his gaze. "Why?"

"I took them out of your jeans pocket. You were probably too frozen to feel them."

She picked up the plastic card. "This looks like a hotel key." Rotating the slim rectangle to read the reverse side, she shrugged. "No name, though."

"To save money, some hotels rarely imprint their name on a key, especially a mom and pop establishment. For us, no name is a good clue. We can stay away from the large hotel chains." He shook a finger at the table. "The flash drive has me curious.

How about we look at the contents in the morning?"

"All right." She munched on a cracker. "The soup tasted good. Thank you."

"You're welcome." He placed the bowl and spoon in the sink.

She made no attempt to rise.

A lazy gaze wandered the length of him until pausing on his bare legs. He anticipated her question before she asked. "A murder suspect put a bullet through my calf. The shot splintered the small bone and ripped the muscle in two." With both hands, he gripped the counter behind him. The incident still raised his blood pressure. The damn perp sought his fifteen minutes of fame, and, like always, the media obliged. "I've been on medical leave for a while, but desk duty starts next week. I can't wait. This convalescing shit is for the birds." He pushed away from the counter and forced a smile. "You, I'll admit, broke the monotony of my boring routine."

Lips twisting, she grunted. "You might be sorry. I could be running from an abusive husband." She inspected the fingers on her left hand. "No ring marks, though."

"The observation hadn't escaped me, but a lot of married people don't wear a ring. You might be one of them." He extended a hand to help her stand. Not that she needed assistance, but curiosity forced him to see if the surge returned, especially while he stood on a linoleum floor.

She clutched the pants waistband and took his hand.

Damn. A jolt of electricity shot right through his fingers and straight down to his toes. What the hell was going on? How could one woman's touch play havoc with his libido?

Dropping her hand, he led the way into the living room. "When we arrive at the station tomorrow, I'm hoping your family filed a missing person's report. If not, the DMV database should tell us who you are. But first, more rest. We'll look at the flash drive over breakfast and pray the contents give us some clues."

"Okay." Tugging on her waistband, she headed for her bedroom. "You know, Lance. I begged more than a half dozen people for help. They ignored me, like I didn't exist. How can people be so heartless?"

Sighing, he rubbed the nape of his neck. "That's how the homeless are treated, Pixie. They are a sad fact of life in a big city. People feel if they ignore the problem, it'll disappear. Never does, of course."

"But you helped me."

The tone of her voice made him uncomfortable. Hell, he was only doing his job. He forced a smile. "Let's say you caught my attention in a unique way." He pointed toward her bedroom. "In case you haven't noticed, your clothes are on the dresser. I presoaked the stained blood on your sweatshirt, and I don't have any idea what smeared your sneakers, but everything turned out clean."

"Thank you." Stifling a yawn, she paused in the doorway and, glancing back, bit her lower lip.

Since her gaze scanned him, he checked the condition of his robe. Satisfied with the secure sash, he met her gaze. "Something on your mind?"

"You approached me with a gun."

And probably scared the hell out of her, too. "I'm a cop, Pixie. I keep my off-duty weapon in the nightstand drawer. My primary weapon stays with the captain until I return to duty." He stiffened. What the hell possessed him to reveal such sensitive information? But the words escaped before he shut his trap. *Idiot.*

"You're a nice man, Lance. Thank you."

Yeah, nice. His mother raised him to be nice. What was the old saying? *Only the good die young.* He should turn into a bastard to live a long and healthy life. Grumbling to himself, he headed for his room. This time, he paused in his doorway and shook his head. He usually kept a tight lid on his emotions and always analyzed the facts while placing them in their proper perspective. Not so with this woman. She had him confused and downright curious. Her beautiful eyes held him captive, and he reacted not as Lance Barnes, the detective, but as Lance, the man, with every protect-and-shelter instinct activated. One way or the other, she required help, and without realizing, she picked a damn good cop.

He entered his room.

After hanging his robe on the door hook, he flopped onto his bed and stared at his nightstand. Until he uncovered more about her, he should choose his words carefully. She could turn into his worst nightmare.

Opening the nightstand drawer, he withdrew his gun and slipped the weapon under his pillow.

Chapter Five

For the longest time, she lay awake staring at the ceiling. Daylight seeped through the closed curtains on the room's one window, but she remained in the comfy curve of the mattress. Her mind felt clearer, and her body had a chance to rest, but the empty void remained. Why had someone clobbered her then dumped her in an alley? Had she said something to piss someone off? She sat up in bed.

Other than a dull ache on the side of her head, she experienced no serious after-effects from being semi-frozen. Toes wiggled okay. Fingers bent easily. She had bruises all over her body, presumably from being tossed around like a rag doll, but considering death as an alternative, she felt lucky to be alive. *Time to face another confusing day.* Throwing off the covers, she slipped from the bed.

Curiosity more than anything propelled her feet toward the window. Last night, darkness hid the view, but with morning daylight, she had no trouble seeing an alley below with unmelted snow covering several dumpsters. A solid brick wall on the other side blocked any type of view, not even a window to spy on a neighbor.

Thoughts of her own home life filtered into her mind. Did she live in a big city like Baltimore or a small country town like…what? Nothing floated into mind. Was she homeless? But she had a hotel key in her pocket. Hopefully, she hadn't picked the item off the street, thinking a plastic card could be useful. And how about family? Was anyone looking for her?

Before last night's shower, she had scanned her body for a tattoo with an *I love you, Jack* or some such saying to give a clue. A husband maybe, or lover...unless the tat covered her lower ass. The bathroom mirror was too high and small to see everything. She considered banging her head against the wall to jar loose her memories, but she'd just give herself another headache.

Sighing, she dropped the curtain and turned toward the dresser to grab her clean clothes. Pressing the clothes to her nose, she sniffed. The fresh floral scent of the detergent was a welcomed change from garbage. While dressing, she took in her surroundings.

The room had a makeshift appearance with furniture assembled with a screwdriver. A man's idea of quality, more likely. Last night, two mismatched lamps of the yard sale variety illuminated the space. The dresser was simulated oak and the nightstand simulated maple. A padded, white vinyl headboard accented the full-size mattress. Nothing matched except for the pillows and sheets. Fully dressed, she exited the room and headed for the bathroom.

After refreshing her face, she stared through the mirror and gingerly fingered her hair. Not what she'd call a street person's hairdo. The strands were expertly styled and shaped her face in an attractive fashion, and the best feature of all, a simple finger-combing drew the cut together better than a brush. Her teeth—oh, yuck! In desperate need of a toothbrush, she opened the medicine cabinet. Nothing but first aid supplies and men's toiletries. To the right of the cabinet, above the toilet, hung a narrow shelf where a half-mangled tube of paste, a toothbrush, and a note waited. Smiling to herself, she picked up the note. The handwriting was a blur. Bringing the paper closer to her nose blurred even worse. So, she stretched the paper to arm's length. *For you, Pixie.*

Pixie. What a name. The man was so damn sweet. This big hunk of muscle rescued her from a horrible experience, and whatever name he used suited her just fine. After all, how many cops invited victims to their homes? A dog or cat, she understood, but a woman with no name? He took a chance when no one would, even for one night. If she hadn't trusted her gut, she'd still be wandering the streets. What to do about tonight bothered her, and the thought of another unknown tightened her throat. The doctor said somewhere along the way, her memories would return. With any luck, soon. Smacking her lips at the freshness of a clean mouth, she replaced the brush and tube onto the shelf then exited the bathroom.

When she reached his bedroom, she stole a quick peek through his door. The room had twice the space of the spare bedroom with the same hodgepodge of assembled furniture. Every inch of the king-size bed had the appearance of an army marching on the sheets with the spread half-way on the floor. On the other hand, her small body barely disturbed the bottom of her sheets. *Well, he is a big guy.* No doubt, he re-tucked all his bedding every single morning.

The aroma of sizzling bacon tantalized her taste buds and drew her away from his door. She followed the scent to the living room where a cushiony sofa stood in the center of the room and faced a large screen TV hanging on the wall. The end tables were the assembled kind, but at least, they and the lamps matched. Nothing hung on the walls. No knickknacks to dust. A small table to the right of the TV held a stereo and, underneath, a bunch of CD's and DVD's. Magazines and newspapers cluttered one end of the tan sofa. His convalescing corner, she surmised, since the remote for the TV and stereo were within easy reach on the end table. Open draperies, exposing an array of windows, and the wall-to-wall rugs were color-coordinated in blue and brown and probably came with the condo. Overall, a nice place, minimally decorated and definitely clean.

Lance hobbled from the kitchen with a tray full of scrambled eggs, bacon, and little sausages. He met her gaze with a smile. "Hey, morning! You're right on time."

At the sight of him, her breath hitched. A black T-shirt hugged his muscular chest while powerful arm muscles strained the short sleeves. Thick thighs bulged under snug blue jeans, and with his jet-black hair falling over his forehead and pale blue eyes as bright as a summer sky, he caused a woman to forget how to breathe. *Nothing wrong with my sexual attraction.* At least desire hadn't been knocked out of her skull.

Flashing a half-grin, he placed the tray on a round coffee table where two plates and mismatched mugs waited on opposite sides of an opened laptop. On an oven mitt, a steaming coffee urn waited. She salivated—hopefully, over the aroma of the food and not him.

Straightening, he wiped both hands on his thighs. "Any headache?"

Since her tongue refused to cooperate, she shook her head. *Mustn't let him see me drool.*

Lance waved toward the sofa. "While we eat, we'll look at the flash drive."

With her gaze on the open laptop, she wrung her hands. "I'm half-afraid to see what the drive contains. I'm praying I'm not a witness to some mob murder and on the run." *God forbid.*

He chuckled. "Let's hope the drive contains more than your grandmother's favorite recipes."

If she had a grandmother. She frowned at the computer.

"Come on, Pixie. Sit." Lifting the plate of scrambled eggs, he poised the spoon over her dish. "Say when." He spooned a third of the portion before she stopped him. He repeated with the bacon and sausage. "Coffee?"

Nodding, she lowered her butt onto the sofa as he passed the cream and sugar. Did she even like coffee? She sipped the hot brew. "My coffee is fine as is, Lance."

After loading his plate, he slid alongside. "Before we start, eat a few mouthfuls."

Oh, my God. The food smelled wonderful, but he smelled even better. His spicy cologne circled the sofa like a cloud. How could she *not* lunge at the man? *I need a distraction.* Holding her plate in one hand and a fork in the other, she wolfed her eggs in record time.

He frowned at her near-empty plate. "You're supposed to chew your food, not swallow the stuff whole. Do you realize what you're doing to your digestive system?"

No, but eating forced her mind off *him.* "Sorry. I'm nervous." In truth, she should concentrate on her situation and not Lance Barnes. She dabbed a napkin on her mouth. "I'll suck on a sausage while you eat. How's that?" Using her fork, she jabbed one.

Gaze flashing, he clenched his jaw. "You don't suck on a sausage in front of a man. The visual implication is way too suggestive." Turning, he shoveled in a mouthful of eggs.

Her cheeks flushed. How could she be so naïve? Without knowing her own history, maybe she should keep her yap shut. After all, they were a man and a woman under one roof. Shit happened. She cleared her throat. "I didn't mean anything, Mr. Barnes."

"No, you probably didn't." Sighing, he rested his fork on his plate and shot her a quick glance. "I'm on edge, Pixie. I keep debating whether I've made the biggest mistake of my life."

"I know I haven't." She smiled because she meant every word. With her luck, he'd take the comment the wrong way and toss her to the street. She inwardly sighed. Her brief stay was over anyway. Tonight, she faced another unknown. Where would she go? Who could she trust? After only one night, she felt safe with Lance, but verbalizing her fears would be wrong. He had no need to babysit a woman shrouded in mystery. *I should get a grip on my emotions.* Otherwise, she'd go into hysterics. Flipping her gaze to the computer, she bit her lip. "Let's get this flash drive over with."

Nodding, he plugged the device into the USB port.

A screen popped open, showing the drive's contents of only one file. Squinting, she leaned forward to read, frowned at the blurriness, then pulled back. "What's it say?"

Eyes wide, he stared. "Can't you read?"

Shrugging, she shook her head. "I probably need glasses."

Brows furrowed, he pointed to the screen. "*Q&A jhlecture.*" He moved the cursor over the file and clicked.

A video showed a packed lecture hall full of eager, young faces with pens busily scribbling on notebooks.

"Doctor Null?" The camera whirled in the voice's direction as a young man lowered his arm. "With your vast language research, have you uncovered the reason behind so many different dialects within one country?"

The voice off-camera left no doubt as to the speaker. Mouth gaping, she pointed at the monitor. "I'm Doctor Null?" She repeated the name in her head. Not an iota of recognition.

Plate in hand, Lance waved his fork. "Shhh."

The same voice replied to one question after the other, always off camera. Holding her coffee mug close to her nose, she listened while her thoughts raced. She *knew* the answers. How could she when her identity disappeared from her mind?

Leaning on his knees, Lance bit into a strip of bacon. "Obviously, you taped the lecture for a reason. The students are questioning you on language and ethnics." His head tilted toward her. "Ring any bells?"

No bells, no whistles. Zilch. "None."

Half an hour later, the video ended. She and Lance reclined on the sofa with mugs in hand.

She nodded toward the screen. "The video didn't tell us much."

After a sip, he shook his head. "On the contrary, the recording told us a lot. Since you carried a hotel key, you are likely a guest speaker. The students are all college-age, so you're at a lecture hall at one of our universities. The camera caught the clock on the wall behind the students with the time as eight-forty. I'm guessing eight-forty at night since guest speakers rarely lecture early in the morning."

The analytical cop. She'd made an excellent choice by swinging at a man with a sharp eye.

"Let me see if I can find a Doctor Null on the Internet." Placing his mug on the table, he typed.

Within seconds, her face popped onto the screen. She gasped and leaned forward. "That's me!" The website heading boasted impressive black lettering large enough for her to read. *Doctor Dana Null, PhD, Anthropologist with a specialty in languages.*

Wow. She finally knew her name. A PhD even. But so much was missing. Why couldn't she remember?

Lance pointed at the screen. "Nice picture." Smirking, he cocked his head. "I can't call you Pixie anymore."

"You can if you want." She'd said the words absently as she scanned the computer screen. Everything looked so damn fuzzy. "My website photo doesn't show me wearing eyeglasses."

Gaze narrowed, he studied her. "Maybe you weren't reading when the blow struck." Placing his elbows on his knees, he returned his gaze to the screen. "Your website says you speak sixteen languages. That explains your strange conversation with the neurologist. You must be talented." With a finger on the touchpad, he tapped to access her professional data. "You're a native of Pittsburgh, a graduate of the University of Pittsburgh, and you lecture around the world." He wagged a finger at the screen. "Doctor Klavoff said you had a Pennsylvanian accent, and he hit it dead on."

Brows furrowed, he chomped on a strip of bacon. "Once we arrive at the precinct, we'll access the Pennsylvania DMV database. The records will tell us your address and, possibly, a link to your family." With his mouth twisting to the side, he faced her. "That's good news, Dana."

Yeah, good news. She had a name. Big deal.

"Here's your lecture schedule." He pointed.

To view the screen better, she nudged her butt toward the edge of the sofa but, again, nothing but a fuzzy blur. "Read it for me, Lance."

"You were at Johns Hopkins the day before yesterday. Somewhere along the way, we'll uncover who conked you on the head and left you in an alley."

"And why." She placed her empty mug onto the table. "I wish I could remember."

With a gentle smile, he patted her knee. "More likely, a robbery. But don't worry. You'll remember in time. We acquired a lot of clues." He disconnected the drive and placed the device by her plate. "We now know who you are. That's a great start." He picked up the bacon plate. "Here, take the last slice."

"No, I'm full." Moaning, she buried her face in her hands. "What a mess I'm in." His help felt so nice. He made her fear of the unknown bearable. She dreaded the idea of being handed over to another stranger, but with her name came an address and perhaps parents or husband. Hell, she wouldn't know them either. At least,

Lance proved easy on the eyes, and his voice soothed her nerves. He turned into the lifeline she needed.

"This is new to me, Dana." He stacked the empty dishes.

She lowered her hands. "What is?"

"Your company for breakfast. I've been alone so long, I forgot how to talk to someone in the morning. I usually grumble at the morning news." Grinning, he met her gaze.

Her stomach somersaulted. Given the opportunity, she'd stare into his blue eyes all day. They were so beautiful...and mesmerizing. If she had any particular talent for reading within the inner depths of his gaze, she'd like the skill to surface. Something emanated from them, and damned if she understood what.

"Hey!"

Oh, shit. Caught. She jumped. "What?"

"You're staring at my lips. Are they crooked?"

No, absolutely perfect. They appeared soft and tempting, but openly staring and wondering how they tasted should be the farthest thing on her mind. Diverting her gaze, she cleared her throat. "Sorry. I'm being rude."

"I can't call that rude. If a piece of food is on my mouth, I'd like to know."

To hell with food. She wanted her lips on his mouth. Shaking herself, she reached for the stacked plates. "You cooked. I'll clean."

Placing a hand on her forearm, he stopped her. "Don't take this the wrong way, Dana, but I want to kiss you, too."

Her breath hitched as a surge of heat shot straight to her core. What wrong way? He was a handsome, single man who made her feel safe and protected. Would she be dumb enough to argue? *Hell, no.* And a thrill coursed through her. They shared a mutual attraction, and her heart performed a happy, little dance. If he threw in his sexy smile, she'd melt at his feet. With a mouth going bone dry, she blinked. "What do you mean?" She inwardly groaned. The sensation of heat urged her to grab hold and never let go, not play hard-to-get.

He leaned close. "You might be married."

Who cares? For a taste of his lips, she'd take this memory to her grave. Locking onto his gaze, she moistened her lower lip. "Yes, I know."

His mouth brushed hers with a feather touch. He lifted his head and paused.

If he believed she'd push him away, then he should have his head examined. All right, yes, she didn't know him…didn't know herself, but with him so close without full body contact tested every ounce of her self-control. How could she feel so strongly toward a man she'd met only yesterday? *Well, I took a chance swinging. I might as well see if my luck holds.*

Placing a palm on his smooth cheek, she met his parted lips. A shiver raised goose bumps under her sweatshirt, and every nerve ending tingled to life. Even though he kept the kiss light, he activated a yearning that rose like a furnace from deep within her belly. She savored every second and, against her better judgment, deepened the kiss, relishing the smell of the spicy aftershave and the taste of bacon on his tongue. He never lifted his hands from his lap. She hankered for some real closeness but fought like mad not to wrap her arms around him. Yes, she could be married. Hell, a mother even. Heart thundering, she suckled his upper lip before pulling away to look into a dark gaze. "Thank you."

A black eyebrow cocked. "For what?"

"For making me feel less alone."

Jaw twitching, he tucked a strand of hair behind her ear. "Someone is looking for you."

She wasn't so sure. How had she lost so much of her life with one blow to the head? Feeling moisture behind her eyes, she cleared her throat and pointed toward the laptop. "I don't suppose my website has any personal information."

He turned to the screen. "I don't see anything. The website is definitely a professional one."

The doorbell rang.

Heart rate skyrocketing, Dana scooted to the end of the sofa. "Please don't tell me you have a girlfriend."

He grinned. "As a matter of fact, I do."

A woman entered with the use of a key.

She appeared in her late fifties and wore a pale pink sweat suit, as if going for a jog. Dana's racing heart slowed as a pair of inquisitive brown eyes locked onto her.

While closing the door, the woman flashed a wry grin. "Well, no sense me asking what the thump was last night."

Chuckling, Lance tossed his napkin onto the stacked plates. "Dana, meet my sweetheart, Thelma, my housekeeper and neighbor one floor below. Thelma, this is Dana, and don't let your imagination run wild."

"Too late, dear boy, because it's about time." Her gaze twinkled. "Pleased to meet you, honey." She elevated a small shopping bag. "You were low on

Scotch. Leave those dishes. I'll take care of them."

Slapping his knees, Lance stood. "I'll explain everything later, Thelma. Right now, I'm heading to therapy. Dana's coming with me." He extended a hand toward Dana. "My therapy only takes an hour. Afterward, we'll head to the precinct, okay?"

What choice had she? She slipped her hand into his, and a flow of strength tingled through her fingers. Her lost memories frightened her beyond description, but his simple touch supplied her with the confidence to continue.

Limping to the closet, Lance grabbed a jacket and, holding it open, motioned for her to slip her arms into the sleeves. "This should keep you warm. I'll stop by the cleaners for my overcoat on the way. Let's go."

"Wait a minute." Thelma raised a hand in the air. "The temperature's at thirty-two degrees. Wear something."

"I agree." Dana zipped the jacket to her neck. "I'd hate to see you die from pneumonia because I dirtied your coat."

"Women," he mumbled but smiled. "I'll be fine."

Dana pointed at the umbrella canister, which was nothing more than a flower-painted bucket. "Your cane?"

With a smirk, he grabbed the cane. "I don't use the cane while I'm home." He nodded toward the table. "Take the flash drive and hotel key."

Yes, dare not leave anything behind. Her heart sank.

Chapter Six

At the physical therapy office, Dana waited in the lounge area while Lance disappeared behind the doors. The walls vibrated with activity—feet thumping on treadmills, weights banging onto the floor, balls bouncing, and voices grunting. If the walls were any thinner, she'd see who did what.

Three other people lounged with her. Two played on cellphones, and the third, an old codger, bobbed his head and snored. Thankfully, he occupied one of the chairs with armrests so he wouldn't topple over and hit the floor.

On the side table to her left, she sifted through the arranged magazines—nothing but a boring selection of fitness and nutrition mags with the occasional Wonder-Patient cover thrown in. Without glasses, she'd strain to read the print, but other than a magazine, what could she do to divert her mind from Lance's soft lips? She could have suckled on him all morning. Huffing out a breath, she yanked a muscle magazine from the table and flipped through the pages, concentrating on the pictures of beautiful bodies—men, women, and even children. Abs on the women and children were a complete turn-off, but the men...totally lickable.

Her thoughts again drifted to Lance. Last night, when she spotted him with only his boxer shorts, she damned near peed on the floor. He had a centerfold body, perfect for some of these fitness mags. Add a little oil and…*oh, yipe*. She shouldn't let her mind wander in his direction. They'd say goodbye soon enough. She had to face reality and accept the fact she'd soon be on her own. If this mental void stayed with her forever, she'd manage somehow. With a PhD after her name, she obviously had a good head on her shoulders, and the website said language specialist. A career, at least. Sucking in a breath through tight teeth, she tossed the magazine onto the table.

Ten minutes later, Lance hobbled out, limping more than usual. As he jerked his overcoat off the hanger, he grimaced. "I overdid the workout."

She stood. "Want to sit for a bit?" Oh, God, he smelled of sweat and spicy cologne. All man. She nearly swooned.

"I'll rest at the office." He headed for the door. "Come on. We've six blocks to walk."

"Why don't we grab a cab and return to your place to put an ice pack on your leg?" She zipped her jacket.

"No!"

The word snapped from his mouth, and she jumped, eyes wide.

He winced. "I'm sorry. I hate being an invalid."

"I'm not exactly happy with lost memories." She followed him out the door.

As he walked, Lance kept his lips pressed tight. Even with a face set in granite, his eyes showed the pain of every step, and he leaned on his cane a little too heavily. He refused the cab with the claim the walk loosened his leg. She doubted his logic but let the statement pass. He was the one suffering, not her. She took in her surroundings.

Nothing impressed her about Baltimore. She passed by a few shops, a half dozen restaurants, and brick row homes with marble steps indented with age. Some homes had a narrow alleyway between them while others were wide enough to place trash cans along the side wall. A dismal gray clouded the sky, and the majority of leftover snow had a blackened sheen from car splashes. Overall, she found not a speck of beauty.

"Oomph!" She'd plowed into Lance's back. *Like hitting a brick wall.* Cheeks flushing, she stepped to the side. "Sorry."

"You need to watch where you're going." He narrowed his gaze. "Are you always this curious?"

"How the hell would I know?" She rolled her eyes at her own tone. With a sheepish glance, she sighed. "Sorry." *Dammit. I've become an apologetic idiot.*

His mouth quirked. "Don't be. I'm irritable."

Well, duh. With every step, he grimaced with pain, but nothing stopped his hurried pace to reach the precinct. Her heart sank. How more obvious could he be? He wanted her out of his hair. Yet, he refused a cab, which would be quicker and more relaxing for his leg. *Go figure.* Rather than force him to rest, she propped a sneaker onto a fire hydrant to retie a shoelace—just for spite.

Gaze glaring, he jerked to a stop. "Don't pamper me, Dana."

"Hey, do you want me to trip on my own shoelaces?" The guy didn't miss a trick. She dropped her foot to the sidewalk and faced him. "You can't rush an injury. You'll do more damage."

He growled. "What are you, a doctor?"

"As a matter of fact, I am." She grinned. "Not one who can help with your leg, though."

Shifting on his cane, he shot her a one-eyed glare. "You're too damn cute."

"Why, thank you, kind sir. You're—"

"Don't you dare call me cute!"

She caught the hint of a smile touching his lips. Maybe he didn't receive compliments often, but cute was too mild a word for him. She chuckled. "I can't call you anything until I find out if I'm married."

Snorting, he continued along the street.

Slower this time, for which her legs responded with gratitude. Keeping to his hurried pace took a bit of an effort. She nudged his arm. "I got a smile out of you."

"No, you didn't."

Despite his protest, the granite had cracked, and his gaze sparkled. She mentally patted her back. Shivering against a swift breeze, she stuffed her hands into the jacket pockets. "Do you always walk everywhere?"

"Usually. I keep my car parked in the condo garage. If I'm doing something work related, I'll use a department vehicle." He glanced over. "For the record, I hate Scotch. Thelma likes to take a sip before cleaning."

A shot of hard liquor would be welcomed right about now. Damn, the cold bit her skin like she wandered naked on the streets. She'd also love a thick pair of socks so her toes wouldn't fall off. Too bad Lance's feet were too big. "Thelma seems nice."

"She is. She lost her husband a few years ago. Great guy…like me." He shot her a sideways look.

She smiled. Yes, he was a great guy—easy to talk to and comfortable to be around. Had she such a man in her life? *With my luck*? Probably not. "Can I ask you something?"

"Go ahead."

"What if we were—um—going at it on the couch when Thelma walked in? Don't you have some sort of signal to tell her you're busy?"

A laugh erupted from deep within his belly.

He wiped a stray tear. "You are the most refreshing woman I've met in a long time, Dana. But to answer your question, Thelma cleans twice a week, and she never shows before nine in the morning. I'm out the door by seven thirty. My dates will leave with me."

Not like she planned on losing control while around him, but should the opportunity arise, she'd rather not be interrupted.

On reaching the precinct, Lance escorted her straight to the photo room. With the DMV database up and running, he requested a Pennsylvania search of her snapshot. Since the room and outside hall buzzed with people from all walks of life, Lance directed Sergeant Hansell to send the results to the detective bureau.

"Over here, Dana. We're heading to the fourth floor."

Placing a hand in the small of her back, Lance led the way to the elevators.

She couldn't for the life of her figure out why his hand felt so good. His warmth, she supposed, since his jacket barely kept out the chill. Or maybe his touch raised a simple craving for human contact since she couldn't shake this overwhelming feeling of being alone.

Voices exploded from the room opposite the elevators.

In one quick move, Lance shoved her behind him, which nearly caused her to lose her balance. Since his size represented a wall more than a human body shield, she leaned to the side and caught a glimpse of the disturbance. A Vietnamese couple—an elderly man and woman—ranted about the hoodlums terrorizing their store. They spoke with thick accents in barely discernible English to a uniformed officer who sat at a desk with hands gesturing for them to slow down.

Nudging Lance aside, Dana held up a 'one-moment' finger and strolled into the room, keeping her gaze steady on the older couple. Bowing in the traditional oriental fashion, she encouraged them to speak in their native tongue. She translated while the wide-eyed cop typed on his computer. The officer, pausing from his report, interspersed with questions, and she relayed the answers. Afterward, the couple shook her hand and bowed their thanks. She turned to Lance who stood watching from the doorway, his gaze unreadable. "Sorry. They needed help."

His half-smile touched his lips. "You just made new friends." He jabbed a finger on the Up button, and the doors opened. "Come on before someone else puts you to work." He ushered her into the elevator.

She disembarked on the fourth floor where a large room stretched before her. Desks grouped in pairs faced each other, and every group had one or two white boards perched on a stand covered with photos and hand-written notations. Some photos were gruesome enough to turn her stomach.

Lance motioned for her to follow, and he limped to the far end where a woman stared at a computer screen.

After a quick double-take, the woman stretched her

lips into a broad smile. Brown eyes bright, she stood and hurried around her desk. "Hey, I missed you yesterday. The boys told me you stopped by." She hugged Lance then nodded toward the floor. "How's the leg?"

With a grunt, he settled his hip on the edge of the desk facing hers. "I won't be wearing shorts anytime soon." He shifted his gaze to Dana. "Dana Null, meet Lieutenant George Cavello, my partner."

"Georgette," she corrected with a hand outstretched. "The men forget I have boobs."

Lieutenant Cavello had a "don't mess with me" physique boasting of strong shoulders and arms. While not as muscular as some of the women in the fitness magazine, she looked capable of fighting her way out of anything. She had long, dark hair pinned off her shoulders with a silver clip. A striking woman with high cheek bones and full lips, she possessed height and a hand grip worthy of an arm wrestler. She wore a pantsuit that hugged womanly curves. The handshake complete, Dana dropped her hand to her side and flexed her fingers to ensure all bones were intact.

Stepping to the side, Georgette turned to Lance. "So, what's up? You here for another visit?" She retraced her steps to her seat and sat.

Lance explained the purpose of Dana's presence with an emphasis on her education and credentials while Dana stood in his oversized jacket feeling like a lost soul. Throughout, Georgette shifted her gaze from her to him, her expression about as taciturn as a good poker player.

When Lance finished, her gaze riveted onto Dana.

Feeling uncomfortable under such scrutiny, Dana

stared at nothing in particular and fidgeted. She wasn't sure the woman believed her partner. After all, how many times a day did someone walk through the precinct doors complaining of memory loss?

While chewing on her lower lip, Georgette closed the black folder on her desk pad. "As preposterous as the story sounds, I trust my partner's judgment, but I hardly understand his actions. He's about as cynical as they come, so him trusting you in his home goes against character." She reclined in her chair and shifted her gaze to Lance. "I'd say you have quite a mystery on your hands. So, what happens now?"

"We wait for the DMV search." One brow raised, he nodded toward his partner's two boards. "You working two homicides at once?"

"Unluckily, yes." She shot him a one-eyed stare. "I know you're curious, but we can't discuss our cases in front of non-department personnel."

Without so much as a flash in Dana's direction, he wagged a finger at his partner. "Dana has surprised me several times already, George. Despite her memory loss, she has a brain in her head. Why don't you remain silent and let her talk?"

Yo, whoa! A direct challenge. *What the hell for*? Thinking back, she hadn't done anything extraordinary, and she certainly hadn't the analytical brain of a cop…well, not that she knew. Big deal, she spoke a bunch of foreign languages. Biting her lip, Dana glanced from Lance to the case boards before settling her gaze on Georgette. "I don't know what Lance expects me to do."

"He sees something in you, honey, and he's made me curious." The lieutenant waved toward the two boards. "Tell me what you see."

Since the contents on the boards appeared better from a distance, Dana remained in her position alongside the desks and pointed toward the board on the right. The focus centered on a photo of a decent-looking blonde woman with arrows drawn from her picture to four others, all male. "The young woman hasn't any familial resemblance to anyone in the other photos. Three men, being close to her age, are possible beaus, so I'm guessing she's a wife or girlfriend to one of them. The old guy in the right corner doesn't fit. He has, at least, thirty or forty years on all of them. A grandfather maybe, but again, no familial markings." *Oh, wow*! She sounded just like herself in the video— all matter-of-fact and to the point. She cleared her throat and pointed. "Are these all DMV photos? They don't look like mug shots."

With a quick glance at Lance, Georgette rocked in her chair and folded her arms across her chest. "DMV. Mug shots are okay, but I detest looking at crime scene photos all day long." She swiveled. "Go on, Doctor."

Hmm. What else? While staring at the photos, Dana tapped her chin. "The woman strikes me as attempting to look suave and sophisticated by overdoing her makeup. The diamond studs in her ears and the diamond necklace match in design and look expensive. The younger men fit the run-of-the-mill variety, but the older guy has an academic look with his eyeglasses and bow tie. He strikes me as a man who'd have the money to shower a woman with diamonds."

Georgette gave her a long look. "Conclusion?"

Scanning all the faces in the photos, Dana bit her lip. "I'm going out on a limb and say she's married to the older guy, and the other three men are friends with benefits."

Lance smiled at his partner. "Well?"

Shaking herself, Georgette chuckled. "Dead on." Grabbing a folder on her desk, she withdrew a photo and showed it to Dana. "I was about to hang this on the board. What can you tell me about her?"

The photo revealed a woman with brown hair, older than the blonde, but with unmistakable similarities. "They're sisters. This one is older, maybe by four years."

Leaning forward and squinting, Georgette studied the picture. "I don't see a resemblance."

Dana swung a pointed finger between the two photos. "The cheekbones, Lieutenant. Same size and shape. Also note the prominence in their ear lobes."

Gaze twinkling, Lance winked at Dana but turned a serious expression to his partner. "Is she right?"

Georgette laughed and, again, sat back. "Yes, on all counts." She pointed to the board. "An unknown assailant stabbed the blonde as she alighted from her car in her own driveway. The attack occurred the night before last. She's sort of a prima donna and married to the elderly—but wealthy—gentleman. I've a classic wealthy-old-man, young-wife murder. His third marriage, and her first." While studying Dana, she rocked her chair, creating a series of squeaks. "How about the second board?"

Shifting her gaze to the center photo, Dana focused on a male, middle forties, with arrows pointing to male and female photos. "He likes being outdoors and has a well-groomed appearance. His brother is in the right lower corner. Note the similarities in the nose. The woman on the upper left is of similar age so maybe his wife or girlfriend." She paused as she scanned the grouping again. "Nope, nothing else."

Georgette narrowed her gaze. "How do you know he likes the outdoors?"

After two days with a befuddled brain, her analysis of the photos created a sense of normalcy. Dana wasn't sure how. *Big deal.* She had knowledge, which didn't help one bit toward her personal life. She waved a hand. "His skin shows the beginning of sun-related wrinkling, especially around his eyes. More than likely, he doesn't wear sunglasses and squints. His brother has a whiter skin tone, so he's an indoors man."

Lance extended both hands, palms up. "Well?"

Smirking, Georgette rocked in her chair. "Someone bludgeoned the guy on yesterday morning's jog. He's a real estate broker with a list of dissatisfied customers a mile long. Lots of suspects in both cases but no proof— yet." She smiled at Lance. "I'm impressed. If I fail to solve these cases by the time you return, I'll let you have a go at them. In the meantime, your own little mystery needs attention." She nodded toward Dana.

"Yo, Lance!" An older man approached, his gaze fixed on Dana. In his right hand, he carried some papers. "You found her."

With a brow cocked, Dana exchanged a glance with Lance.

Sliding off his desk, Lance faced the man. "Dana, this is Detective Bob Fuller. He works in missing persons."

Wow. Someone reported her missing? For the first time in days, her hopes soared. So did a strange tightness in her chest. The unknown was about to slap her in the face.

Detective Fuller handed Lance a sheet of paper. "This report came to me first. The guys told me you requested a copy."

Lips tight, Lance read the paper, nodded, then handed her the sheet.

Her DMV report. The details listed a Pittsburgh address and birth date. She was thirty-two years old. Returning the paper to Lance, she tilted her head and smiled. "Guess you can't call me a teenybopper anymore."

Fuller handed Lance a folder. "Two reports filed. The first came from her fiancé in Pittsburgh. The guy was bound and determined to drive out here and search the city himself. I told him to stay put until we completed a preliminary investigation." He tapped the folder in Lance's hand. "The second report came from the Red Wolf Hotel where she had a room." He glanced at Dana then shifted his gaze to Lance. "You're homicide division. So, why don't you let me handle her case?"

Panic clutched Dana's throat. She wouldn't blame Lance for passing her along, but…*please, oh, please, don't toss me aside. Not yet*. Little by little, bits and pieces of her life emerged, but the uncertainty of everything tied her gut into knots. Not wishing to sway his answer, she avoided eye contact and held her breath.

Lance cleared his throat. "She's an assault case, Bob. Still not homicide, but since she fell into my arms, I'll handle all the reports."

Closing her eyes, Dana released a slow breath. She trusted Lance, and no one else would do. Fully intending to thank him, she opened her eyes only to see him frowning at the papers in the folder. Detective Fuller had already disappeared, and Lieutenant Cavello rocked in her squeaky chair with a smile in her eyes.

The initiator of the first missing person's report finally hit, and Dana widened her eyes. "I'm engaged?" She glanced at the empty ring finger on her left hand. At least, she wasn't married with seven kids. But really now, how could she forget her fiancé? Wouldn't some recognition pop into her brain? Maybe when he walked through the door, he would be the catalyst to return her memories. *I can only hope.* She shifted her gaze to Lance who had not removed his attention from the folder.

With a wry grin, Georgette tapped a pen on her desk. "Problem, partner?"

Lance's frown deepened into a scowl. The expression formed a deep V between his eyes.

A throaty chuckle rose from Georgette's throat. "I guess not."

Lance threw the folder onto his desk. "I'm going to the men's room."

"I'll go with you." After walking several blocks in the cold weather, she could use a restroom visit. "Hey, wait up."

Blue eyes blazing, he whirled. "I don't need you to wipe my ass!" He hobbled away.

Heart jumping straight into her throat, Dana stared after him.

"My, my, he's getting temperamental in his old age."

Dana turned to the lieutenant, whose dark eyes twinkled. "What happened?"

Chuckling, she sat forward. "He got a little upset

when Bob mentioned your fiancé. I never thought I'd see the day." She gestured with a nod. "The ladies room is past the elevators on the left." Her desk phone rang. Frowning, she glanced at the caller ID and then fingered the receiver before shooting a quick glance at Dana. "Excuse me, honey. This call is important."

Talk about confused. Bad enough her brain struggled to piece together fragmented memories. She didn't need her emotions acting the same way. Shaking her head, she headed for the ladies room.

Once finished and exiting, she found Lance leaning against the wall. The scowl had disappeared, but he still had an odd look on his face, something akin to disgust.

Crooking a finger for her to follow, he led her to the elevators and, with a fist, slammed the elevator button. "I'll get a car from the garage, and we'll head to the hotel."

Georgette strolled by while dangling an empty coffee cup from her finger. Gaze twinkling, she leaned toward him. "Don't you want to notify the fiancé first?" She winked at Dana.

Face tight, Lance peered at his partner. "Let's see if the hotel jogs a few memories." He jerked a thumb over his shoulder. "And the lunch room is the other way."

The exchange between the two partners left Dana more confused than ever. When the elevator doors closed and descended, she nudged his arm. "About Georgette's case boards…"

A smile curled one side of his mouth. "I noticed how you always look around wherever you go. I'm guessing you take in more than you reveal. That trait's an insatiable curiosity. As an anthropologist, you see beyond what the average person sees, and you proved my point by what you said to George."

Was she curious? Well, hell yeah. Every time she collided into Lance, she had her gaze riveted on something else. Maybe she wasn't so clumsy after all.

A short elevator ride later, the doors opened to an underground parking garage. After signing a clipboard and lifting a set of keys from a peg board, Lance walked toward a black sedan. Once assuring she buckled in, he maneuvered the car through the garage and then into traffic before he spoke. "Do you remember a fiancé? No, of course, you don't. I'm sorry I asked." With a quick glance in her direction, he loosened his grip on the steering wheel and sighed. "Your hotel is only a few convenient blocks from the Johns Hopkins University complex."

Dana had no idea what caused his mood change. He switched from hot to cold like a spigot turned. If he found her bothersome, why hadn't he passed her off to Detective Fuller? Maybe his leg hurt more than he cared to admit. Pain irritated lots of people.

While staring out the side window at the passing streets, she released a long breath. If part of her memory returned, she sure as hell hoped she regained her understanding of men.

Chapter Seven

The Red Wolf Hotel hadn't the convenience of a national chain with a parking lot out front for ease of check-in—not like Dana remembered staying in a hotel anywhere, but the establishment had a convenient spot at the street curb with a sign *No Parking—Hotel Check-In Only*, which, of course, a service van occupied.

Lance avoided the hotel's across-the-street parking lot with its too-close-together slots and glided the sedan to the curb about a half-block up the street. After a quick look around the neighborhood, Dana alighted, and when Lance came alongside, she strolled toward the hotel entrance.

Besides the hotel, the city block consisted of several eateries, a coffee shop, a bakery, and small breakfast nook, which was called The Breakfast Nook. One townhouse had a strange insignia over the door. A fraternity, no doubt. Several other houses displayed signs *Room to Rent* in the windows. Being close to a university afforded an excellent opportunity for homeowners to make a little extra cash from those students who disliked dorm rooms.

Her gut tightened with every step along the pavement. She recognized nothing of the area, and the hotel drew a complete blank with its ornate red canopy stretching from curbside to the main entrance. The building itself, constructed of red brick, nestled among shops with a wide alley on the left side, and a sign warning *For Deliveries Only*. Raising her gaze, Dana counted five stories with a bunch of windows adorned with white shutters. Two automatic doors allowed access into the main lobby, but she hesitated to approach.

Lance placed a hand on the small of her back. "Anything familiar?"

The heat of his hand helped to steady her nerves. Giving him a wan smile, she shook her head. Not a damn smidgen of memory surfaced. Sucking in a deep breath, she entered the building.

A splattering of reds and browns decorated the lobby with a mural of a howling red wolf prominently displayed on the wall. People milled about, most talking amongst themselves or studying a city map. Some children crowded the small gift shop to the right of the main entrance, their eager gazes scanning the candy display. At the reception desk, a female clerk assisted a couple inquiring about a room for the night.

A young man sauntered from a side door and spoke to the desk clerk. He wore a bright red blazer with a wolf emblem on its breast pocket. As his gaze caught hers, he snapped his head for a quick double-take. With an audible gasp, he gripped the counter. "Doctor Null!" He ran through another side door, rounded a corner, and approached, his gaze scanning her from head to toe. "You're all right!"

His name tag said Gary, Assistant Manager. The poor guy stood no taller than her and, at a guess, had no meat or muscle under his clothes.

Stepping between them, Lance showed his badge. "You're the one who filed the report?"

Since Gary's height was no match to Lance, the young man craned his neck. "Yes, sir. I hadn't any idea where she went. That evening, she arrived after her lecture. We talked for a while, but the following morning, the maid said the doctor hadn't slept in her bed. Even more worrisome, her purse and luggage were still in the room."

Gary intertwined his fingers and stood like a schoolboy expecting to be commended for a good job. Despite the childish stance, he displayed a practiced professional air. While she appreciated that her luggage and purse hadn't been lost to oblivion, she struggled to grasp some sort of connection to this man. Because of his pale hair, blond eyebrows, and white lashes, he fit the definition of an albino—except for the olive tinge to his skin. With such an unusual color combination, she should remember him, but her mind drew a blank.

"We've had several occasions where a guest failed to return for a night." Gary shot a sideward glance at Dana. "Sometimes, guests meet in the dining room and—um, you know."

Lance rolled his eyes. "We catch your drift. Go on."

"Anyway—" His gaze surveyed the lobby. "When I failed to hear from her by late afternoon yesterday, I called the cops." He turned to Dana. "I left everything in your room, Doctor Null, but your laptop and camera equipment are gone." He faced Lance. "I put those facts in the report, too."

"Doctor Null has no memory of what happened, Mister—"

"Cary. Gary Cary, Assistant Manager."

He grabbed Lance's hand and shook.

Comparing the size of Lance to Gary provided her with a good idea how she looked alongside Lance. Maybe the detective's kind face wasn't the only attraction. His physique and height instilled a sense of security, something akin to guardian-of-the-meek and all that crap. With any luck, her fiancé would be big and strong like Lance and not small and wimpy like Gary. If she learned one minor detail about herself over the past twenty-four hours, she liked big men.

After dropping Lance's hand, Gary turned a pair of colorless eyes onto her. The irises hadn't a hint of pigment, as if she stared into glass. Her scalp prickled.

Gary tilted his head toward her. "I'm sorry to hear about your memory loss, Doctor Null. If I can do anything…"

Yeah, create a miracle. She shot him a half-hearted smile.

Lance tapped his cane on the linoleum floor. "You can answer a few of my questions."

Squaring his shoulders, Gary intertwined his fingers. "Sure. I'm here to help."

"Does she use this hotel often?"

"She's used us several times in the past three years." With a quick glance at Lance's cane, Gary nodded toward the sofa. "Do you want to sit?"

Lance looked at Dana who shook her head. He shifted toward Gary. "How do you know about her camera equipment?"

"She showed me the stuff once and how the voice activates the motor. Compact, too, in its own carrying case." He flashed Dana a smile.

Releasing a quiet sigh, she shrugged in return. The equipment sounded expensive, but what would she know? Material objects could be replaced. Too bad she couldn't buy a few memory cards to plug into her brain.

Placing his cane under his armpit, Lance slipped a notebook and pen from his overcoat's inside pocket and scribbled. "Mr. Cary, did you see anyone follow Doctor Null to the hotel?"

"Not into the lobby." He fidgeted and shot a glimpse at the automatic doors. "If someone followed her, maybe he stood outside and waited." One brow cocked, he turned toward Dana. "You always liked the coffee shop across the street. Maybe you ran out when I wasn't at the desk."

"Gary, I need your assistance!" The female clerk waved him toward the desk where a well-dressed man in a black overcoat tapped on the chest-high counter.

Dana jerked at the sight of rotund man. Why? He was a stranger, but his stiff stance and twitching jaw muscles reminded her of someone. Glancing around as if expecting to see an impatient wife, she frowned at the image that made no sense and refocused on Gary.

Nodding toward the desk clerk, Gary cleared his throat. "Do you require anything else, Detective?"

Lance shook his head. "If I have any more questions, I'll let you know." He returned his notebook to his inside pocket.

After reaching into her rear pocket, Dana waggled the plastic door key at Gary. "Does this still work?"

"It should. Room 301. Elevator to the left." With a polite smile, he hurried to the desk.

Fighting the urge to head straight out the front doors, she turned to Lance. "Shall we, Detective?"

****

Lance punched the third floor elevator button with

a little more force than necessary. All right, yes, he'd been on edge since the mention of her fiancé. Hell, he kissed her, knowing he leapt too far ahead of himself. How could he be so friggin' stupid? Without question, six weeks of boring convalescing contributed to his momentary lapse in judgment. A sad excuse, of course, but for a man with no real home life, he found Dana a welcomed distraction. She represented an unusual case, one to stir his stagnant brain and dispel his oh-woe-is-me syndrome.

The elevator doors opened, and he followed her inside.

Who the hell am I kidding? Once the dirt disappeared, the woman was too beautiful to resist. Every time she bit her lip, she stirred something deep inside his chest. Over the years, he'd seen plenty of women display vulnerability, but no woman gripped his heart so quickly. Every time the look passed onto her face, he had this powerful urge to wrap her in his arms and shield her from the evils in the world—at least, until her fiancé arrived...assuming he took the time to call the man. Maybe later...or tomorrow.

Gary Cary was another one who prickled the hairs on his scalp. The damn twerp ogled Dana like spareribs on a grill...unless the sight of Gary's wardrobe triggered a subconscious revulsion. The young man wore a red blazer and tie, red argyle socks, and even a red belt with a wolf buckle. Brown trousers and white shirt offset his colorful outfit, but hell, the man might as well have a neon sign for the hotel hovering over his head. Most business men donned subdued colors, but Gary was like a flag on two legs. Lance inwardly shuddered.

Dana pushed the button for the third floor and then traced a finger along the wolf emblem on the closed elevator door. "I feel like I need a rifle on my shoulder."

He snorted. "All we need is a little girl wearing a red cape and traversing through the woods while the big, bad wolf hides behind a tree." He scanned the ceiling corners. No security camera. "I'm sure the hotel does a good business whenever an event occurs at the university. Location-wise, it's perfect."

The elevator lurched to a stop. Once the doors opened, he covered the door sensor with his body and blocked her exit. With a finger lifting her chin, he locked onto her gaze. "I want you to do things slowly. Look around. If anything triggers a reaction, no matter how minor, tell me. Understand?"

A pair of wide green eyes stared, and those sensual lips, parted and moist, tempted him. With such a simple look, had she any idea how she excited a man's hormones? Sure, he'd love to kiss her again, but Lance Barnes lived by a concrete set of standards. He would not intrude onto another man's turf, no matter how alluring.

"Yes, sir."

Huh? Oh, yeah, she answered his question. The damn woman made him forget his train of thought. He waved her out of the elevator.

Moving his gaze up and around, he scanned for the location of security cameras. A unidirectional one covered the sole elevator and both wings to the rooms. A little red light showed the device operational. Good so far.

She pointed to the sign on the wall listing room

numbers and arrows. "Room 301 is to our right."

Letting her set the pace, he followed, keeping several feet behind to avoid distractions. As with most hotels in the middle of the day, housekeeping carts crowded the hall. By now, the majority of visitors had checked out, but some voices flowed through a few closed doors. One floor above, the sound of little feet running along the corridor told of unleashed energy.

Midway down the hallway, Dana paused by the floor's vending area.

Snapping his gaze right and left of the opening, he stepped alongside. "What entered your mind, Dana?"

Brows furrowed, she shook her head. "I don't know. For some reason, the area seems important."

Positioned within a rectangular recess, the ice maker and several soda and snack vending machines sat opposite the emergency stairwell. While the hall had carpeting to lessen noise, the alcove had gray tiles for easy cleanup. No camera hung within the small space. If Dana entered the recess for ice, she'd be off-camera. Either way, whether entering or exiting, her attacker would be visible on tape from the hall camera.

Brows raised, she faced him. "What are you thinking, Lance?"

He nodded toward the vending machines. "Suppose you were attacked while getting ice? You weren't dressed for the outdoors. Even if you ran to the coffee shop across the street, you'd wear a jacket and take either your purse or wallet."

She shrugged. "Maybe someone stole my jacket."

"A possibility, but I'd like to think you're sensible enough to put on a pair of socks before running outside. Let's continue to the room."

Red-and-brown patterned carpeting covered the hall floor, but cream wallpaper lined the corridor. The latter helped give some brightness to neutralize all the damn red. Room 301 stood at the end on the right, and as he approached, he noted the camera mounted in the corner. The little red light indicated a device in operation. *Two security cameras to record what happened.* Since security video often proved a godsend for the police, he made a mental note to check the responding detective's report.

Using the card key, she opened the door.

With the hope of escaping all the red, he followed her into the room, but the hotel motif continued. A red spread covered the single queen-size bed with white pillow cases for accent. Red-and-brown drapes hung on the windows and, again, the cream wallpaper helped offset the darkness. Wolf labels adorned the amenities in the small bathroom, including the tissue-box holder—red, of course. He expected to see a wolf staring from the ceiling, but thank God, no.

By the closet, her suitcase rested on a luggage rack, unlocked. He lifted the top to see neatly folded clothes. Her black purse sat on the dresser.

Walking over, she unzipped the main compartment, peeked inside, and extracted a wallet, opening the flap to inspect the contents. "Cash and credit cards are still here." She retrieved a cellphone near the purse. "Dead. Hopefully, I packed the charger."

Strolling to the bed table, she lifted a silver wristwatch, turned it this way and that, and then slipped it onto her wrist.

He leaned a hip against the dresser. "If you are a

creature of habit—as most people are—you use the same hotel, carry the same luggage, and probably eat at the same restaurants. Someone studied your routine and pounced."

Frowning, she faced him. "Why?"

"Your camera equipment, more likely." He waved a hand about the room. "You were incapacitated, so the thief had ample opportunity to take everything. Yet, only your camera and laptop are gone. We have theft with a specific purpose."

"But why assault me? Why not wait for when I left the premises for something to eat?" She flopped onto the corner of the bed. "Hell, I was out like a light. They had enough opportunity to steal everything in my room. Yet, they took the time to dump me in an alley in God knows where." Jerking, she jumped to her feet and whirled. "They thought they killed me!"

Forcing himself to keep his face neutral, he studied her. "You keep saying *they*, Dana. Do you know that fact for sure?"

She stared back. "No, I don't know anything for sure. Probably a figure of speech." Her shoulders slumped.

Still peering, he pushed away from the dresser. "A dead body causes too much of an uproar in a hotel. So yes, I'm guessing you had to be disposed." He nodded at the night table by the bed. "Any rings?"

Glancing over, she shook her head. "Not even a tingling."

Aw, damn, she was cute. He couldn't help but smile. "I meant real rings, Dana, the kind you put on a finger. Like an engagement ring. Check your purse."

"Oh." A pink glow rose onto her cheeks. "Sorry."

Grabbing her purse, she dumped the contents onto the bed and rummaged through them. "A class ring." She read the inscription. "University of Pittsburgh." She slid the band onto her right ring finger. "Perfect fit."

Taking a position alongside, he shifted through the purse contents. The usual woman's can't-live-without necessities—compact, lipstick, tissues, and tampon. "Obviously, your engagement ring went with the laptop and camera equipment."

She picked up the eyeglass case. "Here're my glasses. Maybe now I can read without squinting." Removing the glasses from the case, she slipped them on then glanced up and down before grabbing the hotel's TV channel list from the night table. "Yup, these are definitely reading glasses." She replaced the glasses into the case and dropped it into the purse.

Holding out a hand, he stopped her from grabbing the rest of the stuff and retrieved an airline ticket. He scanned the printed information. "You flew in from Pittsburgh on February twentieth, and if I remember from your website schedule, your lecture occurred on the twenty-first. According to your ticket, your return flight was the next morning after your lecture. That's definitive. Your attacker had a limited time frame." He frowned. She lectured at two of Baltimore's largest universities and possibly several of the smaller ones. The suspect pool could include anyone she encountered along the way.

"What are you thinking, Lance?"

Too much, unfortunately. He curled his lip into a slight smile. "A detective's mind at work, Dana. Here." He handed her the ticket.

Taking the paper, she gathered the rest of the purse

contents then zipped the bag. Moving toward the closet, she yanked on the tiny knobs to open the collapsible doors. "A suit and overcoat are hanging in here." She fingered the material on the suit. "Nice. I have good taste." Sighing, she faced him. "I can stay at the hotel, Lance, and wait for my fiancé."

A wave of…something swept through him at the mention of her fiancé. His gut tightened, and he clenched his teeth so hard he swore he'd crack the enamel. He forced a smile. "If that's what you want."

Her face changed into a mixture of emotions, none of which lasted longer than a millisecond. Internally, he wasn't any better, and analyzing the conflict within his chest proved futile.

Stiffening her shoulders, she walked toward him and extended a hand. "I want to thank you for all you've done. I'd like to repay you."

She wore a smile about as phony as a four-dollar bill. He glowered at her outstretched hand. "I don't think staying is the right move."

Stepping back, she dropped her hand. "What do you suggest? Another hotel?"

"Protective custody. At my place." *What the hell*! His mouth spoke before his brain considered the consequences.

Their gazes locked.

She shook her head. "You've done too much already, Lance."

But he wanted to do so much more. As an assault victim, she needed help, and he had a bona fide reason to work her case and find the perpetrators. Deep down, an innate desire to discover the real Dana Null churned within his gut, not what people read on her website. He stuffed his hands into his coat pockets. "I'm not one to leave a case unsolved, Dana. While I can't keep you around until your memory returns, I *can* use the opportunity to question every bit of memory that pops into your mind. The best way to accomplish the job is with you nearby." He paused to cock his head. "Unless, of course, you feel more comfortable in a hotel. Either way, I'll make arrangements with your fiancé."

She covered her face with both hands. "I won't know him."

"You might. Anything can trigger your lost memories." Hell, she needed someone to watch her back. What if her fiancé appeared as a total stranger? What then? The cop in him couldn't say *adios* and wipe his hands of any further involvement. To give Dana some space, Lance hobbled to the opposite side of the room. "You can stay here, Dana. I'll place a guard at your door." Even if he had to be the one to sit in the hall himself. "The choice is yours."

Tears clouded her eyes. They had turned so brilliantly green, he swore they transported him to a forest. Had she any idea how beautiful she was and how she caught a man's breath? If and when she regained her memory, would she change into a classic snob? *God, I hope not.* He loved the naïve side to her personality and her unassuming air. But, with a PhD after her name and her extraordinary language skills, she'd have a fiancé of equal stature. Lance Barnes wouldn't stand a chance.

For now, he'd give her anything she desired. Throwing his cane onto the bed, he limped toward her and wrapped her tight in his arms. Molding into him, she trembled in his embrace, and his heart melted. He kissed her hair. "You have every right to be scared, Dana. I'm offering a sanctuary until you feel confident to leave." He sniffed the herbal shampoo in her hair. His shampoo. He hadn't realized how nice it smelled, but he needed a distraction.

Just feeling the smallness of her body against his heavy overcoat prompted a rise in a part of his anatomy where friends shouldn't go. Swallowing hard, he gripped her shoulders and held her at arm's length. "We'll return to the precinct, and I'll call your fiancé. Let's hear what his plans are." Loosening his hold, he used a finger to lift her chin. Fighting like mad to ignore her incredible green gaze, he smiled. "Look on the bright side. You can wear your own clothes and your own overcoat."

He let his gaze drift to her lips. So tempting. As a cop, he'd encountered many beautiful women, some the drop-dead gorgeous kind, but none influenced a reaction like Dana's quiet beauty. He struggled with the need to stay professional versus his desire to throw her onto the bed. Dropping his arms, he again stuffed his hands into his coat pockets.

Life was so friggin' unfair.

Using both hands, she wiped the tears dripping onto her cheeks. "You're a nice man, Lance."

He cringed. "Yeah—well, you know what women say about nice men."

"No, what do they say?"

Oh, hell. Fighting the urge to swing at something, he retrieved his cane from the bed. "Never mind. Gather your stuff. If you packed socks, put them on. I don't want your cute toes to fall off."

Rather than watch her rummage through her

suitcase, he meandered toward the window. The drapes were opened to let in the daylight, and he had a clear view of the alley below. City building codes specified emergency exit doors and fire escapes as an integral part of every construction. The opposite building had an exit door toward the rear of the alley. This structure, being a hotel, would have several doors—one for fire escape and others for deliveries. He turned. "Can you give me more details about the alley, Dana—besides rats?"

Sitting on the bed, she kicked off her sneakers and slipped on a pair of socks. "Dark. Smelled like garbage."

"How about dumpsters?"

Pausing, she tilted her head. "None. A bunch of trash, loose and in plastic bags. Pieces of broken furniture."

To confirm what he'd already observed, he turned back to the window. Not this alley then. The one below was too clean and organized. The width allowed enough space for a large delivery truck. A car would have no trouble pulling alongside the side door to dump a body into a trunk. His jaw twitched, and he inwardly cursed.

"I'm ready."

Rotating to face her, he froze, and his heart thudded.

Standing in her own overcoat, she resembled the woman on the DMV report. The black coat fit her curves, as if tailored to her body. With his jacket draped over her arm, she slipped her purse over the shoulder of the other arm. A grown woman. And yesterday, he mistook her for a teenager. *Some friggin' detective I am.*

Coughing to assure an intact voice, he retrieved her packed suitcase and followed her out the door. "Before we leave, we'll stop at the front desk and talk to Gary Cary."

On the way to the elevator, she again paused at the ice machine, her brows in a deep frown.

Twice is too much of a coincidence. Alert, he tapped the floor with his cane. "Tell me what entered your mind, Dana."

"Diamonds." She stared into the alcove. "And chlorine."

Taken aback, he narrowed his gaze. "Your engagement ring, and what, bleach?"

Her hand tightened around her purse strap. "I'm not sure about the bleach, but the image of the diamond flashed white and not what I'd call sparkling."

He entered the alcove and, looking high and low, searched for anything resembling a diamond. "Maybe you hit the floor and saw a stray ice cube. People drop them all the time." Swiveling his head, he sniffed. "I don't smell chlorine in here." Setting the suitcase along the hallway wall, he opened the stairwell door. The landing and steps were spotless and well-lit, but a faint chlorine odor irritated his nose. "I'm guessing your assailant struck while you stood by the ice machine. After that, someone carried you down the stairs to a waiting car by the service entrance."

Clutching the rail, Lance directed his gaze up the staircase and then down. "Whether your attacker considered you dead or not, he couldn't leave you here to cause a ruckus. I'm thankful he didn't finish you off once he dumped you in the alley."

Over the years, he'd investigated dozens of cases where camera footage brought a perpetrator to justice. If Dana's assailant hid in the stairwell and, at the opportune moment, assaulted her, he or she should be on camera.

Continuing toward the elevator, she pressed the Down arrow then faced him. "What do you mean about women and nice men?"

Glancing upward at the elevator's floor lights, he smirked. "Women want excitement so they pick men who personify the bad boy. All they ever receive is pain, whether physically or emotionally." The damn elevator must be stuck on the top floor. He met her gaze. "I've seen the scenario enough, Dana. Women aren't interested in a guy like me. I'm too dull."

"The nice-guys-finish-last syndrome?"

"If we finish at all." He shrugged. "Girls ignored me in school. Now, they ignore me because I'm a cop. I don't go out of my way to impress women."

"You impressed me."

"But you have no idea of your type of man…yet. I'd like to meet your fiancé to see if he's a biker with a long beard and ponytail." He hoped not, but nothing surprised him anymore.

Her gaze twinkled. "He might be like you—a man who takes pride in his appearance and profession and one who steps in to rescue a damsel in distress."

Yes, he had a sense of pride about himself, but did women appreciate the trait? Salary-wise, his cop paycheck couldn't compare to a corporate big-wig, but he never squandered what he earned. He lived with a frugal mindset and banked money for retirement.

Hurrah, hurrah. The elevator finally moved.

She nudged his arm. "I think you're wearing blinders. You're too attractive for women not to notice."

The elevator dinged, and the doors opened. Another couple stood within and prevented any retort.

So, Dana considered him attractive. A definite boost to his ego. Thinking back, Cynthia Doyle told him many times, but with her, he had this hang-up about her making far more money. Dana fell into the same category. Hell, she lectured at some of the top universities in the world. In all probability, her fiancé rolled in dough.

After she exited the elevator and approached the lobby, she patted his arm. "Why do you want to see Gary?"

"Security cameras."

Her eyebrows rose. "Oh. Smart thinking. I picked a winner by swinging at you."

"Uh-huh." He couldn't hide the smile if he tried.

Placing her luggage by the lobby chairs, he approached the front desk and requested a word with the assistant manager. When the clerk disappeared into a side room, Lance took a business card listing Gary Cary as the manager on duty. He couldn't imagine living through a childhood with such a name. Kids would turn the name Gary Cary into a torture chant. At the time of birth, the guy's parents were probably stoned.

As Gary emerged, Lance slipped the card into his coat pocket. This time, Gary stayed behind the desk and, like before, intertwined his fingers.

Such an odd-looking young man. At a guess, he was in his late twenties with pale eyes, olive skin, kinky pale hair, and a somewhat-gangling short frame. He wasn't feminine in any way, just…not manly. Clearing his throat, Lance nodded toward the inner office door. "I'd like to see the security footage." With luck, the view screens were on the premises and not somewhere across town.

"The cop who investigated my missing person report made the same request, but the camera tapes only record for a twenty-four hour period before starting over." He shrugged one shoulder. "By the time I filed the report, I had nothing to show him."

In this day and age of sophisticated security cameras, why would any business still use *tapes*? Were the owners too cheap to modernize? Frowning, he tapped his fingers on the counter. "Were any other guests bothered that night?"

"We had no reports of anything happening on any of our floors. By the time the detective arrived, the guests near Doctor Null's room had checked out."

The perfect crime? Except Dana survived the blow, but without any memory, the case would go cold. Was she a victim of circumstance, or had the perp waited for the opportunity to strike? He clenched his jaw. If the latter, then Dana was the intended target, and that piece of news didn't sit well at all.

Chapter Eight

After checking out and listening to a hundred of Gary's apologies, Dana stepped onto the sidewalk and took a long, deep breath of the cold air. For some reason, the hotel felt stifling, and all her tension melted as soon as the automatic doors closed behind her. She wasn't sure why she wanted out of the hotel, but Lance's offer to stay at his place filled her heart with gratitude. He provided the safety she craved while the pieces of her life came together—like wearing her own fitted overcoat and reveling in the warmth of socks on her feet. With a purse slung over her shoulder, she experienced a return to normalcy—except for the void in her brain.

The trip to the hotel triggered only a smidgen of memory. Whoever whacked her head stole select objects in her possession, leaving behind a full wallet and cellphone. As Lance stated, theft with a purpose. Were her equipment and ring expensive enough to risk an assault charge? Holding her hand outward, she studied her left ring finger. No tan line of any kind...unless she hadn't worn the ring very long. *A possibility to consider*.

Once settled into the car, Lance reached across the center console and slipped a hand over hers. "Are you all right?"

How could his hand be so warm with freezing

temperatures outside? Everything about him created a fuzzy feeling within her chest. Would anyone else bother with a lost soul?

He squeezed her hand. "Dana?"

Forcing a smile, she met his gaze. The kindness emanating from his blue eyes instilled her with a strong sense of calm and an overall determination to conquer any problem thrown her way. Letting the warmth of his skin seep up her arm, she shifted her gaze to the dashboard. "I came to frozen in that alley, Lance. I had no idea where I was or even my name, and the experience frightened the hell out of me." Saying the words out loud reactivated the terror of waking in the dark alley. The image of the rats' long whiskers and twitching noses staring into her face would be forever imbedded into her brain. She sucked in a shuddering breath. "Stepping from the alley onto the street, I saw no one, not even a passing car, as if the area had a Do Not Enter sign posted somewhere. As I walked, I passed people huddled under blankets or buried beneath cardboard boxes. They ignored my questions."

"I'm not surprised. What did you see when you left the alley?"

Resting her head onto the seat's headrest, she closed her eyes. "Boarded houses. A few burned-out cars. The neighborhood appeared abandoned." His hand tensed on hers. Surprised, she rotated her head to see his jaw tight with lips flattened into a thin line. "What?"

After releasing her hand, he pressed the Start button and put the car in gear before gripping the steering wheel, his gaze straight ahead. "The area you describe is nowhere near the Red Wolf, Dana. You were taken to the slums. Someone went through a lot of trouble to cart you away from the hotel." He braked for a red light. "My gut says you were intentionally targeted, with the camera and computer taken as a diversion. My job is to find out why."

Without memory, the why might never be answered. What had she done to piss off someone? She frowned. "I'm up the creek without a boat."

Brow cocked, he glanced her way. "The phrase is up the creek without a paddle."

Great. She couldn't even remember old sayings right.

The light turned green, and he flowed with the traffic. "By the way, Dana, your hands are like ice. Where're your gloves?"

"In my pocket keeping warm." She hadn't given her gloves a second thought. And rightfully so. Gloves prevented skin-to-skin contact—something she craved during all this mental turmoil.

Ten minutes later, he guided the car into the precinct parking garage. After rehanging the keys and writing the return time on the clipboard, he led her to the elevator, her suitcase in hand. "Once we arrive at the office, I'll call your fiancé and tell him you're okay. When we find out his plans, then we'll decide what to do next. I'm thinking Chinese takeout on the way to my place."

She smiled. "Sounds good. I have no idea if I like Chinese, but I'll find out."

Dana followed Lance to the homicide bureau feeling like a square wheel. The whole atmosphere prickled her skin. Men and women in uniforms or suits crowded the large room, suspects slumped in chairs with cuffed hands behind their backs, and every other person conversed on a phone. An overall dark appearance shrouded the department, despite the decent fluorescent lighting. Desks were either gray or black with chairs to match, and the few windows available to see the outside world existed in the glass-enclosed offices. A few of the female detectives decorated their desks with vases of artificial flowers to brighten the gloom. For the men, a fast-food wrapper accomplished the job.

Lance's partner wasn't at her desk, and no coat hung on the wooden rack nearby. While he settled at his desk to make the phone call, Dana wandered to Georgette's two case boards.

Anita Seeley was the name under the blonde-haired woman. At a guess, she was in her early thirties with heavy eye makeup giving her the appearance of two black eyes. A connecting arrow pointed to her husband, Anthony Seeley, a man old enough to be her great-grandfather. Besides the photos of the three men, the board contained two more—one of the victim's sister and another female, a young woman in her twenties with streaks of purple through golden hair.

The dark-haired man on the second board was Michael Tenemen. He possessed an ordinary face and nothing noteworthy to catch a woman's eye. An arrow pointed to Kathy Tenemen, his wife, a brown-haired woman in her late thirties. Other than names under the photos, details were scarce.

Replacing the phone receiver in its cradle, Lance waved her over. "Your fiancé cried when I told him you were okay."

A pang hit her heart. A man she didn't know loved her. Could she return that love? With her hands still in her coat pockets, she approached the desk. "I hope you told him I haven't a clue who he is."

"I forewarned him, and his exact comment was, 'She'll remember me.' I hope he's right." Lips pursed, he leaned on the desk and studied her. "He'll start out in the morning, and we'll meet here sometime in the early afternoon. Okay by you?"

What could she say...no? She'd rather spend another night with Lance than face a man she couldn't remember. Biting her inner lip, she stood stock-still by the case boards.

"Dana—"

Realizing she stared at a crying woman across the room, she jerked her gaze to his face. "What?"

Scowling, he narrowed his gaze. "If I were your fiancé, I'd be in Baltimore tonight."

She shook her head. "Maybe he's too busy." Hell, she defended a man she didn't know.

"Too busy to see for himself if you're all right?" He huffed out a breath. "Any normal man would be frantic to find his fiancée missing, and no one, not even the Pope himself, can keep him sitting by a phone. And then to hear she's okay and wait to start out in the morning?" Lips pressed tight, he grabbed a stack of papers and pounded them into a neat pile.

What the hell? Maybe her fiancé hated driving at night, or his job kept him glued to a desk. An infinite number of excuses floated through her mind, none of which warranted an angry response...oh, holy crap. A light bulb finally clicked on in her brain. Leaving the boards, she rounded the corner of his desk. "Are you saying he doesn't love me enough?"

He cleared his throat and stood. "I'm sorry I said

anything."

"Oh, no, you don't." She latched onto his arm. "You're a man voicing your opinion. Explain."

His gaze bored into hers. "Yes, all right. If he loved you, he'd be here cussing me out."

Brows high, she released his arm and stepped back. Was he right? Maybe she had an unusual relationship with her fiancé, like a partnership for convenience. Gad, she hoped not. What was a marriage without love? Until her memories returned, she could do without any more confusion for her befuddled brain.

A brown-haired woman stormed from the elevators clanking high heels on the hard linoleum floor, causing every cop in the department to turn and stare. After a few curt words to the nearest officer, she directed a gaze toward Lance. Dana recognized her as Anita Seeley's older sister.

Stomping toward them, she flared her arms. "Where's Cavello?"

Stretching to his full height, Lance blocked her path. "I'm Detective Barnes. Can I help you?"

Lips pursed, she scanned Lance from head to toe. "I want to know why Cavello hasn't arrested Professor Seeley. He killed my sister."

"And your name?"

"I'm Margaret Horton. Cavello is supposed to keep me informed. Where is she?" Her head rotated in all directions.

Lance leaned against his desk. "At the moment, Lieutenant Cavello is out. Why don't you sit and calm down?" With a wave, he indicated his desk chair.

With a huff, Margaret riveted her gaze onto Dana. "I know you." Stepping toward her, she jerked a finger at Dana's face. "You're that language expert who lectured the other night."

Holy shit, if looks could kill. Cringing, Dana backed away.

Lance sprang off the desk and placed his body in front of Dana. "Were you at the university?"

She snorted. "Oh, get real. I've no interest in anthropology, but *she* knows the professor, my sister's husband." Jerking her chin, she snorted. "Knows him very well, I'm told."

Dana snapped her gaze to Lance. "I—huh…er—" Dear Lord, what could she say? She had no idea about any part of her personal life.

Lance crossed his arms over his chest and faced Margaret Horton. "Someone attacked Doctor Null the night of her lecture. She has no memory of her time at the university."

"So, she says." Margaret waved a hand. "The professor likes young women, and he got rid of my sister just to chase *her*." She leveled a sharp fingernail at Dana. "Don't deny the accusation, honey. He always talked about you and broke my sister's heart." Tears welled in her eyes.

The old man and her? Dana shot a quick glance at the board. The professor's photo triggered nothing. Was she involved in a lover's triangle? *No way.* Not with an old man. Margaret snorted some hallucinogenics. But without memory, Dana faced a precarious position. Could Anita's murder be the reason someone whacked her head and left her to die in an alley? Was she a witness or a perpetrator? With a bone dry mouth, she swallowed. "Lance—"

Without acknowledging, Lance gestured toward his

chair. "Mrs. Horton, please, sit."

"It's *Ms*." She flopped onto the chair and sniffed while tugging on her cream overcoat.

Grabbing the box of tissues from Cavello's desk, Dana offered them to the distraught woman.

Scowling, Margaret slapped the tissues from Dana's hand and sent the box flying. "Anita was all I had left. He took her from me, and I'll bet any amount of money *she* was involved." She jerked a thumb at Dana. With a loud wheeze, Margaret extracted a tissue from her coat pocket and dabbed her nose. "Anita married that bastard, even after my repeated warnings." She blew her nose with a loud honk. "He promised her anything she desired. Now, look where she is. Professor Seeley should be behind bars." She tossed the used tissue in the trash bin.

"No proof," said a female voice.

Georgette Cavello strolled over to the coat stand and hung her jacket. Stepping in front of Margaret, she slipped one hand into her trouser pocket. "The DA wants strong evidence, Ms. Horton. Unless you can provide something concrete, you should go home. I'll find whoever killed your sister." Placing a hand under the woman's arm, she helped Margaret to her feet. "Stay away from the professor, and let me do my job. I'll call you."

Tugging on her overcoat, the woman shot a glare at Dana. "What about her?"

Cavello's gaze narrowed. "I'll deal with Doctor Null."

With a nod, Margaret headed for the elevators.

Georgette pivoted toward Dana, her gaze sharp.

Chest constricting at the vision of mealtime behind

bars, Dana retrieved the tissue box and tossed it onto Cavello's desk. The undeniable urge to run hit like a tidal wave, but where would she go? Determined to stand her ground, she shifted her attention from Lance to his partner. "Why do my nerves tell me I need a lawyer present?"

Jaw tight, Lance stood alongside Dana. "What's going on, George?"

In answer, Georgette trudged to her case boards and yanked the photos from the second board and added them to the first. After rolling the empty board behind the first one, she turned to Lance. "I had an interesting day. I discovered these two cases have one commonality." Gaze intense, she faced Dana. "It's you, Doctor Null."

With her heart dropping straight to her toes, Dana gaped. *Oh, God, now what do I do?*

Chapter Nine

A crawling sensation prickled across Lance's skin, like tiny invisible creatures unleashed to throw him into a panic. For the first time in his life, he'd left his comfort zone, threw caution into the wind, and allowed a stranger into his home. What the hell happened to his brain cells? He never once took home a stray—human or animal. George's words opened the earth beneath his feet, and he envisioned a career nosedive. All his hard work, he flushed down the toilet because of one simple act of kindness. Glaring at Dana, he gritted his teeth, and a wave of self-loathing consumed him. Her face changed to the color of a white sheet, and her green eyes appeared ready to pop from their sockets. Georgette's news scared her, and without memory, she had no rebuttal.

Neither did he. Only a gut feeling. He could count on one hand the number of times a woman fooled him. With Dana, his training and field work came into play the second she swung at his face. Now, her involvement in two seemingly unrelated cases raised questions about her assault. How deep was she involved? Had she known the two murdered victims?

Sharing a look between Dana and his partner, he slipped his butt onto the edge of his desk. "You better explain a few things, George."

Palms flat on her desk pad, Georgette leaned over,

gaze sharp. "Before I do, what proof do we have that Dana Null has a true memory loss? Maybe she's an excellent actress."

Lance glanced at Dana who met his gaze, her back ramrod straight. Her face contorted into an expression akin to standing in drying cement. He shifted his gaze to George. "Neurologist confirmed the blow hit in the area where memories are stored. The assailant struck once with a heavy object, and she has a cracked skull as proof."

He tugged on his overcoat collar. Why the hell he hadn't removed the garment with all the stifling heat in the precinct proved how preoccupied Dana kept him. He hadn't expected to stay any longer than making the phone call to her fiancé. "Her temp registered ninety-three degrees, which indicated exposure to the cold for an extended period of time. Garbage stained her clothes, which—for me—confirmed her story about coming to in an alley. I believe her, George, and you know me. I don't take in strangers." He flashed Dana a quick wink.

After mouthing the words, *thank you*, Dana lowered her gaze to the floor.

While twisting her lips to one side, Georgette flitted her gaze from Dana to Lance then relaxed her stance. Sighing, she gave a curt nod. "All right, I'll go with your judgment." Rolling her chair away from her desk, she flopped onto the seat and settled her gaze on Lance. "Let me tell you what I know." Leaning back, she swiveled toward Dana. "Anita Seeley and Michael Tenemen—our two victims—attended your lecture, Doctor Null. Witnesses said they sat side-by-side. Time-wise, Anita's murder took place between ten and eleven in the evening and Tenemen's the next morning around seven. No witnesses available in either crime."

Dangling her arms over the armrests, she swiveled toward Lance. "Circumstantial evidence suggests the professor had his wife killed because of Anita's string of boyfriends, but in reality, the professor didn't give a damn. Anita married him for his money. He married her for sex. They had a simple marriage of convenience with prenups galore."

Moving to the other side of the desks, Dana slid onto the metal chair closest to the board and pointed at the professor's photo. "That explains the age difference."

"Yes, thirty-five years." Rotating toward her, George pursed her lips. "The professor has known you for some time, Dana, ever since your fellowship at Johns Hopkins. He speaks highly of you."

After a glance at his photo, Dana shrugged. "News to me."

Fighting a wave of tightness in his jaw and neck, Lance pinched the bridge of his nose between two fingers. He needed a distraction from his boring routine but not a double homicide. Sighing, he peered at his partner. "What else, George?"

Georgette crossed her long legs. Even in slacks, the movement was sexy as hell.

With her long, dark hair and dark eyes, she turned many heads and never failed to attract a man's attention. Years ago, he argued with the captain about being partnered with a woman, but she taught him so much. She was a damn good detective and one of the best in the precinct. She also became his best friend.

George flicked a piece of lint from her slacks. "The

professor is a self-absorbed man. Anthropology is his life. What his wife does to occupy her time is entirely her choice as long as she is home at night for him." She rocked in her chair, creating a series of squeaks. "He and Anita hadn't much in common. She struggled through high school and never attended any college. Anthony Seeley is a tenured professor and well respected. I can't imagine what their dinner conversations were like."

"And Tenemen?" Lance nodded toward the board.

Georgette covered a yawn.

She had the tired eyes of following a trail for too many hours and not enough sleep. His injury left her without a partner, and he faulted the captain for not providing a replacement to ease her load.

"Tenemen worked as a real estate broker. Nice family and no history of fooling around. In short, he enjoyed his job and time with his kids. However..." Her lips twisted to the side. "He's not without enemies. Striving to maintain his Broker of the Year award, he's sold some true "buyer beware" properties. Several lawsuits are in the works." Uncrossing her legs, she tugged on her earlobe and frowned. "Something in me says he and Anita sat together by accident. No proof, of course. Just a gut feeling."

With a glance at Lance, Dana slipped her fingers into her jeans pocket and handed the small device to Georgette. "Maybe this flash drive will help."

Taking the stick and turning it in her hand, George cocked a brow. "What's on it?"

"The Q and A segment of my lecture. The camera focus is on the audience."

Lance explained about their trip to the hotel and the

stolen camera equipment and laptop. As he talked, he mentally pieced together the facts gathered by Georgette and combined them with his observation of Dana. More than ever, the details revealed an intentional assault on the visiting lecturer. Had she seen or heard something and the equipment stolen to hide the culprits? And since the perp dumped her in an alley, he or she likely took an inaccurate pulse. Not everyone could feel a weak carotid pulse, especially on a twisted neck. Even worse would be checking the radial pulse, the first to disappear. Like Georgette, he had a gut feeling, and he didn't like it one damn bit. "Dana's assault was not a random act of violence, George."

Nodding, Georgette met Dana's gaze. "I agree with Lance. You were assaulted and your equipment stolen because you taped something someone wanted to hide." Slapping her knees, she jumped to her feet and kissed Dana on the top of her head. "For Lance's sake, I prayed you were aboveboard. Let's head to the video room and hope the drive will break the case wide open."

****

My assault wasn't random? After she and Lance removed their overcoats and hung them on the rack, Dana followed the two detectives to a small room in the far left corner where a large, flat-screen viewer hung on the wall. Underneath, video equipment from VHS to DVD filled a long table, along with a desktop computer and two laptops.

While Georgette plugged the drive into one of the laptops, Lance grabbed three stools and lined them in front of the screen.

Dana could do nothing more but stand by and mull

over Georgette's information. As hard as she tried, she could not connect the dots. Her association with two murdered victims wrenched her gut. If the camera recorded incriminating evidence, then two detectives, putting their heads together, should uncover a clue to give her some answers. She had zilch to offer. Without any way to prove otherwise, she expected one of the partners to slap on the handcuffs.

But Lance's tender gaze reassured her, and her runaway heart eased. With one hand, she gripped her purse strap tight against her shoulder while the other latched onto his arm. "All this stuff scares me. What if whoever hit me discovers I'm still alive?"

Gaze narrowed, he studied her. "I've already come to a similar conclusion, Dana, and it's another reason for you to stay with me."

With one brow arched, Georgette grinned. "Another reason? What's the first one?"

Lance answered with a scowl.

Chuckling, Georgette used the remote to activate the flash drive, and the view screen lit up. After several minutes of video, Georgette slipped her hands into her trouser pockets. "The camera's voice activated."

Lance crossed both arms over his chest. "Dana and I took note of the feature earlier."

Despite the three available stools, the two partners stood in front of the monitor, throwing questions at each other while pointing and commenting on the video. Lance's standard posture of crossed arms over his massive chest had an intimidating air, which, no doubt, dropped a suspect to his knees. To a woman, the stance revealed a very masculine physique. Not to ogle the curves of his muscles like a sex-starved teenager,

Dana sat on one of the stools and diverted her gaze to the monitor.

"There's Tenemen." Georgette pointed.

Curious for a better view, Dana slipped off the stool and moved closer to Lance's side.

Tenemen sat in the last row partially hidden by shadows, the seat on his left empty. Anita was nowhere in sight.

Like earlier in Lance's living room, Dana mentally answered all the questions raised by the students. She knew so much about anthropology and foreign languages yet remembered nothing about her personal life. She had a fiancé with no face who was a man she assumed she loved. How had they met? Was he as attractive as Lance and as big? Did he have a good job and PhD? What in the world would she do if a stranger walked toward her?

"There's Anita." Again, Georgette pointed.

Dana jerked her attention to the screen.

The buxom blonde entered through the door and paused on the landing while surveying the crowded lecture hall. She exhibited the posture of a woman waiting for the world to notice, like an actress on center stage. After pouting at the limited available seats, she nudged her way down the row toward the vacant seat on Tenemen's left. Her tight ass attracted the attention of every male she passed.

Grabbing the remote from Georgette's hand, Lance froze the video where the two victims sat. "She missed the entire lecture. Judging from their casual exchange, they don't appear to know each other."

With hands in her trouser pockets, Georgette grunted. "She doesn't strike me as a woman into anthropology."

Dana coughed. "Maybe she suddenly took an interest in her husband's work."

Leaning forward to see around Lance, Georgette lifted one eyebrow. "Seriously? With that outfit?"

Dana almost laughed at the truism of Georgette's statement. Anita wore a top with a neckline low enough to show a lot of cleavage. Her blue jeans molded to round hips and cut into her crotch tight enough to make Dana wince. While every male ogled Anita's ass, Tenemen settled his gaze on Anita's boobs before returning his attention to the lecture. Dana glanced at her own mediocre chest and sighed.

Lance restarted the video. "Who's this?" He nodded toward the screen. "Her photo is on your board."

Pausing by the doors, the young woman with spiked golden hair and streaks of purple shifted a large cardboard box in her arms. Heavy eye makeup weighted her lids, and purple lipstick contrasted horribly with her pale skin.

"She's staring at Anita and Tenemen, and she doesn't look happy." Lance reversed the video and replayed the footage. "Look how she does a double-take when she glances in their direction. She's horrified." He hit the freeze-frame.

"That's Babs McNamara, the professor's assistant." Georgette toyed with the collar on her blouse. "The girl worships the old man and has made no pretense about her dislike for Anita." She whirled a finger at the screen. "Keep the video rolling, Lance."

Babs descended the steps toward the podium and then disappeared from the camera view.

Georgette sighed. "Babs has no alibi for the time of Anita's murder. I don't consider her a strong suspect, but—whoa! What are Anita and Tenemen doing?"

Again, Lance froze the video.

The blonde and Tenemen had their heads close together while Tenemen pointed to the electronic notebook in his hand.

Georgette gave a curt nod. "I'm told Tenemen shows his properties on his notebook. Look, he slipped her a business card." Pursing her lips, she peered at the screen. "Anita had no card in her possession. Otherwise, I'd have connected the two cases right away. She either tossed the card, or someone made sure they weren't linked."

The video ended. Georgette hit the stop button on the laptop and unplugged the drive. Grinning, she gripped the device in her fist. "A nice stroke of luck." She turned to Dana. "Your video was helpful, Doctor. You realize, of course, the drive is now evidence."

Dana shrugged. "No problem. One of these days, I'll figure out why I placed it in my pocket."

After a slap on Lance's shoulder, Georgette headed for the door. "I've a lot of work to do before I question Babs McNamara and Kathy Tenemen. See you later." She paused in the doorway and nodded toward Dana. "Take care of her, Lance." She winked at Dana and left.

Smiling, Lance faced her. "How about that? Your video proved useful after all."

Big deal. The recording confirmed the presence of the two murdered victims at her lecture. Now, the big question, what the hell was going on?

Chapter Ten

After picking up takeout from a local Chinese restaurant, Dana and Lance settled in the kitchen with opened containers cluttering the table. Once sampling General Tso's chicken, orange beef, and lo mein, along with the rice and hot sauce, she fell in love with Chinese food. Not a morsel remained between them. After cleanup, she brewed a cup of tea and relaxed on one end of the couch with the steaming liquid tickling her nose, her shoes off, and feet tucked under her butt. Could an evening be more perfect? *Well, hell, yeah.* Sex would be nice.

Returning from a quick trip to the bathroom, Lance flopped onto the opposite end, grabbed the remote, and focused his gaze on the six-thirty newscast. He chose not to have tea since he claimed the brew tasted like the inside of a wash bucket.

Being with him felt nice. They were nothing more than a couple relaxing to release the troubles of the day. The bolted front door provided security. The drawn draperies over the living room windows allowed privacy. A cocoon of homeyness—one-sided, of course. Like any man, Lance's attention stayed on the television.

Her thoughts drifted to her fiancé. Who was this man she would meet tomorrow? Did they live together? Suppose she hated the man on sight? *Crap.* Far too many questions to consider. She lowered the mug to her lap. "What if I don't recognize my fiancé? What will I do?" She couldn't live with a stranger. But wasn't she in a similar situation? Lance Barnes had picked her up, dusted her off, and taken her home. Her fiancé would be no different.

She shot a quick glance at Lance to see a steady gaze watching her. Would her fiancé possess such warm, expressive eyes or soft, sensual lips? Would he set her heart racing with a simple look or flush heat to her skin with a crooked smile? In all fairness, she shouldn't compare one man against the other. Yet, in her heart, she wanted her fiancé to be like Lance—a man decisive and kind.

With a smile tugging one side of his mouth, Lance draped a long arm over the back of the sofa. "Take each day one at a time, Dana. Your brain already triggered little bits and pieces of memory. Who knows what circumstances will knock a few more loose? Your return to Pittsburgh, perhaps. You know, familiar grounds. Friends and family. More than anything, I don't want you to feel forced into an uncomfortable situation."

The thought of leaving sank her into a funk. Lance had become the life raft that kept her afloat. But she couldn't stay forever. Home was in Pittsburgh, and she must be brave enough to face her world—good or bad. If her memories failed to return, she'd create new ones, starting with Lance.

She placed her mug onto the coffee table. "I don't even know what I do for a living." Sitting back, she frowned. "Big deal, I'm an anthropologist who speaks sixteen languages."

"When your fiancé arrives, he'll fill in the gaps." After dropping his arm from the sofa back, he cleared his throat. "I've been meaning to ask you…"

A flush rose into his cheeks, making her wonder if he ate too much hot mustard sauce. And—*ohmygod*—his ears turned a beet red!

He grimaced. "I don't stock anything in the way of…uh, feminine products. If you need something, you can ask Thelma."

Feminine products? Like—oh! She almost laughed out loud at his obvious embarrassment. For his sake, she kept a straight face. "Thank you. If necessary, I can find a convenience store." Hopefully, she'd be home before her next menstrual cycle—assuming she marked the date on the calendar.

He grabbed the TV remote and punched in a few numbers. "Channel Nine has a hockey game on tonight." He glanced her way. "Care to join me?"

"Hockey, eh? I know nothing about the game, but I'll sit and watch if you explain what's going on." For all she knew, she could be the sport's biggest fan. Rah, rah, shish, boom, bah! Then again, she might be into ballet and opera. Good grief, the thought made her cringe.

Gathering her mug, Lance stood and limped toward the kitchen.

His limp hadn't improved from the morning PT session. She fought the urge to kiss his leg to make it all better, but he wasn't a child with a boo-boo. Her lips would touch the rough skin of a virile man. Not wise.

He returned carrying two beer bottles and a bowl of peanuts. "I have in my hands the best way to relax." He handed her a bottle then held out the bowl. "I buy the peanuts at The Nut Shoppe around the corner from the precinct. They sell the Spanish variety with the red skins, like my dad and I ate during every ball game."

She waved away the bowl. Peanuts on top of all the Chinese food conjured images of exploding intestines. She lifted her beer bottle to the light. "I have no idea if I like beer." She sniffed the uncapped neck. *Hmmm.* Not the most pleasant smell. "Are you from around here, Lance?"

Sliding the peanut bowl onto the coffee table, he settled on the sofa. "I grew up on Staten Island and began my police career at the New York academy." With a wince, he lifted his stocking feet onto a round, cushioned foot stool. "After a few years of street patrol, I took the detective's test and became one hundred and thirty-sixth in line. I'll be old and gray before I earn a NYPD gold badge. So, I transferred to Baltimore, attended the Maryland police academy, and worked patrol. In time, I took the department's detective test and waited for a slot to open in the homicide division. Even if I spent the rest of my days working patrol, the job was still a lot better than New York." He took a swig of his beer. "From the day my parents took us to the harbor, I liked how the city was more wide open than New York. I'm not too far from family, either. My brother lives in Manhattan and my sister in Philadelphia. Both are married with kids."

Dana reflected on the possibility of her own life. She'd like a sister, but a brother would do. Shaking away the thoughts, she forced a smile. "Parents?"

"Both deceased." He shot her a sideways glance. "Do you recall anything of your childhood?"

Not a damn detail drifted to mind. She shook her

head. Rotating to face him, she placed an arm on top of the backrest and leaned her head against her hand. "Ever since I woke in the alley, I've been in a perpetual state of confusion. I remember how to do basic things, like eat with a fork or brush my teeth. My language skills are intact, even though I have no idea what languages I speak. It's like that blow knocked my personal history right out of my head."

"Then maybe you should spend time on your website and read what you said about yourself." His lips curled upward. "My advice is once you return home, seek the help of a good specialist. I'm sure your fiancé will assist."

Maybe. Maybe not. She sipped the beer and puckered. *Uggh*! Bitter. "I can't drink this, Lance." Shuddering, she handed him the bottle.

"No problem. It's more for me." He took the bottle and set it on the table. Snatching the remote, he lowered the volume as the game started.

She stared at the TV, wondering what could be so special about a bunch of guys on ice skates knocking around a black thingy with sticks. "What's his name?"

One brow lifted, he shot her a glance.

"My fiancé."

"Oh." He palmed a handful of peanuts. "Tim Gardner." He paused, gaze narrowed. "Ring any bells?"

Nothing rang any bells. Just once, she'd like to hear a little ting-a-ling. She nodded toward the TV. "Go on. Tell me about hockey."

Lance explained the game in more detail than she cared to know. If anything, the deep resonance of his voice soothed the apprehension building for tomorrow's meeting. Stifling a yawn, she swung her feet to the floor. "I think I'll turn in and let you enjoy the game."

Stretching, he caught her wrist. "Dana—"

His touch shot a strong bolt of heat straight to her core. Judging from the wide-eyed look on his face, he also felt the rush and dropped his hand.

He shifted his gaze to the game. "I have an appointment with the department shrink in the morning. The visits are mandatory after a shooting." He shrugged a shoulder. "You can sleep late, and when I return, we'll head to the lecture hall." He tossed several peanuts into his mouth.

Her back stiffened. "What if my fiancé is waiting at the station? He might grow impatient."

Smiling, he shook his head. "I can't let you go that easy."

Her heart skipped a beat, and she swallowed hard. "What do you mean?" Hell, she croaked out the words.

"You're part of a murder investigation."

"Oh." She should pull her head out of the clouds. Tucking a strand of hair behind her ear, she chuckled. "The old don't-leave-town speech?"

He grinned. "Something like that. Since we uncovered your involvement a few hours ago, we'll need to hear everything possible from you, even with your limited memories. I'm hoping the lecture hall will trigger a few flashbacks."

"All right." She waited, not at all sure why. For another touch maybe or a kiss good night. She longed to taste his lips again, but every beating heart fiber knew she wouldn't stop. She was an engaged woman. Although her fiancé might be a stranger, fair was fair. Slapping her knees, she stood. "I'll see you when you return."

The doorbell rang. With a groan, Lance shot his gaze from the TV to the wall clock and then rose to answer.

A mirror image of Lance Barnes stood on the threshold. The man had gray showing at the temples and a little more weight under the overcoat, but they both had a remarkable resemblance.

"Robert!"

Lance's face broke into a wide grin as he grabbed the man in the familiar male fashion of hand clasps and shoulder butts along with loud slaps on the back.

Waving him inside, Lance turned to Dana with a big smile. "Dana, this is my older brother, Robert. What a great surprise."

Robert's piercing blue eyes scanned her. "I can't believe I'm seeing a woman in my brother's condo." He turned to Lance. "I can go."

Lance grabbed his brother's arm. "Hell, no. It's not what you think. Dana's using my spare bedroom." He waved toward the closet. "Take off your coat. The Rangers are playing."

"Yes, I know. That's why I'm here instead of hiding in my hotel room." He slipped off his coat and tossed it over a chair. "I'm in town for tonight. Business." He sniffed the air. "I smell *lo mein*—unless Dana is wearing a new kind of perfume." He turned to Dana, gaze twinkling. "Nice to meet you. I'm glad I didn't expect to stay."

She smiled in return. "You can. I won't mind sleeping on the couch." Both men blinked. She glanced over her shoulder just in case something hadn't crawled out of the woodwork. She lifted her chin. "I think the sofa is quite comfortable."

Robert spread his lips into a wide grin. "You're cute. No, Dana, I'm having breakfast with my business associate in the morning and then flying home. I'm here to watch the game."

"Since I was already on my way to bed, I'll say good night."

Before entering the hall, she glanced over her shoulder to see both men staring. Wow. Two handsome men, and she headed to her bedroom alone. Was she crazy or what?

****

Mouth agape, Robert clutched Lance's arm. "Separate bedrooms? My God, Lance, she's gorgeous!"

Typical for his brother to dive straight to the point. Frowning, Lance snapped his gaze from Dana's direction. "She's engaged."

"Then why is she here?"

Lance explained, not in fine detail but enough to make his brother understand Dana's connection to a current homicide case.

Snorting, Robert strolled toward the sofa. "And you're saying her fiancé is waiting until tomorrow? What is he, nuts? If I was in his shoes, I'd be pounding on your door."

"My thoughts exactly." He couldn't wait to meet the guy and hear his excuses for not hurrying to Dana's side. Dana deserved to be wrapped in the man's arms and comforted, not put off until daylight. Muscles twitching at the fiancé's misdirected concern, Lance limped toward the kitchen. "Let me grab you a beer."

"There's two on the table." Robert pointed.

"One's hers. She hated it."

"Uh-oh. Strike one." Grinning, he flopped onto the

sofa while tugging the tie loose from his neck.

Once settled, they talked throughout the game. Since they both played competitive ice hockey to stay in shape, Lance argued about the offensive moves while his brother countered with defensive tactics. Robert was the oldest of three siblings, but even so, his forty-one years looked more like fifty. His brow revealed more creases, and the laugh lines around his eyes formed permanent crow's feet. Something troubled him. During a commercial, Lance jabbed a fist into his brother's shoulder. "Everything okay?"

Robert shrugged. "My detective brother. Nothing passes you." Sighing, he took a long swig of his beer then smacked his lips. "No, everything is not okay." He stared at the bottle. "Johnny's stuttering. The pediatrician wants us to wait a year to see if the phase passes, but the impediment is affecting his grades." Still staring at his bottle, he rested his elbows on his knees. "The kids make fun of him, and every morning, Mary struggles to get him off to school." He scrubbed one hand over his face then glanced at his brother. "He's cutting classes."

"Uh-oh. Not good. How old is he now?"

"Eleven. Mary's done some research. He's at the age where the stuttering continues into adulthood. We think the doctor is full of shit."

Lance slapped his brother on the back. "Then a second opinion is warranted."

"Already done. Johnny's working with a speech therapist, but I don't see any improvement yet." While staring at the TV, Robert sipped his beer. Afterward, he wiped his mouth with his thumb. "Research says a stuttering gene can be passed in families."

Straightening, Lance gasped. "Uncle Harold!"

Robert chuckled. "Yeah, it took me years to figure out why the poor guy mumbled." He settled against the back cushion. "I don't want Johnny to follow Harold's route. My son's already angry because he stumbles on his words. He changed from gregarious to introvert overnight and sulks most of the time in his room."

Being the youngest of the three, Lance never understood their uncle's behavior. Every time his father took them for a visit, Uncle Harold left to work in the garage or had something to do in the attic. The old guy seemed nice enough, but his wife, Aunt Gladys, was the sociable one. He'd hate like hell to see his nephew follow in Harold's footsteps. Forcing a smile, he slapped his brother's knee. "Give Johnny time with the therapist. The problem won't go away overnight. Is this specialist the best in New York?"

Robert lifted a shoulder. "I don't know. I made a few inquiries, but the whole matter boils down to how well Johnny gets along with the therapist. He's rebellious, and if his grades continue to spiral, he'll repeat the school year." He passed a hand through his dark hair. "Mary's beside herself, and I'm not handling the news well either." Reaching toward the coffee table, he paused with his hand over the bowl of nuts. "These were dad's favorite." He grabbed a handful.

"They're mine, too." Lance tapped his brother's bottle with his own. "I'm glad you gave me a heads-up about Johnny. I'll know what to expect the next time I visit." Facing the TV, he jerked, brows high. "When did the Rangers score?"

Chapter Eleven

Too dark. Sounds...muffled, squeaky, like rats. Vibrations, too. They rattled her teeth. Fractured memories. Except the diamonds, and something blue. Why blue? And why me? Who are you? Get away from my face, damn you!

Flailing her arms, Dana bolted upright in bed, flitting her gaze around the dark bedroom in search of those beady little bastards with the pointed snouts. Her heart beat a mile a minute and threatened to pound right out of her chest while breaths puffed through her lips like a marathon runner. At least this time, she hadn't done a nosedive onto the floor. After slowing her breathing, she flapped her moist top away from her chest and then flopped onto her pillow to stare at the ceiling.

Nothing made sense. Her subconscious mind stirred images but provided no explanations. Were the vibrations from a moving car? She remembered one deep jolt jarring her into semi-consciousness. A pothole maybe? That violent shake knocked something close to her nose. Yes, an oil-stained rag, and she pushed it away. That detail could only mean...she gasped. No restraints! And what the hell did blue mean? The color of the car? *Must tell Lance in the morning.* He might fit the puzzle pieces better than her befuddled brain. Rolling to face away from the door, she pounded her pillow and closed her eyes.

Not ten seconds later, a thump startled her. Muttered obscenities followed. Rolling over, she peeked at her partially opened bedroom door. The hall remained dark, but the distinct sound of tormented moans forced her to slip from the bed and investigate.

The glow from Lance's bedroom allowed sufficient illumination to see him hobbling around the living room, cursing between tight teeth. Each step created a deep grimace on his handsome face. From the look of his severe stride, he struggled to put weight on his bad leg. She approached. "Lance, what's wrong?"

After a quick glance in her direction, he limped faster. "I stubbed my toe. Go to bed."

"Then you shouldn't wander around in the dark." A stubbed toe wouldn't cause such an exaggerated gait…unless he broke the bone. She rubbed her eyes. "Want me to turn on a light?"

"No!"

Yo—whoa! What the hell hit him? "You're having a leg cramp, aren't you?"

"Yes. Go to bed."

Like she could sleep with him mumbling and grumbling. Not to mention how good he looked with bare chest and a pair of boxer shorts over a tight tush. Even the sight of his broad back had her fingers itching to touch. Shaking away the thoughts, she took a few more steps toward him. "Let me rub the muscle."

He turned sharply, his gaze intense. "Dana, go away. I'm fine."

Nothing more than male ego. Even if blood gushed from an artery, he'd still claim to be all right. "Let me help *you* for a change."

"I don't see no MD after your name. Go to bed." Releasing a hiss, he shot her a glare. "Out of all the men and women leaving the precinct, my cane told you I was an easy mark. Admit it, Dana. You thought I was a big pushover."

Dana rolled her eyes. "Yeah, right. I picked the guy with a handicap so he'd bash in my skull." Sighing, she shook her head. "Need I mention you handled yourself adequately with one hand, Mr. Detective." Taking a position on the opposite end of the sofa, she leaned toward him. "I didn't stand in the street to analyze everyone stepping out the door, Lance."

He scowled. "I could have hurt you. I'm not proud of the scrape on your cheek."

"You were defending yourself."

Mumbling, he hobbled toward the front door.

A stubborn mule. She hadn't any magic skills for leg cramps—that she recalled—but she couldn't let him hobble around in pain when a nice, gentle massage would do the trick. She moved toward him but stopped. "I'll admit I took a big chance. Suppose you were the worst pervert on the force?" She tilted her head. "Even in my confused state, I liked what I saw and acted. I wasn't wrong."

Grunting, he limped around the perimeter of the living room and then, as he neared, shot her a sideways glance. "And now? Are you sorry?"

"Are you kidding?" She smiled. "You went out of your way to help me. I'll never forget all you've done—unless someone comes along and bops me on the head again."

He strained a smile, but his face switched to a grimace. Cursing under his breath, he hobbled another full circle around the living room.

When the light from his bedroom hit his calf, shadows emphasized the surgical scars and misshapen muscle. Small wonder he hadn't lost his leg.

"I'm not the man I was, Dana. So, don't give me any of that hero shit. I won't buy it."

"Because of one damaged leg?" Resting her butt on the sofa back, she crossed her arms over her chest. "The rest of you looks pretty good." Better than good, but she kept the words to herself.

Shooting her another glance, he narrowed his gaze. "Don't pacify me."

"Pacification is not the word on my mind." Too bad he couldn't read the direction of her thoughts. This hunk of meat limped around nearly naked, and if she had her way, she'd be on him in two seconds flat. He oozed sex with muscles bulging from every exposed part of skin. She should bite her tongue and control her raging hormones. The poor man suffered from a leg cramp, and here she lusted to hump him.

Around the sofa again, he stopped and scanned her from head to toe. "Why are you still wearing my pj top?"

She glanced down. "I'm sorry. Do you want it back?" She reached for the buttons.

"Not this minute, damnit!" Grimacing, he bent to rub his calf.

"I'm wearing panties this time."

Straightening, he scrubbed both hands over his face. "Damn friggin' leg." He completed another perimeter walk.

She inwardly smiled. Some memories might be gone, but she sure as hell understood sexual tension.

The air crackled between them. His powerful male scent inspired thoughts of long, slow kisses through the night.

Passing her, he glanced over his shoulder. "Why don't you wear your own pj's?"

"I will…eventually. I happen to like this top."

"Why?"

She shrugged. "It's yours."

He drew his brows together into a deep frown. "What the hell does that mean? I never wear pj's."

"Your comment isn't worth a field of beans."

Stopping, he stared. "The expression is a hill of beans."

She threw both hands into the air. "Whatever. All I'm saying is this feeling of being alone isn't fun." She grabbed the two small lapels on her top and tugged. "Do you mind if I hold onto some semblance of belonging?"

He sneered. "You don't belong to me. You belong to someone else."

Given another time and place, she'd debate his statement, but the poor man hadn't stopped hobbling in pain. "Let me rub your leg, Lance."

"No!" Groaning, he buckled over the sofa back. "This damn calf won't quit." Sucking in a deep breath, he straightened and eyed her through narrowed lids. "All right, you can help, but I can't let you touch me."

She suppressed a laugh. "Fine." With two hands, she placed fingers on opposite temples, closed her eyes, and hummed.

"What the hell are you doing?"

"I'm rubbing you telepathically." She opened one eye. "Is it working?"

He grunted. "You're being ridiculous."

"Me?" She dropped her hands. "Then, give me one good reason why I can't touch you."

With eyes like slits, he leaned toward her. "Because I want you, damnit, more than any woman before you. Despite this damn cramp, I'm having a hell of a time fighting the urge to put myself inside you. But you're engaged, Dana. I can't let myself weaken." Wincing, he gripped the sofa, eyes clamped shut.

Well, she hit dead-on about the sexual tension. He wanted her. *Good.* But his loyalty toward her fiancé exceeded anything she felt. *Does that make me a terrible person*? How could she even fathom being engaged with a near-naked hunk like Lance around? With one hand, she ran her fingers through her hair and sighed. "If you start screaming from pain, the neighbors will think we're having sex anyway. I'll rub your calf." Stepping beside him, she knelt on the floor.

A vague memory of hands massaging her feet popped into her brain. Who or when drew a blank. Pushing the thought aside, she blew warm breath onto her hands then began a gentle massage. The muscle felt like a hard knot and, without question, refused to ease. "If you feel a rise from my fingers, don't worry. I'm an adult. I've seen men before." At least, she remembered basic male anatomy.

After several minutes with his moaning and groaning filling the air, he released a long breath.

The muscle in his calf finally relaxed. The bullet wound aside, his legs showed strength with black hair covering defined muscles. She liked the feel of the coarse hair beneath her fingertips and the roughness of his skin. He might consider himself damaged goods, but to her, he was all man.

"You can stop, Dana. The stabbing pain is gone."

Not in the least willing to remove her hands, she continued for another minute. Sitting back onto her heels, she dropped her hands to her lap.

Glancing down, he released a heavy sigh. "I overdid the therapy this morning because I'm sick of the cane. I want to throw the damn stick into a burn pile."

She ran a finger along his scar, and a tremor traveled across his skin. "You have a nasty hole in your leg, Lance. You need time to heal." Clamping onto the sofa back for support, she stood.

He might argue, but he made a nice picture of manhood. Boxer shorts. Broad chest. A light touch of black hair enhanced the broadness of his chest while muscles flanked his waist as if they were shields to protect the kidneys. His tush—tight and round—drew her gaze from the enticing bulge in the front. Sexy as hell, every inch of him, and her lady parts practically begged for some attention.

Clutching onto her shoulders, he snapped her gaze to his face. "Time is not on my side, Dana. Your fiancé will be in Baltimore tomorrow, and I want more than a casual taste of your lips."

The heat in his blue eyes revealed the depth of emotion coursing through him. Her heart thundered against her rib cage. Locking onto his gaze, she swallowed hard. "Now is as good a time as any."

Dropping his hands, he backed away. "No."

Shit, shit, shit. His rejection squeezed her heart. She picked a man too friggin' noble, but he had every right to worry about her fiancé. What if the man stood taller with more muscles and an uncontrollable temper? And what about her own behavior? Hormones before common sense? Lowering her gaze to the rug, she shook her head. "All right, you win." She might as well live with the sexual frustration and hope her fiancé was a drop-dead gorgeous hunk who'd hump her until kingdom come.

"Dana."

She kept her gaze on the floor. "What?"

Stepping close, he grabbed her shoulders and crushed her against his chest.

He captured her mouth like she would escape. Hard chest muscles rippled against her breasts and sent the sensation of power straight to her core. Her knees weakened. Heat poured from his tight embrace and warmed the chill of her forgotten robe. She never felt anything so wonderful.

She slid her hands along his back muscles until stopping at the shorts' waistband. Then—what the hell—she inched her fingers under the material to squeeze his butt. *Ohmygod*. She grabbed solid rocks. She slipped her hands toward the front of his shorts.

"No, Dana. We shouldn't do this." He clamped onto her wrists and, with one swift movement, lifted her into his arms and pressed her against his chest.

What the hell! But he stifled her response with his mouth, and she relished his taste, greedily probing for more. This back-and-forth crap was for the birds. Right or wrong, she wanted him and for as long as he chose, maybe longer if she had her way. "I'm not married yet."

"But you might love him very much." Entering her dark bedroom, he lowered her onto the bed and sat alongside, nudging her to move over. He touched her chin. "You are beautiful, Dana, but I can't let anything progress between us. I won't let you live with something you'll regret."

Even in the dark, she saw the hungry gaze scanning her face. "No regrets, Lance. I want this." She placed both hands on his cheeks and lowered his face to her lips. The kiss was short-lived.

He pulled away and buried his face in her neck. "What we're doing is wrong."

Somewhere in the back of her mind, she knew he spoke the truth. Where the hell were her scruples? Had they been knocked out of her head along with her memories? She fingered his chest hair. "I hope my attraction for my fiancé is as strong as what I feel for you. The funny part is we just met yesterday."

Lifting a lock of hair from her face, he toyed with the strands. "I don't understand the attraction either. All I know is I want you in my bed, and I'm fighting a primal urge like mad." Leaning over, he suckled her lower lip. "When your memories return, I'll have a fair shot."

A gaze scanned her face. Then, he smiled and straightened.

She placed an open palm on his bare chest. *Like touching a sun-kissed boulder.* "You're a man of strong principles, Lance. I hope my fiancé appreciates your restraint." She brushed a finger across his lips, savoring the softness.

Clamping hands on both sides of her head, he kissed with a greed that returned all her desire to the surface. Damn him. Just when she pushed her arousal to the back of her mind.

Releasing her, he stood. "Good night, Pixie."

She stared at this beguiling man with an erection tenting his boxer shorts. What woman had the willpower to resist such a blatant display of manhood? Muscles and strength oozed from every pore, forcing her to swallow the saliva accumulating in her mouth. But he was right. Sex with another man would change the dynamics of her relationship with her fiancé.

Clamping her eyes shut on the image of what could have been, she turned onto her side and prayed her fiancé was man enough to satisfy the urge growing in her belly.

Chapter Twelve

The next morning, Lance took his usual chair in the psychiatrist office and talked about nothing in particular. After weeks being asked the same questions, what more could he say? He was shot. He survived. Case closed. Sure, since the gunshot, his systematic routine fell by the wayside, but he adjusted. Normally an eat-work-sleep man, he struggled with the constant disruptions. Like physical therapy three times a week and the once-a-week psychoanalysis. In between, he made several visits to the surgeon who repaired his leg.

Today, he leaped one important hurdle. The shrink cleared him for active duty. Hallelujah! If he could kick his heels, he would, but he settled for a fist pump outside the doctor's office door. The captain was his next hurdle. The old man demanded all his officers run five miles without breathlessness. Lance couldn't run yet, but until then, he'd settle for desk duty. In no time, he'd be on board with his partner. Mood light, he hit the Down button on the elevator.

Toward the end of the session, the psychiatrist remarked on Lance's attitude change. Lance had a habit of sulking through every visit, but in retrospect, he agreed with the doctor. Dana caused the change. She dispelled his self-pity mentality. Last night, her hands on his calf worked like magic. He almost searched on her website to see if masseuse was part of her doctorate.

Dear Lord, the feel of her hands aroused him to the point of embarrassment. No way could he hide the bulge in his boxer shorts, and why should he? Her desire glowed in her green eyes, and her voice conveyed the huskiness of a willing woman. Only his honor stopped him. Damn, fool honor. As if another man wouldn't jump her the first chance he got.

Lance exited on the ground floor.

After stepping through the medical center's glass double-doors, he hobbled out onto the sidewalk where George waited in a precinct car. Before dropping his butt onto the passenger seat, he kicked off the snow from his leather boots and then flashed her a big grin.

Lowering the fan on the heater, she smirked. "Your face tells me you heard good news."

"I can begin active duty when the captain approves." He buckled his seatbelt.

Shifting the car into gear, Georgette checked the side mirror and eased into traffic. "As much as I miss you, Lance, do you want to return so soon? Since you have a houseguest, you might want to spend more time with her."

Judging from last night's episode and the mixed feelings churning in his gut, he disagreed with George's suggestion. How could two people hunger for each other in just two short days? He barely controlled his urge to ravish her. Clearing his throat, he stared out the side window. "Before the day is out, she'll be riding into the sunset with her fiancé. Work will be the perfect activity to…" His tongue twisted.

George braked for a red light. "To purge her from your mind?" She cocked her head toward him. "I guess you'll be glad when she leaves." The light changed, and she flowed with the traffic.

"Damn right. She's disruptive." So much for his good mood. For some inexplicable reason, speaking the words hurt. Deep in his heart, he knew the statement was one big lie.

"I think you're full of shit." George turned a corner.

Damn clairvoyant woman. He scowled. "What?"

"You aren't letting her go that easy, are you?"

He tugged on the seatbelt. The damn strap threatened to cut off his carotid artery. "She's engaged."

"If she remembers, you mean." She eased left at the next corner. "All I'm saying is don't push her out the door into the arms of a stranger. We don't know who did what to her or if they'll try again."

Yanking on the bunched overcoat under his butt and getting nowhere, he gave up. "I'm hoping her fiancé jars loose a few memories. If he doesn't, he won't leave the precinct with her unless she gives the okay."

"Good. You had me worried. I'm sure she won't stay forever." She braked for another red light. "I should mention one point." Leaning toward him, she tapped her nail on the console between them. "Dana's assault is the key to my case. My gut tells me so, and I'd like her to stick around for a little while. If necessary, we can put her in a hotel under guard if she's interfering with your bachelor ways." Winking, she eased the car forward.

Dana would never be in his way, but in reality, he couldn't keep her long term. She had a life of her own in Pittsburgh, maybe a family, and certainly a fiancé.

Once her memory returned, she'd see the stark differences between them.

Georgette glided the car to the curb in front of his condo building. "Let's keep her video under wraps, Lance. Tell her, too." She shifted into Park.

"Not a bad idea." He unbuckled his seatbelt and twisted in his seat. "Did you talk to Babs McNamara?"

"Of course." She drummed her fingers on the steering wheel. "For a girl seeking a PhD, she acts a little too flippant. If you happen to meet her on your trip to the university, let me know your opinion." She touched his arm. "You need to fall head over heels in love, Lance. You'll experience an incredible feeling."

He rolled his eyes. "Where the hell did that statement come from? We were talking about McNamara." Damn women and their romantic notions. Couldn't a man live a solitary life without some matchmaker butting in? "You know full well I'm too career-oriented for any relationship."

"Then, high time you considered the possibility. Nothing relieves the stress of our job than having someone at home waiting who cares and loves you." She gestured with her head at his car door. "Go on. I'll call when her fiancé arrives."

Once Georgette's sedan disappeared from view, Lance stood by the condo entrance and surveyed the activity around him, not in the least anxious to head inside. Last night, a light snow blanketed the city, sending people out onto the sidewalks to either shovel or sweep with a broom. Shop and home owners alike pushed the new white fluff toward the curb to combine with the mounds of blackened crud not yet melted. Snowfall in the country painted a peaceful scene with visions of sleighs and snowmen while children built forts and had snowball fights. Snow in the city turned black within hours from car exhaust, smog, and asphalt splash-back. No beauty whatsoever.

Lucky for Baltimore, the Chesapeake Bay added warmth and protected the residents from more severe weather. Maybe Pittsburgh received the brunt of last night's storm, and Dana's fiancé slid into a ditch along the interstate. Not a bad thought to lift his spirits.

A car with a wheel flapping crawled by, the driver obscured by tinted windows on all sides. Black sedan, four door, and late model. A yellowed plastic cover hid the license number. During his street patrol days, he'd go after the driver for two violations of city law, namely the darkened windows and hidden plate. But those days were over.

Turning, he entered the condo building but hesitated in front of the elevator doors. He and Dana had limited remaining time—a matter of hours, in fact—and he wasn't sure what emotions churned in his gut. He wanted her gone but then wanted her to stay. Was confusion part of every man/woman relationship? If so, the idea of anything between them should be squelched while he still had some sanity left in his befuddled brain.

He jabbed the Up button for the elevator, and the door opened. On the ride to his floor, he mulled over Dana's impending visit with her fiancé. Ten to one, she'd recognize him and be off to Pittsburgh before dusk. But was Georgette right? Could Dana's assault be the key to two murders? With no concrete evidence, how could they keep her in Baltimore? Maybe he shouldn't jump ahead of himself but take a wait-and-see position. He exited the elevator and, with key ready, approached his condo door.

Music penetrated through the walls. Judging from the twang, the genre could be none other than country and western. He slipped his key into the lock and entered. The sound flowed from the kitchen along with off-key singing. After dropping his cane into the umbrella canister, he opened the closet to hang his overcoat and crossed the living room to investigate.

Dana stood in front of the sink, belting out the song…in Spanish. Her narrow hips swayed in rhythm, and she looked so damn carefree. If given the opportunity, he'd watch her for hours, but his groin stirred. Shaking his head at his body's betrayal, he tapped on the wall.

Turning, she wiped her hands on a towel and lowered the volume on the counter radio. Then, she smiled.

His heart melted. Her lovely smile traveled straight to her eyes.

"Hey, how'd it go?" She tossed the towel onto the counter.

"Good." With arms folded across his chest, he leaned against the doorjamb. "You were singing in Spanish."

She snickered. "And I knew all the words to the song. Go figure." She pointed to the place settings on the table. "I made lunch. Hungry?"

"Always." *For her*. He forced his mind from her cute little ass and strolled to the table.

An odd feeling surfaced to add to the mound of confusion already clouding his head. Women had stayed overnight plenty of times. Some even prepared breakfast, but for the first time ever, he entered his home, and a meal waited. Everything felt right. A beautiful woman stood at the sink. The aroma of tuna and cheese filled the kitchen, along with the fresh scent of dinner rolls. His mouth watered—for her and for food. If dessert included great sex, a man couldn't ask to be anywhere else.

Was this overwhelming sense of peace what Georgette meant? A wife and family? Someone to listen to his troubles and share meals and the events of the day? The closest he came to any serious relationship involved Cynthia Doyle, but she packed her things and left when he failed to commit. He'd give the same speech to Dana. So, whatever the hell circled his heart, he'd shake off the feeling soon enough.

With the use of mismatched oven mitts, Dana placed a casserole dish onto a folded towel in the middle of the table. "I couldn't find a hot plate thingy and didn't want to burn your table." She tossed the mitts onto his microwave. "I substituted crackers for croutons, and you might need a little more pepper." She nodded toward his chair. "Let's eat." She slid onto the opposite chair and grabbed a serving spoon. "Your brother seems nice. Are you from a large family?"

"I'm the youngest of three." After pouring iced tea into their glasses, he pulled out a chair and dropped onto the seat.

"Aw, the baby of the family. A handsome baby." She waggled her eyebrows and grabbed his plate.

Even without her lips stretching into a smile, her gaze twinkled with laughter, revealing a glimpse into her inner soul. When happy, she turned into the most breathtaking woman in the world and activated a pool of heat deep in his groin. Last night, while wearing a serious expression, she rubbed his calf, yet desire sparked in her gaze. He fought like mad to resist her, but when her lips parted and pupils dilated, he nearly ravaged her. Common sense prevailed. No way in hell would he let her regret their mutual lip-lock.

She spooned ample portions of the casserole onto his plate and set it before him. "Is Robert in town often?"

"Not often enough." After picking up his fork, he hesitated.

"Don't wait for me." She filled her own plate.

He forked some of his food. The flavors of tuna with melted cheese caused a groan to escape from his throat. Add the crunch of the crackers and…wow. "Great tasting stuff." He forked more, shoveling the food into his mouth like a starving Neanderthal.

"Thanks. I used what you had in the cupboard, and Thelma stored these little rolls in your freezer. *Manga*." She slipped two napkins from the holder on the table and handed him one. "Last night, I had another nightmare. I distinctly remember having my arms and legs free."

No restraints. The word amateur floated into his mind, and what better proof that the perp rushed Dana from the hotel. He swallowed and met her gaze. "That's definitive, Dana. What else?"

"Potholes. One woke me—sort of." She chewed, her gaze focused over his shoulder. "I smelled an oily rag, and I remember something blue. That's about it."

"A blue what?"

Shrugging, she directed her gaze onto her plate. "I've no idea." She stabbed a forkful of casserole. "So,

137

what's troubling Robert?"

Mouth full, he shot his brows high.

She chuckled. "Don't look so surprised. I saw a man struggling to contain his emotions...you know, like you."

Beautiful and astute. He smiled. "You're quite the detective." He explained about Robert's son and then gulped a large portion of his tea. "Stuttering isn't the end of the world, of course, but Robert and his wife, Mary, are concerned." He finished the last bite on his plate then grabbed a dinner roll and slabbed on some butter. "I never used tuna in a casserole. Most of the time, I open a can for sandwiches. I'm impressed." Placing the roll on his napkin, he dragged the casserole dish toward his plate, spooned another hefty portion, and tapped the serving spoon to drop every last morsel. "Did you make this recipe from memory?"

With her napkin, she dabbed her mouth. "I searched online. I'm glad to see I can cook."

"Me, too." He smiled, but she already turned her attention to her plate, lips pouting. Leaning across the table, he cocked his head to draw her gaze. "Still worried about your fiancé?"

She toyed with her food. "Big time." Her brows drew together. "What if I never regain my memory?" She shot him a quick glance. "What will I do?"

Reaching across the table, he patted her hand. "Give yourself time to fall in love again. Don't worry about rushing into anything." He wished he could say or do something to ease her fears, but she faced an uncertain future. *Best to move the conversation in a different direction.* He refilled their tea glasses. "I phoned the Department of Anthropology at Johns

Hopkins. The receptionist provided the location of the lecture hall you used. We'll head over to the university after we're finished, and Dana—" He waited for her to meet his gaze. "No mention of your video to anyone, understand?"

She quirked her lips. "Keeping the enigmatic clue under wraps, eh?"

"Just a little ace in our pocket." Damn, even a slight curve to her lips made his hormones jump. He diverted his gaze. "George will call when your fiancé arrives." Maybe his phone picked today to die. Better yet, maybe a massive traffic jam closed the interstate and stuck Tim smack dab in the middle.

His gut tightened. What the hell was wrong with him? He was a career man and bachelor, a man dedicated to his work and set in his ways. A woman in his life represented a change in direction and was not part of his overall plan.

His mind was a jumbled mess.

All Dana's fault.

"Okay."

Huh? He'd lost his train of thought…again. Shaking himself, he glanced her way to see her staring at her food. "What's okay?"

"For Georgette to call."

"Oh, that."

He understood her concern. Tim Gardner might trigger some memories, or he might not. Either way, she had to face him. She couldn't stay in Baltimore forever.

For some reason, the image of her walking out the door depressed him like hell.

Chapter Thirteen

After signing for a department car, Lance drove Dana to the Johns Hopkins University complex. The full-sized sedan handled the roads well, especially in this weather, with patches of black ice surprising a driver. En route, silence surrounded them. From time to time, he stole glances her way to see if she showed any recognition of the passing streets. Nothing. Her gaze flitted with her normal curiosity, but her face showed no light-bulb moment. Nearing the School of Anthropology off North Charles Street, she straightened in the seat.

"Recognize anything, Dana?"

"I'm not sure. The walkways look familiar."

She bit her lip in her sexy little way, and he almost missed the parking lot. If she wasn't careful, she'd feel a hunk of man on top of her. He pulled into one of the open slots and killed the engine. Giving his most encouraging smile, he opened his door. "Let's hope for the best." No return smile, but at least, she stopped biting her beautiful lips.

Like any renowned institution, the campus grew in all directions as added curricula required additional buildings, more dormitories, and an abundance of parking lots and multi-level garages. In a city as old as Baltimore, parking space remained as scarce as green grass. Many students took public transportation or used bicycles. Even more walked. He should count his lucky stars to find a vacant slot so close to their destination, even if the lot was across the street.

Nearing the curb, he caught her arm, his expression stern. "Remember. You are to relay any flash entering your mind, no matter how trivial."

With her gaze fixed on the buildings across the street, she sucked in a large breath. "Yes, sir."

After a break in traffic, he followed her to the opposite curb.

Students from all walks of life rushed to classes with backpacks on shoulders and cellphones to their ears. Some fool kids wore spring jackets or none at all, even though the temperature hovered in the mid-thirties. They'd probably catch pneumonia, and then some fool lawyer would sue the university for not providing heavy jackets for stupid children. *No friggin' common sense anymore.* He scanned the area.

Many of the university's buildings were built in a traditional box-shape and constructed of red brick with white window trim and flat roofs. Some contained two or three floors and were either large or small, depending on its purpose. Interspersed among them stood a more modern structure with glass doors and prefab walls. The entire area had a nice, open feel with trees, grass, and, of course, interconnecting walkways.

Following the directions received from the Department of Anthropology receptionist, Lance led Dana to the modern building, which included two large lecture halls. As before, he encouraged Dana to walk ahead while he lagged to the side to prevent a distraction. Anything could trigger a memory, even a gesture as routine as grabbing a door handle.

Moving slowly toward the concrete steps, she glanced right and left then at the big structure with the double-door entrance. Her expression remained solemn with not an iota of recognition flashing.

Once stepping inside an empty antechamber, Lance pointed toward the double doors on the right with the sign *Lecture Hall #2* embossed on a gold plaque.

Leading the way, Dana swung open the door. He followed her into a large classroom with the standard stadium-style seats, tapering to a podium equipped with a microphone. Each row of cushioned chairs had a Formica writing surface with the exception of the last row.

A sense of déjà vu swept over him. As a student at New York State, he'd spent many hours in lecture halls for his criminology courses. Some of his professors held the students captive with interesting ways of conveying information, but far too many put everyone to sleep. Old Professor Williams challenged him the most and convinced a frustrated Lance Barnes to persevere. If not for the old guy, Lance might have taken a walk before the end of his second year.

While standing on the top step, Dana stared at the wooden podium and the large view screen covering a section of a wide blackboard. She glanced over her shoulder with a lift to her brow.

He winked in response. "Go on. I'll wait here." He settled into one of the uppermost seats against the wall, the same row where the two murdered victims sat.

With slow steps, Dana descended and meandered toward the podium.

Something about the way she carried herself struck him, with her head high and back straight, like she belonged in this type of room. Subtle elegance flowed with her movements, even in her long overcoat. *Nothing clumsy about her now.* He couldn't take his gaze off her.

Standing behind the podium, she turned toward the seats and stared past him, which was damn difficult since the wall rose behind him.

Alert, he straightened in his seat. "What, Dana?"

Dropping her gaze, she shook herself. "I'm not sure. I recall an argument in the doorway."

"Directed at you?"

"I don't think so." Moving toward the left of the podium, she wandered to a long metal table covered with different types of projectors. She tapped a fingernail on the surface. "I had my equipment on this table."

Slow but sure, her mind filtered through the confusion and recaptured some memories. *Give Doctor Klavoff a medal.* She'd be herself in no time. To draw her attention, he thumped his cane. "What else, Dana?"

She put her thumb and forefinger together to form a zero.

Somehow, Dana's lecture connected her to two murder victims—one male and one female. Her assault and the theft of her equipment meant she'd filmed a clue someone wanted to hide. The killer could be anyone in the audience, and knowing his partner, Georgette had her hands on a list of the attendees.

The bang of the lecture hall door snapped his gaze from Dana. An elderly man stumbled through carrying an overloaded briefcase and an armload of loose papers, flapping with his hurried movements. He had a disheveled appearance with a blue bow tie askew and silver hair resembling a wad of gray cotton candy. His dark suit hung on him like he'd lost a lot of weight. Lance recognized him from Georgette's case board—Professor Anthony Seeley, the female victim's husband.

A perky young woman followed, her arms equally loaded with loose papers—Babs McNamara, the professor's assistant. Her spiked golden hair with the purple tips had the same disheveled appearance, as if she and the professor got caught in a wind tunnel. At least, her blue jeans and T-shirt showed a presentable student appearance.

Gaze focused on the podium, Seeley abruptly stopped, forcing Babs to sidestep to avoid a collision. He fluttered a pair of gray bushy eyebrows. "Dana! How nice to see you." He descended the remainder of the steps and plunked his armload onto the table. The papers promptly slid to the floor. With only a glance at the mess, he approached Dana and grabbed her hands. "You should have told me you were still in town." He shook both her hands at once. "I'm so sorry I missed your lecture, but the feedback was as wonderful as usual." He dropped her hands, smiling. "You're welcome to stay for my lecture."

Wide-eyed, Dana stared at the man. No recognition passed onto her face, and she glanced at Lance.

The professor, following Dana's gaze, locked onto Lance, and his expression changed to the classic deer-caught-in-the-headlights look.

Seeley shook himself. "So sorry. I passed right by you."

Yeah, another totally oblivious citizen. Welcomed fodder for a thief. Lance stood and limped down the steps. His damn calf muscle pulled, but his physical therapist stressed the need to stretch the leg. Who the hell ever said pain was good? Some masochistic idiot, no doubt. Nearing the podium, he extracted his badge from his coat pocket and flashed the gold shield toward the professor. "I'm Detective Barnes from Baltimore PD. Doctor Null sustained a head injury that impaired her memory."

The professor shot his gaze from Dana to Lance then returned to Dana. "I don't understand." He cocked his head and placed his face close to Dana's. "You don't know me?"

Eyes wide, Dana backed away. "No, sir, I don't."

"I'm Professor Seeley, head of anthropology. Of course, you know me. I schedule your lectures every year." He turned to Lance and waved toward the woman behind him. "This is my assistant, Ms. McNamara."

The girl nodded a brief acknowledgment but said nothing. Instead, she plunked her armload of papers onto the table and squatted to retrieve the papers from the floor.

Lance bent over Babs. "Did you attend Doctor Null's lecture?" Since Dana's video revealed Babs in attendance, he used a common detective ploy to catch the person in a lie.

Babs threw him a nonchalant look. "Yes, I was there. The professor had a faculty meeting so I checked on the progress."

"And what did you see?"

"See?" Frowning, she stood and piled the papers into a neat stack on the table. "Well—" She chewed on her lower lip, gaze distant. "A packed lecture hall." She smiled at Dana. "Doctor Null's lectures are always a delight."

Lance couldn't remember his professor's lectures being anything but long-winded. Of course, a beautiful woman like Dana would hold every male's attention and not necessarily on the lecture. He slid his gaze from Dana to Babs. "You saw her camera equipment?"

"Sure. She always tapes her lectures, mainly the question-and-answer sessions to post on her website."

Clearing his throat, the professor adjusted his eyeglasses. "I don't see what any—"

Lance held up a finger. "Someone assaulted Doctor Null the night of her lecture and stole her laptop and camera equipment. Since two members of her audience were murdered—one of whom was your late wife—the footage must contain a clue."

Seeley blinked. "Oh, dear, most unfortunate." His gaze shifted from Dana to Lance. "I'm also acquainted with the second victim, Michael Tenemen. And now you implicate Dana in all this. So sad." He clucked his tongue.

Her face as blank as a sheet of paper, Dana's back went rigid while watching the professor. Had the professor triggered a memory, or had his insinuating words hit a sore spot? Lance narrowed his gaze at Seeley and Babs. "Who knew Doctor Null stayed at the Red Wolf Hotel?"

Babs positioned herself alongside the professor. "Everyone knew. She always stays at that hotel whenever she's in town." She toyed with a blue rubber band bracelet on her left wrist. "The students love her and often walk with her to the hotel…in better weather, of course." She turned to Dana. "I guess you're not there anymore, huh?"

Dana let a polite smile slip onto her lips. "No. I'm temporarily with Detective Barnes."

Lowering his head, Lance hid a grimace. Maybe he should have told Dana to be a little more discreet with her whereabouts.

The professor gasped. "Good heavens, my dear. You must stay with me. I've plenty of room."

Lips tight, Babs yanked his arm. "Aren't you a bit premature, Professor? You just lost your wife."

Without removing his gaze from Dana, he shook off his assistant's hold. "Nonsense. Dana and I have known each other for many years, even before Anita. You bought me this blue bow tie, remember?"

That piece of news caught Lance's attention. How far back, and how chummy were they? The professor's simple statement involved Dana more than anyone realized. Did she participate in the murder of the professor's wife, and then her co-conspirator whacked her on the head to eliminate a potential witness? What about Tenemen? Had she known him as well?

Stiffening, Dana sidestepped toward Lance. "I can't accept your offer, Professor. I don't know you."

Seeley pursed his lips. "Yes…quite right. My apologies. Should your memory return, you'll understand."

Even if she didn't, Lance understood all too well. Despite Dana's engagement and the recent death of his wife, the old man had no qualms about making a romantic move on Dana. Had she encouraged him, or was the guy so brazen he believed he could latch onto any woman he desired? Resisting the urge to thump the professor's foot with his cane, Lance stepped in front of Dana. "Why are you here, Professor? You deserve a

147

grieving period."

Seeley jerked his gaze from Dana and coughed. "Grieve for Anita? Hardly, young man." He shrugged. "I'll miss certain aspects of our marriage, but our union turned into another huge mistake. We had a prenup in place—a necessity after my first wife." He forced a smile, showing a set of coffee-stained teeth. "An old man can't marry a young woman and expect her to remain faithful. I allowed Anita to do as she pleased, as long as she stayed disease free."

How nice of him. Maybe the old guy owned stock in an erectile dysfunction pharmaceutical company and popped the pills like candy. Lance coughed. "Excuse me, sir, but you're a little too open-minded in my book."

Babs huffed. "She didn't deserve him. Anita constantly embarrassed the professor and the entire department. She played all her little games right under his nose to make him jealous."

Jealous enough to kill? Facing Babs, Lance narrowed his gaze. "Like what?"

Twisting her mouth to the side, Babs scuffed her red, high-top sneakers on the wooden floor. "Oh, you know, like flirt with men and kiss them in public or bend over to show them her tits. The woman was a piece of trash." She turned to the professor. "I'm sorry, sir. She wasn't any older than a lot of us, yet she kept her nose in the air and treated students like scum."

The hall door opened. A woman rushed in, looking a little windblown with brown hair sticking in all directions. Her gaze locked onto the professor.

Lance cocked a brow. Well, well. The plot thickened. Another face from Cavello's board.

"Mrs. Tenemen!" The professor tripped on a few steps to meet her halfway. "What can I do for you?"

"Your office told me where you were. I want Michael's manuscript."

He shook his head. "I'm not carrying his packet."

Babs stepped forward. "The manuscript is on the professor's desk. If you want to wait until after the lecture, you can return to the office with me."

Narrowing his gaze, Lance studied the assistant. Did her job description require running interference for the professor, or was Seeley the typical, absent-minded academic who couldn't remember to tie his shoes? Judging from the man's lack of reaction, probably both.

Kathy Tenemen checked her watch. "I have to pick up the kids. Can you drop the envelope at my house?"

"I don't own a car, ma'am. I can mail the manuscript."

While biting her lip, the woman glanced from Babs to Seeley. "No, I'll stop by tomorrow. Leave the envelope with the outer office." She turned to leave.

"Wait a minute." Lance hobbled over and flashed his badge. "How long have you known the professor?"

Seeley cleared his throat. "Because of a layman's interest in anthropology, Michael and I met some years ago, but I've only met his wife twice, both brief."

What the hell was wrong with these people? Kathy Tenemen and Professor Seeley both lost a spouse, but neither looked in mourning. No black clothes. No red noses or puffy eyes. Not a damn smidgen of grieving.

With a bang, the hall doors again flew open. Students flowed through chattering as they took seats.

Babs grabbed an armload of the loose papers and rushed to distribute them before the pupils took a seat.

Whirling, Kathy Tenemen ran out as if she would turn into a pumpkin. The professor hastened to raise the white view screen.

Lance smiled at Dana. "Time for us to go."

On the way to the parking lot, Lance's cellphone chirped for a text message. After reading, he sucked in a large breath through a tight throat and met her gaze. "Your fiancé is at the precinct."

Chapter Fourteen

No avoiding him now. Jitters threatened to consume every cell in her body, starting from the inside out. Her throat mimicked the Sahara, her palms Lake Mead, and her feet…well, forget the feet. Dana couldn't keep them still if she tried. She paced the width of the precinct elevator, as if searching for a way out. Thankfully, no one else rode with her and Lance. She'd be stepping all over their toes.

Oh, God, help me. She was about to meet her fiancé, a man from her past and one who might provide answers. Would she recognize him? Even worse, would she *like* him? Above everything, she should refrain from comparing him to Lance and give the guy a chance. Just because Lance became her knight in shining armor and the man who saved her from disaster didn't mean her fiancé wouldn't do the same. *So, remember. Don't compare.*

Lance chuckled.

The deep tone sent a flush of heat straight to her core. Yep, so much for not comparing. She glared at the floor buttons above the door. Why wasn't the elevator stopping at every floor? What were they in, some kind of express?

"Relax, Dana. He's not your execution squad."

She increased her pacing. "I'm so scared."

"Of course, you are. You're confronting the

unknown. But look on the bright side. He could snap your memories to the forefront, and all your troubles will be over."

The elevator jerked to a stop. *Oh, joy. We're here.* Fists tight, she plastered her back to the wall.

He patted her shoulder. "Take a deep breath."

Deep breath? She sucked in the entire volume in the elevator and half-expected Lance to drop from lack of oxygen.

The doors opened. *A now-or-never time.* Glancing at Lance for one last ounce of encouragement, she stepped out.

From a bench near the vending machines, a man jumped to his feet and rushed forward.

He was small in height, a few inches taller than her, with brown hair and eyes, and average in the looks department. He wore an expensive silk shirt under a black leather jacket, tailored trousers, and patent leather shoes that she swore no man wore anymore. A gold watch glittered on his wrist, and a solid gold chain peeked from his open shirt collar. He reeked of money, which surprised her since his face resembled that of a high school senior. Would she marry a younger man for his money? Was he even old enough to shave?

Approaching with arms outstretched, he wrapped her tight to his chest. "Dana, sweetheart, you had me so worried. You didn't return any of my calls." Releasing his embrace, he took her head in his hands and kissed her.

Stiffening, she couldn't respond. She didn't know this man, and he sure as hell hadn't created an increase to her heart rate.

He released her head and slid his hands to her

shoulders, a frown forming. "What's with the scrape on your cheek? Did you fall?"

No way would she tell him how she and Lance met. "I have a crack in my skull, too."

He twisted his mouth to the side. "Yeah, about that. Someone told me you had no memory."

Stepping forward, Lance cleared his throat. "I'm Detective Barnes, the man who called. You must be Tim Gardner. Perhaps you two would like to go into the lounge to talk." He gestured with a wave toward an open door.

Jutting his chin, Tim draped one arm around her shoulders and glared. "I'm taking her home."

And be alone with a stranger? Throat constricting, she backed away, forcing Tim's arm to drop to his side. She ducked behind Lance, using his body as a shield.

Tim widened his gaze. "Dana, what are you doing? It's me!" He reached.

Placing a hand on Tim's shoulder, Lance stopped him. "No memory, Mr. Gardner. I suggest you talk for a while."

Tim shrugged off Lance's hand. "We've no time for such nonsense. Her father wants her home."

"I'm sure he does, but talk first." He pointed toward a glass-encased lounge opposite the elevators. "See if you can stir a few memories."

Fighting the overwhelming urge to run and hide, Dana led the way. Tim hadn't triggered a smidgen of memory. Her doubts about him increased tenfold while her gut jumped around so badly she swore she'd need a bathroom. Taking a deep breath, she entered the room.

The lounge possessed a clean but worn look with one long sofa and several wooden chairs. Side tables were here and there, and in the corner stood a large cardboard box overflowing with colorful children's toys. Casting a quick glance at Lance who stopped outside the door, she almost ran to drag him inside.

Instead, he winked and closed the door.

All the anxiety from the elevator increased. Feeling trapped, she wanted to run. And her gut—oh, Lord—felt like the breeding ground for Mexican jumping beans. Would she ever remember this Tim Gardner? What if love never resurfaced? What should she do?

Taking her hand and nudging her to sit on the sofa, Tim settled alongside and released a long breath. "We've known each other all our lives, Dana. Please tell me you remember *something*."

She shook her head. Glancing down at their joined hands, she fought the urge to yank hers free. The man made her feel too uneasy with all his touching. "Do I have family?"

"Your mom and dad. Me. Some aunts, uncles, and cousins. You're not alone." He patted her hand. "Once we're home, I'll take you to the best doctor in Pittsburgh."

Even his hand felt like a cold fish slapping her skin. She peeked toward the windows to see if Lance loitered nearby. Hell, he should be in here with her. He was her safety net and the man who provided the calm she craved. *I'm being unjustifiably critical.* Tim deserved a chance. She caught sight of a brown head popping from the children's box—a teddy bear. "Do I have pets?"

"No, I'm allergic."

Holy crap. Brows rising, she faced him. "We live together?"

"Well, no." Gaze focused on the floor, he coughed. "Your parents are against any cohabitation plans."

A puzzling response. Since when did parents dictate living arrangements for two engaged adults?

He shifted on the cushion. "You travel too much for pets, Dana. Once we're married, you agreed to cut areas of your busy schedule to raise a family." Meeting her gaze, he squeezed her hand then glanced down and gasped. "Where's your ring?" Leaping to his feet, he ran to the door and threw it open with a loud bang. "Detective, get in here!"

His sharp tone attracted the attention of every cop passing. Several turned from the vending machines and approached the windows.

Minus his overcoat and waving aside his fellow officers, Lance limped inside. "What's the matter?"

"Her engagement ring is missing."

"So are her laptop and camera equipment, none of which she can describe."

Red-faced, Tim clenched his fists. "I bought her a fourteen thousand dollar ring."

Frowning, Lance leaned on his cane. "Then, I'm glad you're here to describe everything. Come with me. I'll put you together with the larceny detectives."

After Tim and Lance left, Dana stared at the open door. More confusion than ever seeped into her brain. An expensive engagement ring couldn't be purchased with pocket change, so her impression of Tim having money was dead on. Since she still wore her overcoat, she fingered the edging. At a guess, good quality wool. And the suit she packed into her luggage had the feel of expensive jersey. Maybe she had money, too.

A few minutes later, Lance returned alone.

Smirking, he rested his butt onto the fat arm of the sofa, facing her. "You were wearing an expensive engagement ring, Dana. Tim's calling the jeweler for the diamond's registration number." He tilted his head. "Any memories popping up?"

"Nothing. I'm frustrated and disappointed." Shoulders slumping, she bent over, grasped both sides of her hair, and tugged. "My life is a mess." Dropping her hands, she straightened and shot him a glance. "Tim acts like an important man."

"Yeah, funny that."

The strange modulation in his voice surprised her. She studied him. "You're hiding something. What's his age?"

"Your age—thirty-two."

She gaped. "But he looks so young."

His smirk returned. "So do you. I thought you were a kid."

Under different circumstances, she'd consider his comment a compliment, but something deep inside bothered her. What attracted her to Tim? His size? Money? Was she so hard up she settled for a guy whose voice shook the tiny hairs on the back of her neck?

Tim re-entered the room, lips pursed. With a gaze flashing, he locked onto Lance. "Don't you have bad guys to catch?"

Lance waved aside the comment and remained on the arm rest.

Growling, Tim stopped in front of Dana. "I described everything. The cop had the gall to say the thief probably re-cut and remounted the diamond by now. He's talking fourteen grand down the toilet— thanks to this inept police department." He stuffed his hands into his jacket pockets. "The camera was expensive, too…the best money can buy." He took her hand and urged her to rise. "We can't do anything more here, so we might as well go. If we're lucky, we'll be home in time to join your folks for dinner. I'll call and tell them we're coming." Releasing her hand, he extracted his cellphone from the jacket's inside pocket.

Panic choked her airway. Clutching her throat, Dana shook her head. "I can't go anywhere with you. I don't know you."

Fingers poised over his phone's keypad, he stared. "You can't stay here. You belong with me."

Jutting her chin, she folded her arms across her chest. "At the moment, I belong to no one."

Tim cocked a brow. "You know that statement isn't true."

Lance tapped his cane on the floor. "What's the hurry, Mr. Gardner? The more you push, the more uncomfortable she'll be."

Glaring, he huffed. "Her father wants her home."

Yeah, a father she couldn't remember. Did Tim intend to drag her out of the precinct? Then what? And why wasn't her father with Tim? Maybe his face would jar a few memories. Tim's sure as hell didn't.

Lance scratched his ear. "Yes, you mentioned her old man already. However, she is the only one who can provide details about her assault. We haven't any viable leads, and whatever she provides will be a tremendous help." He leaned on the cane. "Besides, she's smack in the middle of a double-homicide investigation."

Gasping, Tim grabbed her arm. "Dana, is this true?"

Disliking the tightness of his grip, she uncrossed

her arms and yanked free. "Unfortunately, yes."

Tim's gaze shot from her to Lance. "Her father will say something about all this. He's an important man in Pittsburgh."

Dana started. *He is*? Too important to take a ride with Tim? She shook herself and, with two fingers, tugged Tim's jacket sleeve. "Take it easy. They're hoping some memories return, and I'll provide clues. Good cops are on the case." She dropped her hand.

"Like *him*?" Tim thumbed a gesture at Lance. "The guy's walking around with a cane. He's a damn invalid."

Holy shit, if looks could kill... Lance's gaze cut Tim into pieces. All six foot two of him stood and stretched to full height, like a bear on its hind legs. And Tim, no taller than Dana, hardly paid Lance a second glance. Dana stepped in front of Tim. "That comment was cruel. Detective Barnes has a bullet hole in his leg and is on medical leave, but he's helping me all the same. Without him, I'd still be on the street, possibly dead."

Sneering, he shot Lance a sideways look. "All right, I'm sorry."

Yeah, he looked real sorry. *Why the hell am I engaged to a man with such a large chip on his shoulder?*

Tim again grabbed Dana's hand. "Let's go to your hotel to talk. In private."

Why must this man always latch onto me? One might think her a child unable to fend for herself. Again, she jerked her hand from Tim's grip. "I'm not in a hotel. I'm with Detective Barnes."

Head snapping, Tim gaped. "You're staying with

him?"

Back stiffening, she lifted her chin. "He was kind enough to take me in."

"Take you in?" He threw his hands in the air and paced a circle in the small lounge. "I don't believe this. Not only have you lost memories, but your common sense as well." Pausing to pinch two fingers on the bridge of his nose, he dropped his hand and faced her. "You're a PhD living with a lowlife, Dana. This situation can't be good for your reputation." Sighing, he approached and took her by the shoulders. "He's taking advantage of you, honey. None of this stuff had to happen if I accompanied you on your trips." He caressed her arms. "From this point on, I go with you."

Grateful for the overcoat to shield his touch on her skin, she narrowed her gaze. "Unless some memories return, I won't be traveling anywhere." Tim insulted—not once, but twice—the man who helped her, the very man who still stood like an angry bear ready to pound his victim into the ground. Lips tight, she backed away. "Common sense told me to trust the detective. I feel more comfortable with him than I do you."

Stepping alongside, Lance patted her shoulder but directed his gaze at Tim. "We couldn't put Dana on the street to fend for herself, Mr. Gardner. Her concussion and memory loss places her in a vulnerable state. If she wants to stay longer with me, she's more than welcome. And don't worry." He thrust his face close to Tim's. "We lowlifes know our boundaries."

"You are not a lowlife." Dana stomped a foot. The whole conversation was giving her a headache.

A red flush rose onto Tim's cheeks. Fists tight, he whirled to face Dana. "I can't allow you to stay another night with a strange man. You're my fiancée, and your proper place is by my side." He ran fingers through his hair. "Look. To ease your mind, we'll use *two* hotel rooms."

Dana locked gazes with Lance. Did he want her to accept the offer? *Tell me something, damnit. I'm pleading.*

Lance flashed his sexy, little smile.

Her stomach somersaulted. She'd rather stay with Lance than go to a hotel with bossy Tim Gardner. She barely tolerated the man.

Again thumping his cane, Lance faced Tim. "We have only your word she is your fiancée, Mr. Gardner. I'd like to see a copy of the announcement from a newspaper, or perhaps a photo of her in your wallet or on your cellphone."

Tim dropped his jaw. Shaking himself, he slapped his lips shut then whipped out his phone. "Yeah, I have a picture. I didn't think to keep the paper printout." Scrolling through, he stopped and shoved the phone in Lance's face.

"That's from her website." Lance twisted his lips to the side. "I'm talking a lovey-dovey kind of photo."

Gaze darting from Lance to Dana, he shook his head. "I don't have one."

"And why not? You're engaged. If I were in your shoes, I'd carry a half dozen or more to show the world." Sighing, he shifted on his cane. "You see my problem, Mr. Gardner? I can't let her walk away from police protection if you're a virtual stranger."

A warm glow settled around her heart. Lance's words created the overwhelming calm she needed. He could have passed her off to Tim, but he kept his promise.

Tim's nostrils flared. "I'll call her parents and tell them I'm having trouble with a big asshole. You can deal with her father yourself." Lips twisting into a sneer, he snorted. "You don't want to mess with Howard Null, Detective."

"I'll welcome the challenge, Mr. Gardner. Tell him to bring a family photo to prove who they are. Until I know Dana is in safe hands, I won't release her."

Jaw twitching, he glared. "You can't hold her against her will."

Brows raised, Lance cocked his head toward Dana. "Are we holding you against your will?"

She stepped closer and smirked. "Hardly."

A red flush brightened Tim's cheeks, and he stepped into Lance's space. "You have no right to do this."

Lance wagged a finger. "In the eyes of the law, I have every right." Bending, he leaned on his cane. "You display a volatile temper, Mr. Gardner. If I released Doctor Null and something happened, I'd be negligent. I don't care to mar my spotless record." Straightening, he withdrew his wallet from his rear pants pocket. Opening the flap, he extracted a business card, grabbed a pencil from a side table, and scribbled on the reverse side. "My address and cell number." He thrust the card at Tim. "Let me know when her parents arrive."

Dana watched the men's facial exchanges with something akin to awe. Lance remained calm with an air of indifference while fire shot straight out of Tim's eyes. Volatile temper, indeed.

Snatching the card from Lance, he flashed his gaze

toward Dana. "Doesn't your cell work, or did they steal your phone, too?"

"My phone's at Lance's place, charging." She'd forgotten to grab the device before she left this morning. Not like she had anyone to call.

"You should carry your phone at all times, Dana." Grunting, he jerked his head toward Lance. "I've no intention of calling him. I'll communicate with you alone." He glanced at the address on the card. "I'll take your parents to his place and let your father ream his ass." He faced Lance. "Does this damn city have a five-star hotel?"

Lance cocked a brow. "If you're talking expensive, yes. Right off the interstate. If you drove down East Baltimore Street, then you should backtrack the same way. You'll see the hotels."

Narrowing his gaze, Tim jabbed a finger on Lance's chest. "I know what you're doing. She's my fiancée, and I intend to keep it that way. Hands off, hear me?"

While expanding his chest, Lance glanced at Tim's finger. "You shouldn't touch a police officer, Mr. Gardner."

Tim dropped his hand. "You stay away from her."

"Whatever you say."

Whirling, Tim grabbed her shoulders and planted a kiss on her lips.

Damn this man and his grabby hands. She pushed on his chest. As before, she felt nothing, except for repulsion. Shouldn't she, at least, remember his lips?

Gaze intense, Tim held her at arm's length. "Don't you dare let him touch you. You're mine. He's a leech after your money." He dropped his hands. "I'll call you later." He stormed out of the lounge and toward the elevators.

Brows high, she turned to Lance. "I have money?"

He laughed, gaze twinkling. "Dana, you are so precious."

She went from cute to precious, which, theoretically, had the same meaning. But hearing Lance use the word gave her a warm feeling to counter the coldness she felt near Tim. What's more, the tension of meeting Tim hadn't helped the throb developing in her head. With two hands, she rubbed her temples. "I don't like him."

"Don't pass judgment too quickly. Most men have this caveman mentality toward their women."

Meeting his gaze, she frowned. "You mean act like an ass?"

"Sure. Male possessiveness." He grinned.

Aw, he was precious, too, but she still wanted to punch a wall. "I'm not an object to be possessed."

Georgette strolled into the lounge. "We're all objects of possession, dear. Male or female, makes no difference. We mark territory with engagement rings or wedding bands." She waved her left hand. "All symbols of keep away. A fourteen grand engagement ring says a lot." Grunting, she crossed her arms over her chest. "Not bad for a man with no job."

Lance shot Georgette a glare.

"Oops. You haven't told her?" She snickered. "Sorry, Dana. Lance asked me to check on Tim." She leaned against a table cluttered with puzzle pieces and nodded at her partner. "Shall I fill her in?"

"You better," he growled.

Chuckling, Georgette pushed away from the table

and approached. "Tim lives with your parents, Dana. Yet, you own a condo on the other side of the Allegheny River. From what I can tell, you're quite a distance from your parents. This tidbit of information struck both of us as odd."

The scenario sounded strange to her, too. Shouldn't she be the one living with her parents? She tapped the side of her head. "I need my memories. None of this makes sense." Dropping her hand, she slid a sideways glance at Georgette. "And you said he doesn't have a job? How's he paying for a five-star hotel?"

Lance shrugged. "I suspect your parents will foot the bill. Or you. Tim hasn't any type of recordable income. No bank account either."

Good grief. Was this information for real? Why would she marry a moocher? And Tim lived with her parents. Why?

Too much was missing.

She shifted her gaze between the two partners. "Maybe I threw him out."

Lance shook his head. "He's used your parents' address for years, Dana. Whatever is going on doesn't sound kosher. I want some concrete answers before I'm comfortable putting you in his care."

Even acting in a professional capacity, Lance looked out for her. Because of him, the warm glow returned. If her memories refused to resurface, well, so what? A future with Tim didn't thrill her. She'd rather strike out on her own. Although... They were only engaged, not married. She could end their relationship. He might cry and beg, and too bad. Maybe some day, she'd remember why she accepted his ring.

Lance's cellphone rang. Excusing himself, he

limped toward the door and answered then whirled back. "Well, of course, her cell clicked to voicemail. The damn phone's charging at my place. No, we're still at the precinct." Glancing at Dana, he rolled his eyes. "Yes, all right, I'll tell her." He disconnected. "Tim called your parents. They're flying out of Pittsburgh and will be here by this evening."

A low chuckle rumbled in Georgette's throat. "I noticed my partner sent Tim way across town when a five-star hotel is right around the corner."

Dana snapped her gaze toward Lance. Was he inconveniencing Tim just to spend more time with her? True or not, the thought lifted a heavy weight from her chest, and she suppressed a smile. Whatever happened tonight, she'd have Lance by her side.

Chapter Fifteen

Dana no sooner entered Lance's condo when her cellphone played a series of bell tones from the spare bedroom. Since she knew no one on her contact list except Tim, she took her time heading to the night table where the device rested. As expected, the ringing stopped. Looking at the display, she sighed at the voicemails waiting. Granted, twenty-two calls accumulated by the time power returned to the phone, but these last seven were from this morning. While shaking her head, she returned to the living room to hang her coat. "Seven voicemails, all from Tim. Can you believe this guy?"

Without answering, Lance took her coat and hung it with his own in the closet.

Ever since he left the precinct, he'd become quiet. Not like she blamed him. The news about Tim having no job and living with her parents made no sense whatsoever. If Tim lost his job, wouldn't he move in with his fiancée? Or his own parents, wherever they might be? Right now, she had too many confusing facts for her befuddled brain.

After closing the closet door, Lance limped toward the kitchen. "How about some spaghetti and sausages for supper?"

She followed. "Spaghetti is fine. I'll skip the sausage." She stopped in the doorway. "I can make a salad."

"Sounds good."

Opening the refrigerator door, she rummaged through the contents. For a bachelor, the man kept a well-stocked kitchen, which she attributed to Thelma's influence. She found more than enough ingredients to create a tasty salad—romaine lettuce, tomatoes, carrots, black olives, and cucumbers. Two kinds of bottled dressing sat on the shelf in the door—Italian and French. Choosing the former, she placed her stash on the table with a chopping board and knife and set to work.

"I don't do this often, Dana." He turned on the burner under a saucepan.

"What's that?" She stretched for a salad bowl in an overhead cabinet.

Glancing over his shoulder, he shrugged. "Make dinner for a woman."

Well, yeah, sharing a home-cooked meal proved a tad more intimate than dining with takeout. She popped a black olive into her mouth and chewed—tender yet salty. Good. "Do you prefer the woman make you dinner?"

"No. I like to cook. Preparing food relaxes me."

"Ah, then you're not used to having a woman in the kitchen." She poised her chopping knife over the cucumber. "If I make you uncomfortable, I can put up my feet in the living room."

He slid a gaze to her face. "No. Stay."

Damn him. His gaze—sparkling or not—always weakened her knees. She couldn't explain her reactions, but whatever Lance triggered hadn't occurred with Tim. Deep in her heart, she belonged with Lance more than

Tim, and no amount of restored memory could convince her otherwise. While Lance flooded her with inner peace, Tim did just the opposite and aggravated the hell out of her. She couldn't imagine living the rest of her life with such a bossy man. In no time, she'd swallow antidepressants like candy.

Since she needed a utensil to toss the salad, she turned toward the drawer and collided into Lance as he stretched over her to retrieve a box of spaghetti from the cabinet above her head. The brick wall again. Only this time, his chest stopped her.

Their gazes locked, and her breath hitched. Heat flushed across her skin as unfamiliar sensations seized her heart, like a tug of war between want and reason. *What the hell is happening?* Thoughts of dragging him to a bed threatened to override common sense, and she struggled with so many rising doubts. Not of him, but herself and who she was. She had to resist temptation…somehow.

Her cellphone again played the now-familiar bell tones, and she knew instantly who called. *Perfect timing.* Sucking in a breath to get her racing heart under control, she backed away—right into the table. She whirled to catch the rolling tomato. Grimacing at another act of clumsiness, she headed for the door. "I better answer. Otherwise, he'll call all night." Leaving the tomato in the bowl, she ran to the bedroom and snatched the phone before the call clicked into voicemail. If anything, Tim's interruption allowed her a chance to rein in her emotions concerning that big hunk of meat in the kitchen. "Hello?"

"Where were you?"

His tone took her aback. She tightened her grip on

the phone. "In the kitchen. Am I allowed to eat?"

"I want you to carry your phone at all times. Is that clear?"

Was she always such a wuss and cowered whenever he spoke? Plain and simple, the man was a bully,

"Do you hear me, Dana?"

She stiffened her back. "Yeah, I hear you, and no, I won't carry my phone."

"Dana—"

"Stop bossing me around, Tim. What do you want?"

A long pause ensued. For all she cared, the man could froth at the mouth.

He cleared his throat. "Your parents chartered a jet. Neither one is happy with our situation."

She wasn't thrilled either, but Tim probably meant her being with Lance. From the sound of Tim's angry voice, she might be in for a good fight. But something he said… "Whoa, wait a minute. My parents chartered a jet? How much are they worth?"

"A ton, darling. Don't think for one second the detective doesn't know about your parents' bank account."

Her parents were wealthy? Was that the reason Lance allowed her to stay, for a chance at a monetary reward? Men sought an easy life as much as a woman. Hell, Anita Seeley married an old man for his money. Who's to say Lance Barnes wasn't licking his chops? *Oh, God, I hope not.* Her heart squeezed with the thought.

"Hey, you still listening?"

Swallowing more doubts, she shook herself. "Call

when they arrive."

"I'd rather the cop be somewhere else. I don't like his influence on you."

The man had nerve. "This is his home, Tim. We're the ones imposing. Besides, he's been the perfect gentleman."

Tim grunted. "We'll resolve this issue later."

He disconnected without so much as an *adios*.

Resisting the overwhelming urge to scream out her frustration, she threw the phone onto the bed and slipped all ten fingers into her hair. She tugged until a few roots snapped. Satisfied no clumps of hair accumulated between her fingers, she returned to the kitchen to the aroma of tomato sauce and sausages…and Lance's immediate calming effect.

While stirring a pot, he glanced over his shoulder. "Problem?"

She sucked in a shuddering breath. "I can't imagine how I got involved with a man like Tim."

"If you're engaged, you must love him."

"I keep telling myself that." After finishing the salad preparation, she gathered the hodgepodge of ingredients and restocked them in the fridge. Closing the door with a little more force than necessary, she whirled and jammed her fists on her hips. "I wonder if I've always been submissive to his bossiness."

With a stifled laugh, he tapped the spoon on the rim of the pot. "You're not submissive now. And after last night, I'd call you impulsive." Turning to her, he winked. "A nice impulsive."

"Why? Because I rubbed your leg?" She lifted two plates from the overhead cabinet.

"No, because you kissed me—twice."

The thought of his lips brushing hers warmed every inch of her skin. If he hadn't stopped her, she'd have continued all night. While setting the plates onto the table, she hid a smile. "You kissed me back."

"And I loved every second. Here, taste this. I added more garlic." With one hand cupped underneath, he held out the spoon.

She tasted the red sauce, and a hint of basil and roasted peppers intermingled with the garlic. She cocked a brow. "Not bad for out of a jar."

Removing the lid on a boiling pot of water, Lance dumped in the entire pound of spaghetti and stirred. "From the way he acts, Tim is used to bossing you around, Dana." He shot her a glance. "I liked the way you stood your ground."

Well, she wasn't in the mood to be a doormat. Maybe the bump on her head changed her from a submissive woman to one who stood on her own two feet. Even if she lost her memories forever, from here on, she'd be the latter—no matter what.

Clearing her throat, she shot him a sideways glance. "Did you know about my parents' financial situation?"

After adjusting the heat under the boiling water, he stirred the pasta. "George did a little snooping and discovered your father is a corporate bigwig in Pittsburgh, which made us both wonder why Tim lived with them. Without any recordable income, Tim could be the lawn boy or a servant of some sort." He met her gaze. "You have money of your own, Dana. You make three times my salary."

The fact bothered him. His shoulders stiffened, and he stirred the sauce as if his attention depended on its thickness. But three times his salary? Damn, uncovering her employment status just turned into a priority.

After dinner, she paced around the living room, constantly glancing at the wall clock. The damn batteries must be dead or ready to die. Maybe the clock hands were stuck. Tim called ages ago to say they were on their way, and she couldn't sit still. Would she know her own parents? What if her parents proved as big a disappointment as Tim? She would seriously consider jumping from Lance's fourth floor window.

Lance, with his slippered feet propped on the foot stool, stared at the TV while flipping channels with the remote. "Relax, Dana. They're your parents."

Easy for him to say. His whole world hadn't changed from a bop on the head. She stopped behind the sofa and stared at the back of his hair. "If they ask you to leave, please don't. I'm afraid to be alone with them." The pacing resumed.

"You might recognize them right off and go flying into their arms."

"I hope so." She paused to rub her temples. "Oh, hell, let me splash some cold water on my face."

The doorbell rang. Her gut jumped straight into her throat, and she whirled, half expecting the door to open on its own.

After rising and coming around to her side of the sofa, he took her by the shoulders. "Whatever happens, I'll be here."

Her heart swelled with gratitude. She had no memory of any man being so nice. Grimacing at the door, she bit her lip. "All right, I'm ready."

With a thumbs-up, he opened the door.

Professor Anthony Seeley stood on the threshold, looking as disheveled as earlier. She hadn't expected him, and from the raised brows on Lance's face, he hadn't either.

Seeley peered around Lance and caught her gaze. "I'm sorry to intrude, but I found the detective's address on the Internet. I want to talk to you before you return to Pittsburgh."

With a stern expression, Lance crossed his arms over his chest. "You could have called."

Dana almost laughed. The professor's bushy eyebrows fluttered, and the old man stepped back, as if noticing Lance in the doorway. Lance might be a big man, but the professor acted like he was the door.

Seeley cleared his throat. "What I say must be in person."

With a brow cocked, Lance glanced over his shoulder. "Dana?"

She couldn't imagine what brought the professor all the way to Lance's condo. He knew she had impaired memory—unless his memory proved twice as bad. With all the unanswered questions rolling around in her head, she didn't need Anthony Seeley to add more confusion. Sucking in a calming breath, she shrugged. "I guess."

Lance waved him in. "I can't take your coat, Professor. We're expecting Dana's family."

"Oh—yes…that's fine. I'll be brief." Stepping around Lance, he paused. "Will you allow us some privacy, young man?"

Coming alongside, Lance squeezed her shoulder. "I'll wait in the kitchen."

Dana shot him a not-too-far glare, and he winked

in response. She waited for him to hobble away before focusing on the professor. With a wave, she gestured toward the sofa. "Please, sit, Professor."

The old man approached and took her hand to urge her to sit with him. "Do you remember me yet?"

She didn't want to sit, but he nudged her onto the seat cushion and then inched closer as if her eyesight bordered on blindness.

His closeness was way too chummy for a man who just lost his wife. For all she knew, Anthony Seeley could be her grandfather. Fighting like mad not to jump to her feet, she shifted her butt on the cushion in a discreet attempt to place some distance between them. "Nothing has come back yet, sir."

Brows high, he straightened. "Sir? My word, woman, I'm Anthony. We're good friends and work well together." Clinching her hand, he closed the small gap between them. "I want you to join me at Johns Hopkins. You'd be a great asset to the department."

Dana gaped. "You're offering me a job?" She twisted her hand under his bony grip, but his fingers held fast. What was it with grabby men? First, Tim. Now, this old guy. The man she wanted to grab her and never let go was too damn noble.

"Oh, more than a job, my dear. With Anita gone, the house is empty. I want you to reside with me, be my assistant, and eventually take the Chair when I retire."

Reside, as in live in? Words eluded her. Instead, Dana blinked at the old man until finding her voice. "You've made quite an offer, Professor, but what about Babs? She's your assistant."

Seeley waved aside the comment and rubbed his knee against hers. "Babs is young and foolish. She'll move on." He placed Dana's hand in both of his. "Think about my offer, Dana. I'm in no hurry." His thumbs caressed her wrist while a tender gaze locked onto her face. "I've loved you for many years, my dear. Maybe in time, you'll grow to love me. Patience comes with age, and I'm a patient man."

With a blank expression, she stared at the man with a whiff of salami on his breath. Her gut churned and threatened to upchuck her wonderful dinner. She swallowed hard. "You love me?"

"Oh, yes." Loosening his grasp, he patted her knee. "I realize we have quite an age difference, but I can provide for you and make you happy. Children are not out of the question either." Smiling, he released her hand. "We talk a common language, Dana. Our dinner conversations will be quite stimulating."

Was he for real? Had she given this man encouragement? When push came to shove, she was an engaged woman. Maybe he didn't know—more likely, he didn't care. But one important detail bothered her most. Could she be the professor's motive for killing his wife? Unable to breathe or think, Dana jumped to her feet. She needed distance to gather her thoughts, which were so jumbled she barely put them together. This old man couldn't be serious, right? *He's senile.* Turning toward him, she forced a smile. "Professor, I don't know what to say. I've no way of answering unless my memory returns." As good an excuse as any.

He huffed out a breath. "Yes, quite, quite." Nodding, he stood. "I never loved Anita. I pampered her as I did all my wives. You will be the first to be an equal." With one finger, he nudged his glasses up his nose. "My feelings for the women in my past are nothing compared to what I feel for you, Dana." With his gaze locked onto her face, he approached. "Give my offer careful consideration. My position at the university and my money should help influence your decision." He kissed her lightly on the cheek and, with a shy wave, left the condo.

Too stunned to move, Dana stared at the closed door.

Lance strolled in.

She faced him. "Did you hear?"

"I'm a cop, Dana. I eavesdrop." Grinning, he tugged on an ear. "I'll admit, I almost hit the kitchen floor."

"Maybe he's looking for a nursemaid." She shifted her gaze to the front door. "I don't know whether to feel insulted or flattered." Shaking her head, she met his gaze. "He didn't ask if you and I were…um, you know."

"Fooling around?" Gaze twinkling, he chuckled. "I suspect he's a man used to getting his way. I'm sure he'd have you sign a list of stipulations for the marriage." He resettled on the sofa, grabbed the remote, and flipped through a few channels.

Frowning, she watched the television flip from one channel to the next without a pause. How could any program catch his interest at that speed? If she stared any longer, she might go into an epileptic fit. Shifting her gaze to the floor, she swallowed the sour taste in her mouth as the earlier question returned. She winced. "Do you think he murdered his wife for me?"

He paused from his channel surfing. "I don't have all the details on the case." He shot her a quick glance. "In the morning, I'll relay this turn of events to

George."

Clasping her arms around her torso, she shuddered. How the hell could he stay so calm? Well, yeah, sure, none of the circumstances involved him. Everything pertained to her. And where was Tim? Were they lost and driving aimlessly around the city? "I've had too much thrown at me in one day. I don't know how much more I can take."

Chapter Sixteen

While Dana made a mad dash to the bathroom, Lance jabbed the remote's channel button as if the batteries lacked juice. Not like he had any particular program in mind. Anything would do to take his mind off Dana and the suitors lining up for a piece of her ass. She deserved a real man—not a boy with a chip on his shoulder wider than the Golden Gate Bridge and definitely not an old man like Seeley with one foot in the grave.

A glance at the wall clock revealed the time as eight-thirty-five. He should get a grip on his emotions before the friggin' entourage arrived. Could his mind be any more of a jumbled mess? Nothing but conflicting thoughts collided to make him question his sanity. Like relief when she'd be on her way and out of his life, followed by regret for the same reason. Disappointment, too, clouded his heart because she chose a man like Tim when so many options were available. Her parents' visit might be the trigger to restore Dana's memories, and she'd live happily ever after with the man she promised to marry—assuming she recalled why.

When an irritating commercial blasted the sound several decibels higher, he clicked off the TV and tossed the remote onto the coffee table. Not a damn worthwhile program on anyway. Like he gave a shit who lived with whom or what bug the jungle gang ate this week. If he was a drinking man, he'd guzzle half a bottle of whiskey out of sheer frustration. He rubbed the nape of his neck.

Dana needed to go. His attraction toward her grew every second they spent together, and he had neither the time nor patience for a relationship. A homicide detective worked long hours to follow clues before leads grew cold. Because of such dedication, cops suffered a higher than normal divorce rate, and he'd rather not become another statistic. Besides, right or wrong, Tim put the ring on her finger.

The doorbell rang.

Dana ran from the hallway and froze in the middle of the living room, looking like a frightened rabbit with green eyes wide to popping, her gaze riveted on the front door. Standing, he met her halfway and placed his hands on her shoulders. "Stay calm and don't raise your hopes, okay?"

"I want this meeting over and done." Shifting her gaze to his face, she forced a smile. "Thank you, Lance…for everything."

The doorbell rang again. Then, a third time. Rolling his eyes, Lance hobbled over to answer.

With brows furrowed, Tim stood flanked by an older couple, all three of the same height. The man and woman were in their early sixties and well-dressed—the woman with a fur coat and the man in an expensive wool overcoat. The woman stared at Lance while chewing one corner of her mouth, but her husband sneered and checked his gold wristwatch.

Tim flashed Lance a smug look. "Meet Howard and Marta Null."

The twit neglected to mention Lance's name. Funny that. Without a word, Lance waved them in with no intention of asking them to sit or remove their coats. *Two can play this shitty game.*

Marta Null, a fiery redhead with too much jewelry around her neck and wrists, spotted Dana and rushed past Lance. "Sweetheart, what happened?" She wrapped her arms tightly around her daughter.

Dana stood like a stick, arms straight by her sides, and her face pale. Her gaze darted to all three faces in rapid succession.

Pouting, Mrs. Null held her at arm's length. "You recognize your mother, right?"

Dana shook her head.

Her mother slapped a ring-covered hand over her mouth to stifle a cry.

Overcoat unbuttoned, Howard Null approached.

The stocky man had the appearance of a man straight out of a boardroom with an expensive silk shirt and tie under a tailored suit complete with a perfectly trimmed short beard to match his gray hair. The gold watch glistened with diamonds, and a do-as-I-say attitude emanated from a pair of shrewd green eyes— Dana's eyes. But hers were soft and beautiful, a pleasure to watch when a sparkle danced within them. Howard's gaze emphasized a hardness best kept inside a board room. Without saying a word, he repeated his wife's gesture of wrapping his arms around his daughter.

Dana remained stiff, as if frozen to the spot. Her gaze flitted from one face to the other, until a wide-eyed gaze locked onto Lance. He gave a slight nod in encouragement. Whether the gesture helped or not, he wasn't sure, but Howard noticed the brief exchange and frowned.

Releasing Dana, Howard turned to Lance. "Leave us."

"Sorry, sir." Lance positioned himself on Dana's right. "Since Baltimore PD entrusted me with the safety of your daughter, I can't leave. I will, however, stand off to the side."

In two strides, Tim placed himself on Dana's left and leered at Lance. "You're nothing but a cocky ass, you know that?" He reached for Dana's arm. "Pack your bags, sweetheart. We're leaving."

Retreating, she shook her head. "I'm not going anywhere. I don't know you people."

Standing together, with such young faces, Tim and Dana resembled high school teenagers with Mom and Dad close by as chaperones. Lance would bet any amount of money the couple would get carded well into their forties.

Slipping a hand inside his coat, Howard withdrew a photo and handed it to Lance.

Dana's graduation photo. All four of them in one picture. He hadn't any doubts about Dana's parents, but his heart sank nonetheless. Somewhere deep inside, he hoped to send them on their merry way.

Howard tapped the photo. "You asked for proof."

Yeah, proof. Lance handed the photo to Dana who held it with both hands, her gaze intent on the faces.

Grinning, Tim leaned close to her ear. "That's when you earned your PhD."

"Dana, sweetie." Marta patted her arm. "We want you under the care of the best specialist we can find. Your father sent inquiries across the country." She leaned close. "You must get better, honey. We have so much to do before the wedding. The event's set for May the first. Your father secured the country club, and I've all the invitations ready to mail. Plus, your dress fitting is next week, and we can't miss such an important appointment."

Tearing her gaze from the photo, Dana gaped. "We're that far along?"

Lance's gut twisted. He envisioned a wedding hall full of overdressed people in gowns and tuxedos, crystal champagne glasses, and an orchestra...no, a damn philharmonic on stage. The crème de la crème would be in attendance with speeches galore to congratulate the newlywed couple. With an effort, he swallowed the acid rising from his stomach.

Marta stroked her daughter's hair. "You should put some foundation on your cheek scrape, dear. So unbecoming. And for the wedding, you must let your hair grow. We can make a nice arrangement with diamonds and pearls. Right, Tim?"

Tim grunted. "I always liked her hair long, but she cut it to spite me."

Long, short, or bald, no hairdo could diminish the effect of Dana's gorgeous eyes. Lance smiled to himself.

Howard snapped his fingers. "Let's not forget Washington, D.C. They require an immediate answer. She's already wasted enough time."

Gasping, Marta clamped onto Dana's arm. "Honey, you must answer their letter before they give the job to someone else." Releasing Dana, she turned to her husband. "Oh, Howard, what should we do? We can't let such an opportunity pass because of a bump on the head."

Gaze darting from one face to the other, Dana shifted on her feet. "What job?"

Placing a palm over her heart, Marta sighed. "Honey, the president's translator. The job's so prestigious." Her face beamed. "Just think, you can stop this silly lecture circuit, marry Tim, and have lots of babies. He's already contacted several realtors in the D.C. area." She clasped her hands together, closed her eyes, and tilted her head toward the ceiling. "He'll buy a house big enough for us to stay while we attend all the presidential galas. I know—" Whirling toward her husband, she tugged on his coat sleeve. "*I'll* answer the letter. They won't know the difference. Before everything is said and done, her memories will return."

You hope. Lance shook his head. Something told him they didn't give a damn about her assault except for the inconvenience to their own schedules. How had Dana tolerated these people? All right, yes, they were family, but what compelled them to run Dana's life as if she had a simpleton's brain? And why the hell did Tim live with her parents? *Yes, something is off kilter.*

Gaze narrowed, Dana glared at her mother. "Your returning an acceptance letter is not a wise move. What if I don't want the job?"

"Not want the job?" Marta tsk-tsked. "Oh, no, honey, the position is practically yours. You can't refuse." She patted her daughter's arm. "Everything will be all right, dear. Wait and see. In the meantime, I'll accept the position for you."

Resisting the urge to interfere, Lance watched this verbal exchange in silence since they chose to ignore his presence. On several occasions, Dana glanced his way with a gaze flicking between anger and uncertainty. Her fear disappeared. She stood ready to hold her ground against three bullies, and his chest swelled with pride. Catching her gaze, he smiled while rolling his eyes. She responded by curling one corner of her luscious mouth.

With a back going ramrod straight, Tim flicked his gaze between Dana and Lance. Sneering, he grabbed Dana's arm. "Pack your stuff. We'll stay at the hotel tonight, and I won't take no for an answer. Tomorrow, we'll leave for home."

Dana jerked her arm from his grasp. "No."

With a huff, Howard stepped toward his daughter. "The photo proves we're family, Dana. Stop this nonsense and get your luggage."

Marta nudged Dana's arm. "Honey, you can't stay here. This…place isn't quite your standards." Crinkling her nose, she scanned the living room.

Lance followed her discriminating gaze. Everything looked okay. Thelma kept the condo clean. No cockroaches roamed after dark, and no bedbugs crawled in the mattress. The furniture wasn't the highest quality, mostly self-assembly from the home improvement store, but adequate for his needs. He cleared his throat. "This *place* is my home, Mrs. Null."

Tim tugged on his pants belt. "I told you he's a lowlife. Everything in this room is cheap crap."

Green eyes flashing, Dana glared at her family. "Don't you dare insult the man who helped me. As far as I'm concerned, I don't see a damn thing wrong."

Marta grimaced. "Of course, you don't, dear. You're not yourself—and please watch your language. We taught you better."

While shaking his head, Howard approached Lance. "What progress have you made with her case?"

"Hardly anything, sir."

"Why not? Her laptop and camera equipment are worth thousands and her ring fourteen grand."

Crossing his arms over his chest, Lance faced the older man. "Since Dana has no memory of her assault, she couldn't provide any specific details. Our best help came from Tim who described the items in detail several hours ago. Once her memory returns, she might provide a description of her assailant."

Jaw muscles twitching, Howard pivoted toward Tim. "I'll give you the money to buy another ring. With the police report, you can file a claim with the insurance company."

Grasping Howard's hand with both his own, Tim pumped. "Thank you, sir. I appreciate your help."

All three faced Dana, like a firing squad without the rifles.

As if someone threw a switch, Dana's expression changed to stone. A pink flush replaced the paleness in her cheeks, and she jutted her chin, every part of her body rigid.

Her gaze hard, she leveled a glare at all three. "I'm not leaving yet."

Marta waved aside her protest. "Be sensible, dear. You can't stay here. You're an engaged woman, and he, of course, is not your fiancé."

Nudging Tim with an elbow, Howard nodded toward the hallway. "Go grab her things. I assume you'll find them in a bedroom."

Yo, whoa! Now, they crossed the line. The tiny hairs on his forearms prickled. They might push Dana around but not him, and especially not in his home. Lance held out his palm to stop Tim's forward movement. "In the eyes of the law, you cannot force an adult to go somewhere against her will."

Marta and Howard spoke at once. "She's our daughter! We have every right."

"She's a thirty-two-year-old professional and not a child to order around. I recommend giving her another day or so to assimilate what happened tonight. You threw a lot of information her way."

Tim glowered. "She's not herself and needs medical attention. She isn't competent enough to make decisions."

"Hey! I'm standing right here." Dana spread her arms wide. "I'm not comatose, and I've been checked by a doctor. All I need is time."

Howard snorted. "We don't have time. Whether your memory returns or not, you will go through with the wedding."

"Like hell I will."

Go get 'em, Dana. Damn, he was proud. She stood her ground like a pro. But really now, was the man out of his friggin' mind? How could he force his daughter to marry a stranger? Granted, they weren't strangers before her assault, but everything about their verbal exchange disturbed Lance. Dana needed someone on her side, and he'd be damned to let them bully her into submission. After releasing a calming breath, he wagged a finger. "All three of you are pushing too hard."

Fists tight by his sides, Tim stuck his face close, gaze glaring. "Since when does a lowlife cop think he's a psychiatrist?"

The hairs on Lance's head bristled. *Go on. Take a swing.* He'd jam Tim's arm between his shoulder blades until he screamed bloody murder. Fists on his hips, Lance puffed out his chest and stood with legs spread apart, his gaze matching Tim's. "My degree is in criminology, and I recognize what is going on here more than you realize." He slid his gaze from one face to the other. "Your main preoccupation centers on the disruption of some carefully pre-arranged plans. Not once have you expressed concern about Dana's injuries. She has a cracked skull and memory loss, and you're forcing wedding plans down her throat. How can you expect her to accept without protest?"

Marta stuck her chin into the air. "She's a good daughter and obeys her parents."

With a snort, Tim spread his arms outward. "I'll be damned. He has her brainwashed."

Struggling like mad not to throw these people out the door, Lance stepped alongside Dana. "Her injury set her back, but your main concern is to push plans she can't remember."

All three stared. Marta gaped, Tim sneered, and Howard glared. Hadn't anyone ever challenged them? Was their bossiness the reason Dana lived in her own condo while Tim stayed with her parents? Although, the scenario made no sense. These days, engaged couples lived together before the big day.

Tim gritted his teeth. "We won't get anywhere with *him* in the way." He faced Dana's parents. "Marta, Howard, you should return home. I'll stay until Dana comes to her senses."

Arms flaring, Marta paled. "But she *can't* stay here. Look at this place!"

Here we go again. He'd met her type before. Marta Null lived in a pristine home with perfect fixtures which no one could touch. Children were delegated to a basement, adults to a kitchen, while a living room had a look-but-don't-touch splendor to be admired and envied. *Time to knock them down a notch.* "I don't see anything wrong."

Growling, Tim took a position alongside Marta. "No, you wouldn't." He patted Marta's arm. "I'll stay and sleep on the couch."

"That's where I sleep." Lance shot a quick glance at Dana. A bold lie, of course. Anyone using the bathroom passed the two bedrooms along the way. But since their noses twitched at his living quarters, none would dare use his facilities.

Tim puffed out his chest. "Then, I'll sleep with my fiancée."

"Ha! No, you won't." Dana hurried to the other side of the sofa.

Following her, Tim reached for her arm. "Honey, I can't leave you alone with him."

Face tight, she glared at his hand and then crossed her arms over her chest. "You can, and you will, Tim."

The little man's cheeks glowed a deep red.

Twisting his mouth to the side, Howard studied his daughter but said nothing.

Marta—ah, well, poor Marta. Her mouth fell open and stayed locked in place.

Dropping her arms, Dana confronted Tim and, with a finger, jabbed on his chest. "You're leaving and taking my parents with you. Whether you stay in Baltimore or not is your own decision. Right now, I'm tired and heading for bed. Don't bother to call. If you do, I'll turn off the phone. When I'm ready, I'll let you know. Good night."

She stormed toward the bedrooms and slammed the door.

Lance smiled and faced the open-mouthed group. "I believe Dana has made her wishes quite clear." He waved toward the door. "Time to go, people."

Chapter Seventeen

The aroma of fresh-brewed coffee woke him, a rich and wonderful fragrance to activate visions of a coffee shop full of delectable pastries. Shaking away the vision, Lance rolled over to check the time on his digital clock. Two in the morning, and someone decided on a late-night coffee break? Groaning from the tantalizing smell, he buried his head under a pillow.

Three nights of interrupted sleep. If this pattern continued, he'd fall asleep at his desk the first week back on duty. But damn, the coffee aroma filtered through the pillow like the urn sat right beside his bed. Maybe it did. He popped open one eye and scanned the night table. Nope. Sighing, he swung his legs over the side of the bed, threw on his robe, and slid his bare feet into a pair of slippers. Stifling a yawn, he strolled into the hall.

A small night light from the bathroom gave sufficient glow to see. He could walk around blindfolded, but for Dana's sake, he inserted a socket light so she wouldn't bump into any walls. Hobbling toward her open door, he peeked into the dark room to find the bed empty. The hall bath was empty, too. With his mind racing through a half dozen possibilities— from her running after Tim to her hopping onto a bus to escape her overbearing parents—he limped toward the living room.

The image of last night's guests flashed before him. They stood like the three musketeers with swords ready to slash their way through Dana's resistance. Were they always so adverse to her wishes? If so, she fought a never-ending battle alone, even against her fiancé. Once Dana retreated toward her bedroom, they turned their venom onto Lance. Tim and Howard threatened him with all kinds of lawsuits, which, of course, had no validity. Dana chose to stay, and as an adult, she had every right to refuse their demands. With assurances to keep them abreast of any new developments, he finally pushed them out the door.

All right, where is she? Since a brighter-than-usual light glowed from the kitchen, he stepped through the doorway to see Dana curled onto a table chair. Her beautiful green eyes stared into a steaming mug while a stony expression covered her face. The look was so unexpected, his heart lurched.

I'm getting soft. Having her in his condo and sharing his space lured him into a world he had yet to explore. Never once had he considered a life with a woman. Overnight guests stayed on occasion but never beyond breakfast. Dana became an actual live-in, albeit temporary. Yet, he felt comfortable with her, which, in his book, was unusual. Sure, this beautiful and smart woman depended on him, but once her memories returned, she'd resume life as usual. Maybe then, she'd figure out why she agreed to marry an ass like Tim.

He cleared his throat. "Coffee is not what you drink if you want to sleep." Some people argued the point. Georgette, for one. The damn woman drank gallons of high-test and still zonked out in seconds.

Her gaze blank, Dana quirked her lips. "My

memories are back."

Something told him the news hadn't flushed her with happiness. She should be jumping for joy, not looking like an emotionless void. He stuffed his hands into his robe pockets. "Want to talk?"

In answer, her gaze drifted to the mug.

Lance strolled to the counter, grabbed a mug, and poured a cup of coffee. His hand shook. The real Dana Null was about to emerge, and he wasn't sure what to expect. Would she be as snobby as her family and consider a cop as lowlife—as Tim so blatantly defined his profession? In a way, he hoped so. She'd be out the door faster than a speeding bullet. With cup in hand, he leaned against the counter and sipped.

A half-smile touched her lips, and she nodded toward his cup. "You won't sleep either."

"Then, we'll be awake together." He extended a hand. "Let's talk in the living room."

With her lips pressed tight, she took his hand and stood.

Something very fragile struck him, or maybe the word defeated described her best. For a short time, she faced her foes with head high, but now, a vulnerability covered her like a shroud. He had to resist the urge to yank her into his arms and soothe her. Right or wrong, she belonged to another man.

"Thank you for lying about sleeping on the sofa."

Smirking, he squeezed her fingers. "I didn't want Tim here either." Releasing her hand, he turned on a lamp by the sofa then pointed to the cushions. "Sit and talk, Dana. Tell me why you're so sad."

She curled into the corner and, as before, stared into her mug.

He always admired how a woman folded her limbs close to her body, like a spring fitting snugly into its slot. The ability made a woman special, along with the fragility inherent to her gender. Even George. As big and strong as she appeared, she melted in the arms of her husband. Lance settled on the opposite end of the sofa. "What's the matter, Dana? Most amnesiacs express happiness with the return of their memories."

She snorted. "If they're nice ones, you mean." She sipped her coffee then met his gaze. "When Tim and my parents stood united against me, I experienced the proverbial life flashing before my eyes. My three-against-one life, Lance, like a bad dream over and over again."

To keep her talking, he withheld any expression of opinion. "Go on."

She gulped the last of her coffee and stared into the empty mug. "Tim and I grew up together. He lived next door, and his parents and mine socialized—or hobnobbed, if you prefer the word." With a lopsided grin, she cocked her head. "My parents came on pretty strong toward you."

"That they did." He couldn't help but smile. "I take a lot of shit from a lot of people, Dana. Your parents and Tim were a piece of cake."

Sucking in a shuddering breath, she toyed with the edge of her robe. "Anyway, when Tim's parents died in a plane crash, Tim moved in with us. We were the same age and became like brother and sister. Neither of us had another sibling so we turned into best friends and always looked out for each other." She shifted on the seat. "We attended the same schools and functions, but our senior prom became the turning point for me." A lazy smile curled her lips. "Charlie Denison asked me to be his date, and I floated on cloud nine. But Tim went ballistic." The smile faded. "He said I was *his* date then ran to my parents for reinforcement. The three of them hounded me until I relented." She released a sick, little laugh, all the while shaking her head.

"As the years passed, my parents pushed us to marry. Tim liked the idea because whatever my parents said, he obeyed. I fought against the entire concept." She traced a finger along the handle of the mug. "I planned to finish my doctorate and build my translation business. Tim never pursued a career. He graduated high school and worked odd jobs. He stopped working when my dad promised him an allowance." Releasing a puff of air, she met his gaze. "Well, I achieved my doctorate, and they relentlessly pushed for marriage."

She uncurled her legs to place her mug on the coffee table. Shooting him a sideways glance, she shrugged. "I've no intention of marrying Tim. I love him like a brother, nothing more."

Relief swept through him faster than a tornado through the open plains. But despite her declaration, his gut twisted with tension. He slipped his coffee. Gaze narrowed, he studied her. "A fourteen grand engagement ring is a huge commitment, Dana. A man doesn't buy an expensive piece of jewelry unless he's certain the woman will accept." Most men, anyway. The jury was still out on Tim and his ability to pay for such a ring on his "allowance."

Dana's lips spread into a wry grin. "The ring wasn't stolen. I've stored it in a safe deposit box from the day it was given to me. And Tim couldn't afford the ring. My mother paid. She told him I deserved nothing less."

Her words hardly made sense. Was he, in fact, hearing of the most extreme case of emotional abuse? "What about the wedding date and invitations, your gown fitting, and country club? In my opinion, your nuptial preparations are on a traditional path."

She shook her head. "Hard to believe, but they're doing everything without me. I've told them a hundred times no. I don't care how much they prepare. I *will not* marry Tim!" She shot to her feet and paced.

Lance chewed the inside of his cheek until he clamped a little too hard on the soft tissue and drew blood. *Great*. Nothing beat blood mixed with coffee. He followed her agitated steps. "Dana, this whole story sounds preposterous. They can't force you to walk down the aisle."

With a fiery gaze, she turned. "Oh, but they're doing their best. That night, before I left my hotel room for ice, I had another big argument with my mother. My father's bribing me and Tim with a huge endowment. Tim, naturally, is ecstatic." Growling, she stopped to pull her hair. "No matter what I say, they're convinced I'll change my mind and see the benefits of marrying Tim. So, of course, the wedding plans are proceeding as if I'll suddenly agree. Can you believe they had the gall to post an official announcement in all the newspapers?" Her shoulders sagged.

Staring, Lance fell back against the cushion. He'd heard a lot of strange stories in his career, but Dana's deserved the spot at the top of the list. In this day and age, how could parents coerce their child to marry against her will? The whole damn premise sounded so stone-age. "I'm having trouble absorbing this story,

Dana."

"It gets worse." Lips pouting, she again paced. "I've dated off and on over the years, but nothing amounted to a long-term relationship. Every man I found interesting walked away without explanation. Their desertion flooded me with an incredible inferiority complex. My parents insist I'm undateable."

His breath caught. What more must this woman endure? Her parents used everything in their power to control their daughter, even to the point of dissuading her from dating. *Undateable, my ass.* Before he snapped the mug's handle in two, he slipped the cup onto the coffee table and flexed his fingers. What he wouldn't do to grab her now, this second, and kiss her senseless. He coughed. "You're beautiful enough to turn any man's head, Dana."

She stopped pacing and stared, mouth agape. After a slow blink, she slapped shut her mouth. "Thank you. I don't hear such a compliment often enough."

Hell, hadn't she looked in the mirror lately? She was the embodiment of beauty and brains wrapped into a petite body. If given the chance, he'd horse-whip her mother and father. But why such determination to browbeat their daughter into submission? What could they gain from such a union? Fighting a wave of chest tension, he passed his hand through his hair and then faced her. "Have you considered the possibility your parents worked to destroy your confidence so Tim is your only choice?"

Folding her arms across her chest, she wandered around the living room. "Yes, the notion occurred to me right after my PhD. They weren't happy with my achievement, just relieved when my studies ended.

They pushed for me to live with them, but my translation business grew exponentially after graduation. My client base allowed me to afford my own place."

What he wouldn't do to perform a little head bashing. Howard's head in one hand, Tim's in the other. Boom! Then, he'd slap some sense into Marta.

Dana stopped and performed a two-finger squeeze on the bridge of her nose. "Caffeine wasn't a real bright idea."

She looked beautiful in her long robe with the sash untied to show silk pj's. Her feet were bare and hair mussed, and even without makeup, she had the power to excite hormones into action. So, why had so many men deserted her without explanation? Were they all blind? Hell, he'd welcome her to his bed every single night.

He jerked. What in the world was he thinking? For years, he ended his work day at the tavern around the corner with a beer and a sandwich while watching a newscast on the overhead TV. He had no reason to break the habit anytime soon. Although, coming home to a home-cooked meal held a certain appeal, especially if the woman looked like Dana. *Get your head out of your ass, Barnes.* He fussed with his robe. "You have the guts to fight your three bullies, Dana. All you need is to stand your ground."

With a grimace, she faced him and shook her head. "I often wonder if having no family is better than what I have. I'm bound to alienate them."

"What about relatives?"

"Some, but I haven't seen them in years. Dad said they weren't at our social level."

What the hell was wrong with her old man? Every kid needed one cousin as a comrade-in-arms. Lance shook his head. "Best to stand alone than to be shoved into a loveless marriage. Your shotgun wedding, for whatever reason, is convenient for them, not you." He stretched an arm over the back of the sofa. "Any man who pushes for marriage knowing the woman isn't interested should have his head examined. Yes, I'm sure Tim wants the endowment, but his constant hounding won't get you down the aisle." He patted the cushion to his left. "Sit and tell me about the D.C. job. It sounds prestigious."

Frowning, she flopped onto the cushion and threw her head onto the backrest. "I'll be a translator for the president." Rotating her head, she met his gaze. "The state department approached me with the job offer and not the other way around."

"But?"

Looking away, she toyed with her robe's belt. "I'm not into prestige. My translation business gives me more work than I can handle. My lecture circuit drags me away from the computer and into fresh air, but traveling is a hassle I can do without." Shaking her head, she sighed. "The D.C. position requires a lot of travel—Air Force One, of course."

Arching her head over the sofa backrest, she covered her eyes with both hands. "I planned on moving out of Pittsburgh and closer to Penn State where I frequently lecture." She dropped her hands onto the seat cushions with a loud thump. "I haven't mentioned my plans to my parents or Tim, but no matter where I relocate, they'll hound me." She closed her eyes.

Long, dark lashes covered those expressive green eyes, but her full lips held his gaze. She had a subtle beauty impossible for any man to ignore. And why should he fight the feeling? She no longer had a fiancé…and no ties. Without thinking twice, he slipped his arms under her legs and lifted her onto his lap. Right or wrong, he wanted her.

****

Dana said nothing, not a yelp or a single word of protest. From the moment she spied him on the precinct steps, she longed for the comfort of his arms. She just *knew* he would calm her frazzled nerves, even for a little while. And damn, he felt so nice. She rested her head on his shoulder as if she'd done it a thousand times.

Last night, while standing before the intimidating threesome, she experienced a shock wave of emotions. All her memories returned, every single, sordid detail of her miserable life, from her parents' constant manipulation of her time to their accusations of disloyalty to Tim. They planned a wedding she didn't want and pushed her toward a job where they could hobnob with the political rich and famous. Ever since high school, her parents shot to pieces her every plan to make a life of her own. Sheer determination forced her to succeed and build a career with her language skills. One of these days, she'd tell the dynamic trio to take a hike.

Lance's large hand rubbed the back of her neck, and chills traveled the length of her spine. No other man ever took the time to cuddle her so tenderly, not even her father. All her life, she dated man-boys—whether within her social circle or not. They lived without goals or even a place of their own. Lance was a real man with a noble career and roots. Mommy and Daddy weren't standing on the sidelines dictating the rules or paying the rent. He exemplified a manhood she craved. Funny how blind she'd been all these years.

Her trust in him hit hard. With memories intact, she recognized the emptiness of her life, and an ache hit her chest like a tsunami. Her family couldn't be trusted with even the minor details of her schedule, because they'd do their damnedest to interfere. In their eyes, her every decision symbolized an erroneous path and gave them another reason to control her life. Unlike Tim, she supported herself from as early as graduate school and, despite their protests, succeeded in her chosen field.

But she had no personal life. Sure, she partied with girlfriends, but men entered and exited so fast she hadn't a chance to learn their last names. Lance became the first man to offer comfort and security without expecting anything in return. Like now. He had his arms wrapped around her and held her on his lap. She sucked in his spicy aftershave and let the enticing smell chase away all thoughts of her overbearing family.

"This is nice, Dana." He kissed the top of her head.

"Yes, it is." She melted against him and toyed with the edge of his robe. Her fingers itched to slip inside to feel the muscles on his chest. "Sitting here like this is perfect." Also torturous. To ask more of him would be wrong.

"I'm glad you're no longer engaged."

Something in his voice drew her gaze upward, but his eyes revealed nothing. The pulsing against her hip confirmed what her ears heard. Her heart rate kicked up a notch to match the hammering within his chest. *Well, hell.* Hiding a smile, she drifted her gaze to his mouth then traced a finger across his lower lip.

He clamped onto her hand and slipped her finger inside his mouth, never once removing his gaze from her face.

The sensation was incredibly erotic, yet she hesitated to respond, anxious to see what came next.

As if reading her mind, he flashed a gorgeous smile, showing beautiful white teeth. The pulsing against her hip increased, his gaze darkened, and a flood of heat accumulated between her legs.

Locking his hand behind her neck, he captured her mouth.

He tasted of coffee with a slight hint of peppermint from his toothpaste. Her lips separated to allow his tongue to probe, and a stream of warmth shot straight to her core. She relished the taste of him, and she slipped her hand beneath his robe to stroke the hard pectoral muscles. The firmness sent her hormones into a rage, and she squeezed, only to feel the pulsing against her hip turn into a full-blown rod. A shudder traversed through every nerve in her body.

He lifted his head to scan her face.

His blue eyes changed from the paleness of Robin's eggs to the deep blue of the ocean, and a powerful urge to take him on the sofa hit with an animalistic force, as if the bump on her head knocked inhibitions straight out her ears. Not like she practiced any Miss Morality code where men were concerned, but when men left without explanation, they shattered a woman's ego. For a long time, she accepted her mother's "undateable" label. But not anymore. Men like Lance were out in the world. All she had to do was open her eyes.

She stroked the soft stubbles on his chin. "At the hotel, do you remember asking what type of man I liked?" She brushed a finger along his bottom lip, and their gazes locked. "A man like you, Lance."

Chapter Eighteen

God help her. She hadn't realized how much she ached for this man. With the engagement issue out of the way, she cleared her mind and heart and gave herself complete freedom to explore. No guilt. She'd enjoy him for whatever short time remained.

Dana slipped her fingers into his hair and kissed with everything she had. Groaning in response, he stood with her in his arms and carried her to his bedroom. Despite extremities built like steel, he held her with a mixture of strength and tenderness which generated a sob from deep within her throat. He was so unlike any man in her life, and although marginally experienced with sex, she *knew* Lance would be the ultimate sexual partner. For one, she'd never gone to bed with such a big guy, and the vision of his power over her both frightened and excited her hormones. Without question, she felt something for him. She wasn't sure what, but he touched a nerve deep within her soul. She could hardly breath, and her heart hammered so loud she swore the vessel would pop from her chest.

Breaking their lip-lock, Lance placed her on his bed and leaned close to her ear. "I better not get a leg cramp."

She gazed into his darkened blue eyes and grinned. "I'll rub it…along with other body parts."

He pinned her to the mattress and sank his tongue

deep into her mouth. Her thoughts scattered. Heat flushed through her body, making her robe and pj's unbearable. *Too many clothes.* But his weight kept her immobilized, a possession of sorts, and she enjoyed every aspect of his male dominance.

Lifting his head, he twisted his lips into his sexy, little smile, and her bones turned to putty.

Grabbing her wrists, he extended her arms over her head and dropped feather kisses along her cheek and neck. Following her clavicle line, he kissed downward as his fingers unfastened each button on her pj top. Chest exposed, he cupped one breast and massaged while his mouth suckled the other's hard nipple.

The sensation of his mouth and hand doing their magic shot sparks of pure pleasure straight to her core, and she moaned.

He nuzzled her ear. "We have a long way to go."

"Oh, please, take the slow road."

Prior to her assault, she'd blush from such a bold statement, but Lance made words flow from her mouth without thought. Every touch evoked a shiver of delight. Like now. His finger traced the edge of her rib cage, and she rolled her eyes closed from the tickle across her skin. The man had the skill for erotic torture. She arched her back in appreciation. "Maybe I don't want slow after all."

In answer, he lunged at her breast like a man determined to swallow it whole.

Sliding an arm beneath her, he lifted her enough to slip off her pj top and robe.

Inching her pants down but stopping just below the hip, he squeezed her butt and growled into her neck "No panties."

His large hand slithered between her legs and massaged her sex. She damn near hit the ceiling as a fervor too wonderful to describe created a deluge of moisture between her legs. While his tongue probed her mouth, he slid a finger into her moist heat, muffling her gasp. The simultaneous assault triggered a response that awakened a core dormant for too long. Struggling to break her wrists free of his hold and failing, she sucked in a hard breath as an orgasm tightened around his finger. "Oh, my God, Lance—"

"Enjoy it, Dana."

He increased pressure to give her the ride of her life. But she hungered for more than simple fireworks. She needed *him* inside her, pulsing, pumping, and whatever else he had in mind.

She vaguely felt her pants slip down her legs.

After kissing both her breasts, he released her wrists and stood while undoing the sash to his robe. Stripping, he allowed her a full view of his body, not in the least embarrassed where her gaze lingered.

Breathless and dazed at the size of the man about to descend on her, she devoured his nakedness and prayed her vagina could accommodate him. If not, she was in for one hell of a ride.

He rolled on a condom but stopped, his gaze sweeping her body.

She licked her lips. "What's wrong?" *Please, Lord, no second thoughts*.

"You ready for me?"

With his mussed black hair and desire exploding from his gaze, how could she *not* be ready? He smelled of all man, looked like an Adonis with muscles galore, and she couldn't wait to feel him inside her. Then afterward, she'd have a feast and taste every square inch of his gorgeous body. Oh, yeah, she was indeed ready, and she smiled. "For as long and as many times as you want me, Lance Barnes."

****

The aroma of bacon permeated the condo, and she salivated while hurriedly dressing. Great sex created an insatiable appetite, along with sore thigh and butt muscles. So, pancakes with lots of maple syrup and crispy bacon would suit her perfectly.

Nothing beat an all-night lovemaking marathon. She felt twenty pounds lighter—mentally and physically. Naturally, she called their dalliance lovemaking when in reality, they performed plain, old-fashioned sex. Neither muttered the word love…although, on her end, she experienced several moments when sixteen variations of the word stopped on the tip of her tongue. For most of the night, he gave so much and kept her on cloud nine, but the strange feelings churning around in her chest were unfamiliar. No man had ever taken the time to pleasure her with such tenderness, and if push came to shove, she'd easily fall in love. Maybe she already had, but reality squelched any further thoughts. Her stay in Baltimore was temporary. Even if today turned into their last together, she'd never forget the one man who made her feel so lucky to be a woman.

Oddly enough, a buildup of misgivings threatened to destroy her memories of their wonderful night. She had no regrets about sleeping with Lance, and she'd do it again in a heartbeat, but she couldn't hang around his condo forever. She had a business to run and clients to pacify. Despite the two murdered victims from her lecture, she couldn't help Lance and Georgette. And the clues surrounding her assault were as vague as ever.

No, unless ordered otherwise, she'd head home with Tim. Gad, the drive would be agonizing, and she wasn't in the mood to listen to his constant yapping. Maybe she should fly home and leave Tim to drive by himself. *Like I'll avoid the inevitable.* The three musketeers would rant and rave the second she set foot in Pittsburgh. Hell, Lance was right. Her parents and Tim bullied her in their quest for control. Ignoring them or running away wouldn't solve any problems. The solution rested solely on her shoulders—the old, show-a-stiff-backbone-and-fight bullshit.

The revelation lifted her spirits. She'd handle Tim on the drive home then confront all three about their stupid wedding plans.

Heart light, Dana entered the kitchen and froze. While Lance stood at the stove flipping pancakes onto a platter, Tim sat at the table watching him with a snarl. Both men turned her way, and her gut wrenched. *Aw, shit.*

Lance rolled his eyes. "Tim arrived while you were in the shower."

Thank God, they'd agreed to dress before breakfast.

Tim shot to his feet, jaw twitching. "You slept with him, didn't you? Don't lie, Dana. The evidence is all over your face."

She thought she washed her face well enough in the shower. He must be complaining about the smile she couldn't hide. Regardless, she refused to let him spoil her mood. Squaring her shoulders, she walked to the table and snatched a strip of bacon.

"Dana, how dare you? We were saving ourselves for marriage."

Oh, good grief. Poor naïve Tim. As if she'd refuse a night of perfect sex with a real man. Chewing, she faced Tim. "I never made such a promise. I lost my virginity in college." She shoved the remaining strip into her mouth.

Tim's gaze blazed. "You whore!"

Spatula still in hand, Lance swung around and, with his other hand, splayed his palm on Tim's chest and pinned him to the refrigerator, rattling the bottles within. "You do not use that tone with a woman way above your caliber, Gardner. You either use a civil tongue, or I'm tossing you to the street."

Tim sidestepped from Lance's hold and glared. "You slept with my fiancée! Look at her lips. Did you want to bite them off?"

Dana smiled. Yes, her lips were swollen from a night of lip lock, but his teeth bit more than her lips. The memory warmed her, and she glanced at Lance who winked. He returned to the stove while she fought back a grin. "We're not engaged, Tim, and you know it."

Throwing up his hands, Tim paced within the small kitchen. "I can't believe you're screwing with me, Dana. Wait 'til I tell your parents."

Lance tapped the griddle with his spatula. "Her memories returned, Timmy. She told me about your supposed relationship."

Staggering, Tim gaped. "What do you mean *supposed*? Our engagement is real, and she's well aware of the fact. Hell, the ring alone is proof. Right, Dana?"

Debating whether to steal another strip of bacon, she decided against it and licked her fingers. "I said I won't marry you, Tim. I don't care how hard my parents push." She leaned toward him. "The ring's in a safe deposit box at my bank. If you want, you can return it to the jewelry store and get a refund."

"But, but—"

Gaze gentle, she brushed a hand up and down his arm. "You're like a brother, Tim. We might not be related by blood, but I still consider you family."

"We're also best friends and perfect together." He narrowed his gaze. "This guy took advantage of your injury and turned you against me."

For another night like the last, she'd let Lance take advantage any time. She opened the refrigerator and grabbed the bottle of orange juice.

"Your parents did a lot for me, Dana. I owe them."

She met Tim's glare. "You don't have to be their puppet." Retrieving two small glasses from an overhead cabinet, she poured the juice into both.

The word puppet struck her, and she tensed. In the eyes of Marta and Howard Null, she and Tim were indeed dangling by strings. Her parents demanded everything be *their* way and bribed when necessary. The endowment, for example. Dana didn't need the money, but Tim sure did, and he put pressure on Dana to tie the knot. Well, enough was enough. No more of this three-against-one crap. She replaced the orange juice into the fridge.

Tim grabbed her arm. "You know I love you, Dana. We'll enjoy a solid marriage, you'll see. Don't let this guy rob your happiness."

As if Tim filled her with overwhelming joy. How

had she tolerated him all these years? Stiffening, she shrugged off his hand. "Last night, Lance made me feel like a woman. Our night together was consensual." She slammed the refrigerator door.

Tim flared his nostrils. "Your father won't agree."

"Tough. I'm a thirty-two-year-old with a doctorate and career. I stand on my own two feet." Something Tim hadn't done—ever. *All right, calm down.* She pinched the bridge of her nose, counted to ten, then dropped her hand. "Look, Tim. We've had this conversation many times. I won't marry you and don't care about the endowment or my parents' preference for my mate. Case closed."

"You know your mom and dad are afraid you'll grow into an old maid."

She stifled a laugh. "Then, so be it." Better to live alone than marry her *brother.*

Tugging on the collar of his leather jacket, Tim huffed. "You're being selfish, Dana. You're not thinking of me at all. The endowment will make us comfortable for life, but I'm a patient man. Your father won't approve of any man but me. Your history with men proves my point."

Like she gave a damn. Before this Baltimore trip, Tim's comment would cut too close to the quick, but not anymore. He manipulated as much as her parents. She didn't need anyone's approval to live the life of her choosing. As for her history with men…well, maybe her experience with Lance changed her future. Good sex with a great partner definitely boosted her ego.

Snorting, Tim stuffed his hands into his jacket pockets. "Your parents flew home last night. I'll call and tell them your memory returned, and we're leaving

Baltimore. Get your stuff together."

Over the years, she tolerated his bossy behavior to keep the peace. But his friggin' antics had to stop. Scowling, she crossed her arms over her chest. "Sorry, Tim, with my memory intact, Lance wants me at the precinct to make an official report."

Tim gritted his teeth. "Anything to delay, right?" Whirling toward Lance, he pointed a finger into the man's face. "You're a shrewd one, detective. Don't think for one second I'm not aware of your games. I'll come with you."

Lance flashed Dana a lazy smile then redirected his gaze onto Tim. "No, you won't, Mr. Gardner. You aggravate her. I need her with a clear mind." Finished with the spatula, he dropped the utensil into the sink and wiped his hands with a towel. "What do you suggest, Dana?"

That's right. Throw Tim back at me. She squinted at Lance. "I think Tim should return to the hotel and wait for my call. I don't remember very much, Lance, so I doubt I'll need to stay in Baltimore."

For some reason, the statement gripped her heart and twisted. She had no reason to stay. Lance had his career. She had hers. Two separate worlds in two separate cities.

Cheeks flaming, Tim stamped a foot. "This is an outrage, Dana. You'll make out the report, and we'll immediately hop in the car and head home." He pointed toward the kitchen entrance. "Grab your things, and I'll drive you to the precinct." He threw a thumb over his shoulder in Lance's direction. "This crippled lowlife can walk." Puffing out his chest, Tim invaded Lance's space. "My job is to take care of Dana and keep her from leeches like you. Her parents and I are well aware of men after her money."

Smirking, Lance tossed the towel onto the counter. "What better way to keep both of you under their thumbs than to have the two of you married? Lucky for Dana, she returned to her senses."

Exasperation plus. Tim was so dense. Maybe she should move to Antarctica. Were Internet connections available way down in the tundra?

The doorbell rang, followed by the click of the lock.

A few seconds later, Thelma strolled into the kitchen carrying two canvas shopping bags.

Stopping short, she stared. "Oh. Excuse me." With a wan smile, she plunked the bags onto the counter. "This is quite a crowd for you, Lance."

Ignoring Thelma, Tim grabbed Dana by the shoulders and whirled her to face him. "I'll forgive your indiscretion, sweetheart. I'm sure *he* initiated everything, and you, being a weak female, went along for the ride. We'll talk on the way home. Don't forget." He shook her shoulders. "We need to hunt for a home in D.C. I've a great list already. With your qualifications, the oval office will want you to start right away." Releasing her, he turned and glared at Lance. "I'll take her to the precinct now."

"And leave this fabulous breakfast?" He shook his head. "No way, Timmy. She'll eat first. You can grab a hot dog somewhere."

Tim pressed his lips into a thin line. "Like hell. I'm staying."

Throughout his life, Tim's temper generated more trouble than her father could handle. Not serious go-to-jail trouble, but enough for irate parents to call and complain. If he kept taunting Lance, Tim might find himself in handcuffs. Determined to stop Tim before he succeeded with his first-ever criminal record, she stepped between them. "Enough." She grabbed Tim's shoulders and pushed him toward the kitchen entrance. "Go to your hotel, order room service, and I'll call when we're done. Lance and I want to eat breakfast, and you're intruding."

Tim jerked his head at Thelma. "What about her?"

"Yo, whoa!" Thelma held up her hands, palms out. "I'm passing through and not staying."

Glancing over his shoulder, he sneered. "I don't like how you're acting, Dana. You've changed, but I'll go." Stopping at the kitchen entrance, he pointed a finger at Lance. "You keep your hands off her, you hear? Her father will talk some sense into her and straighten her ass." He stormed from the kitchen.

Grinning, Lance met Dana's gaze. "That went well."

Oh, hell. Dana ran to the living room. "Tim, wait"

Whirling, he twisted his lips. "Good. You've come to your senses. He's not right for you, honey."

"Will you shut your damn mouth?" She wanted to scream or, at least, pull her hair out by its roots. Sucking in a large breath, she released the air in one big whoosh. "Look, Tim. Lance and I aren't serious, but I am entitled to a little sexual release."

He huffed. "Aw, hell, you could have asked me."

God, help me. She clamped onto his arm and tugged. "Don't you understand? I think of you as my brother, Tim. I can *never* sleep with you."

He waved aside the comment. "You're talking

minor details. You'll come around on our honeymoon."
He leaned close. "I'm your chosen one, Dana. Your
mom and dad already approved our marriage. Call
when you're done at the precinct." He brushed his lips
against her cheek and left.

Dana stared at the closed door. Chosen one? When
the hell had she slipped into an alternate universe?

Chapter Nineteen

Thelma leaned toward Lance's ear. "What's going on?"

While staring at the kitchen entrance, he curled his lip. "Long story. I'll tell you over drinks someday." He met Thelma's wide-eyed gaze. "The short version is Tim wants to marry Dana." So did the professor and Lord only knows who else.

"And she doesn't want to marry him." Nodding, she glanced at the entrance. "Smart girl. The guy's a jerk." She opened one of the canvas bags on the counter. "Help me put away these groceries so I can leave you two alone. Obviously, you need to talk."

When Tim showed at the front door, Lance mustered every ounce of his police training not to wring the man's skinny neck. Hell, he entered with the same attitude from when he left the previous night—indignant and confrontational. Why was Tim so damn thick-headed? Sure, best friends sometimes fell in love, but Tim's love was clearly one-sided, and love didn't mean pressuring to marry.

Gut clenching, he grabbed the second grocery bag and emptied the contents.

All these friggin' interruptions spoiled his mood. He and Dana had a wonderful night—and morning. Her kisses kept him erect for hours, and she accepted his thrusts with a greed that made him proud. Just thinking about her softness against his skin eased the tension in his chest.

"I bought those cookies you wanted." Thelma tossed him the pack.

Catching the box, he grinned. Chocolate-coconut macaroons. Great with coffee. They stuck in his teeth, but damn, they were a good sugar rush. "Thanks, Thelma."

"So, she's leaving today?"

"Yes." He slipped the cookies into the overhead cabinet.

She cocked her head. "You don't sound too happy."

"Oh, I'm happy enough." *Shit, what a liar*. Dana's leaving gripped his heart like a vise. In a few short days, he'd gotten used to having her around. The woman felt right, but the feeling had to be hormonal. Why else had he this overwhelming urge not to let her go? He'd dated smart, beautiful women many times and, never once, considered keeping them long-term. His career came first. Meeting Dana hadn't changed his mind...well, not specifically. Ever since she entered his life, he questioned his sanity, his career path, and yes, his existence. He loved every second they spent together, and deep down, he wanted that feeling to last. But once again, reality kicked his ass. Lance Barnes worked in a dangerous profession. Women liked their husbands alive and well at the dinner table every night.

Dana re-entered the kitchen with her face scrunched into a frown.

She had this faraway look in her eyes, like she contemplated world peace. Lance motioned for her to sit, but she hardly glanced his way. "Come on, Dana.

Let's eat. Our food's getting cold." He turned to Thelma. "You want some?"

Thelma folded her canvas bags. "I ate already. Besides, you two need some privacy. Tootles!"

Stuffing the two bags under her arm, she waved and left the kitchen. A minute later, the front door clicked shut.

Lance wrapped his arms around Dana and pulled her close. She felt tense. *Well, duh.* A guy like Tim would create a frozen glacier in the middle of a desert. With a finger, he lifted her chin. Her gaze remained distant. "He's gone."

She started, as if noticing for the first time he held her to his chest. A definite blow to a man's ego.

Shaking herself, she wrapped her arms around his waist. "Tim said I've changed, and you know what? He's right."

"In what way?"

Her jaw twitched. "I'm done arguing with Tim and my parents about this stupid wedding. As of today, I have absolutely no fear of taking on the three of them. If I alienate them, then so what? Their marriage plans are about to crash and burn." Gaze sparkling, she squeezed his waist. "You inspired the change, Lance Barnes. You filled me with the strength to stand on my own two feet."

"I doubt I caused anything, honey." He returned the squeeze and, tightening his embrace, swayed her. "You had the guts all along." He kissed her nose. "Let's eat." Before the sway swelled him to a breaking point inside his jeans. Sitting, he grabbed the coffee pot and filled their mugs.

After stacking several cakes on her plate, buttering,

and then pouring on hot syrup, she shoved a cut piece into her mouth and chewed. She rolled her eyes. "These are wonderful. Almost as good as sex." Her face sobered, and she toyed with her food. "My drive home with Tim won't be a pleasant one. I've never seen him act so possessive."

"The endowment gives him a strong incentive." He poured a hefty amount of syrup on his cakes. "How much is your father promising?"

"A million five."

Eyes wide, Lance stopped mid-pour. "Are you shitting me?"

"Hardly." She munched on a strip of bacon.

Some incentive. Why so much? He pursed his lips. "Is there a time frame?"

"Oh, sure. Marriage before the end of the year. Children within two years." She shuddered. "My father detailed our marriage like a board meeting agenda. The whole thing's ridiculous."

And suspicious. The scenario smacked of desperation. Why were they pushing so hard? Lance understood Marta's pea-brained mentality. The woman had a show to put on for a bevy of influential guests. But how could anyone force a woman to waltz down the aisle and marry a man against her will? *What the hell am I missing*? Would they drug Dana in order to fulfill some divine prophecy? Lance studied her. "I don't like any of this, Dana."

She glanced up. "What, the pancakes?"

He loved how her innocence surfaced when he least expected. She could brighten any man's day. He forced a frown. "No, their push for marriage. I'd like to know why they sound desperate." Maybe he should do a little covert checking on Howard Null. As a rule, rich people had ulterior motives for giving away their money. He cut into his pancakes. "You talked about moving to State College. How far is that from Pittsburgh?"

"Not far enough." She chewed.

Even her chewing had an undeniable sexiness. Hell, sitting across from her every morning and evening could be sheer torture. He cleared his throat. "With your memory intact, what can you tell me about your night at the hotel?" He shoved in a forkful of pancakes.

Her face thoughtful, she lifted a slice of bacon. "Not much." She bit off a piece and chewed. "I left my room for ice, and someone whacked me by the machine."

"Did you see anything, like a foot or an arm?"

Swallowing, she dabbed a napkin on the corner of her mouth. "Yes, an arm in a black coat." A pause. "And something blue. Maybe a shirt sleeve."

He waved his fork. "That's good, Dana. Can you remember the time?"

Frowning, she swirled a forkful of cakes in the syrup. "I'm not sure. The lecture ended at nine. Some students helped me pack and asked more questions. I think I arrived at the hotel around nine-forty-five. I had partially stripped for a shower when I remembered ice, so I threw on a pair of jeans and sweatshirt, but before I left the room, my mother called. We argued. I tossed the phone on the bed and ran out for the ice." She cocked her head. "Maybe ten-fifteen."

"Do you prop open the door?"

She shook her head. "I never prop the door."

Stuffing a wad of cakes into his mouth, he chewed.

Not enough syrup. He poured more. "Okay then. Someone entered your room with a key. I doubt the perp took your key and then replaced it to your pocket. He'd waste too much precious time." Unless two people were involved—one to carry the equipment and the other to carry her. Without surveillance video, his thoughts were all supposition, but the idea made sense. Since hotel management and housekeeping had pass keys, he'd check to see if anyone reported a key stolen. "You mentioned diamonds."

"Huh?" She paused in the middle of downing her orange juice. "Oh—right. I saw diamonds when I hit the floor." She drained the glass.

Diamonds. What could they mean? The alcove tile had a nondescript gray pattern. The hall rugs were a black and red motif to match the Red Wolf's theme. But diamonds? None that he could recall. Maybe her blow to the head caused a brief hallucination. Something like stars in her eyes. *Hmm.* He crunched on a strip of bacon while savoring the hickory smoke. "Describe what you did when you woke in the alley."

Reclining, she sipped her coffee. "I saw rats everywhere, so I screamed. Newspapers and trash bags covered me. I kicked them off and jumped to my feet, but then, the alley whirled, and I fell into a pile of garbage." She shuddered and stared into her cup.

"Describe the surroundings." After helping himself to more pancakes, he cut them into pieces. "I already determined you weren't in the alley by the hotel." He pointed to the cake plate. "Eat some more."

Replacing her mug to the table, she forked three and covered them with syrup. "I had a metal fire escape above me. Even in the dark, the staircase looked old and rusted, like it hadn't been used in a long time." She stopped, gaze distant. "I tripped over a plastic crate on my way out of the alley."

"Was an outside fire escape on the opposite building?"

"I faced a solid brick wall and the faded remains of a company logo. I can't tell you what the logo said."

"Was the alley wide enough to fit a car?"

"Gosh, yes. I'd say wide enough to fit a trash truck."

Now, we're getting somewhere. With her memory intact, the case turned in a more positive direction. His pulse quickened. "Describe the street."

Resting her fork on her plate, she stared behind him. "From the alley, I crossed the street to a church. The doors were padlocked with a heavy chain, and black graffiti covered the exterior."

"What about a name on the church?"

She shook her head. "Nothing."

Not unusual. If the church plaque consisted of any metal, someone would pry loose the plate and sell it for scrap. He tapped his fork on his plate. "Abandoned then. That's definitive."

"Why?"

"Because the area surrounding your hotel has newer construction. Metal fire escapes became a part of the past. Most of the buildings—including this one—contain interior stairwells." He hissed. "You were transported to the oldest part of the city."

Mouth agape, she blinked. "I assume we're talking distance?"

"Very much so." Grabbing another strip of bacon, he munched. "From the beginning, I wondered how you arrived at my precinct since neither your hotel nor the university are anywhere nearby." His gaze narrowed. "How *did* you reach my headquarters?"

She quirked her mouth. "I hopped onto the rear of a utility truck, the kind with the big bucket that rises up a pole. Only one guy sat in the cab and had his cellphone glued to his ear. I jumped off when the neighborhood changed to better homes."

Even half-frozen, she used her brain. *Damn brave woman.* She made him proud. He drank his orange juice in one gulp. Smacking his lips at the taste of too much rind, he lowered the glass to the table. "Now, tell me the importance of the flash drive."

She finished the last on her plate and wiped her mouth. "The drive isn't important at all. I always tape the Q & A sessions. Some students ask questions good enough to post on my website. At the first opportunity, I transfer the video to a drive to free camera memory. If time allows, I'll sit on the bed and load the drive into my laptop then edit." Sighing, she wrapped both hands around her mug. "That night, my mother continued her tirade about me not taking more responsibility with the wedding plans. I was so aggravated, I hung up. The flash drive was right next to my door key on the dresser, so I slipped both into my pocket without thinking before grabbing the ice bucket and rushing out the door."

And the phone call's distraction almost proved fatal. The scenario was so common it bordered on cliché. Frowning, he lifted the coffee carafe from its warming plate and refilled both mugs. "Tell me about the lecture, Dana." He replaced the carafe. "Did anything unusual happen?"

"Not that I recall." Leaning her elbows on the table, she placed her cup under her nose. "I remember the argument between two women by the door." She sniffed the rising steam. "One of my helpers joked about tramp and super-tramp." She sipped.

"What was the argument about?"

"I've no idea. The words were kind of huffy, know what I mean?" Gasping, she lowered the cup to the table and met his gaze. "Anita Seeley!"

He leaned on the table. "Are you sure?"

"Yes, one woman was Anita. She entered the hall halfway through my lecture and paused on the landing. Low-cut top and big boobs. That was her, all right."

"Did you see the other woman?"

She pursed her lips. "No. Anita stood to one side, but the other woman hid behind the door."

"How about the student who commented about tramp and super-tramp? Do you have his or her name?"

"No, sorry."

He patted her hand. "That's okay. We'll watch the video again to see if a few scenes jar any memories."

With a cocked brow, he scanned the empty plates on the table. He and Dana polished off a whole pound of bacon and enough pancakes to feed a small army. For a woman her size, she sure shoveled in the food. Smiling at a vision of a plump Dana in old age, he stood while stacking plates. After loading them into the dishwasher, he turned and shot her a one-eyed gaze. "By the way, what's wrong with my décor?"

Dana chuckled into her coffee. "My mother disliked your easy-to-assemble furniture."

Grunting, he grabbed his mug to gulp the last of his coffee. "I'm a bachelor. I buy functional furniture." He stuffed the empty mug into the washer. "My college roommate used stacked pizza boxes for end tables."

Smiling, she rolled her eyes. "My mother would throw a royal fit." Finishing the last of her coffee, she stood and placed the mug in the washer.

The doorbell rang. *What the hell today?* First, Tim. Then, Thelma. Who was next? Marta and Howard Null? Fighting a wave of irritation, he headed for the front door.

A young man stood on the threshold with a large flower box in his arms. "For Dr. Dana Null. Sign here, sir." He thrust an electronic gadget at Lance.

Feeling totally dumbstruck, Lance signed with his finger before taking the flowers. After closing the door, he returned to the kitchen.

Dana fastened the latch on the dishwasher and pressed the Start button. She glanced over her shoulder and raised a brow. "Oh, how nice."

"They're for you." He laid the box on the table. "Not from me, Dana."

Both brows rising, she lifted the lid to expose a dozen yellow roses and a small white card. After reading, she groaned.

Lance read over her shoulder. *Please reconsider. Anthony.*

Dana released a long breath. "At least, they're not from Tim."

Crossing his arms over his chest, he leaned against the counter. "Explain your relationship to the professor."

She lifted the flowers for a sniff then replaced them on the table. "I completed a fellowship at Johns Hopkins under Doctor Seeley's tutelage. He's a knowledgeable anthropologist, and working with him was a great experience. We meshed together from the start. Because of my specialty, he invited me to give a series of lectures, and I've returned twice a year ever since." She fingered one of the roses. "Whenever I visit, the professor and I schedule a dinner date, and we'll talk for hours about cultures." Glancing at Lance, she shrugged. "I like him but more as a respected colleague. I'd never consider marriage." She stared at the wall and smiled. "He's like the grandfather I never had." She returned her gaze to Lance. "On this trip, his faculty meeting prevented our dinner date."

"A convenient coincidence to have his wife murdered on the same evening, wouldn't you say?"

She met his gaze. "A little too convenient, but he has the money to divorce her, Lance. Why ruin his career by killing his wife?"

"Depends on a lot of circumstances, Dana. Divorces can get nasty, even when children aren't involved. Or maybe he thinks he's smart enough to get away with murder." But would the professor hurt Dana, steal her equipment, and then propose marriage? Logic said no.

Rubbing both hands along the sides of her hips, Dana bit her lower lip. "Lance, I—huh…" Breaking eye contact, she headed for the living room. "I'll go pack."

He caught her arm. "No, you won't. We'll find something for the flowers then head to the station. George needs to hear all you've told me."

She stood too damn close, smelling of shampoo and a touch of citrus. If he wasn't careful, he'd drag her back into the bedroom. He dropped his hand. "Let's go."

Chapter Twenty

What the hell is his hurry? Dana yanked her overcoat from the hanger, but Lance already waited in the hallway to lock the door, waving her out.

While locking the door, he spoke over his shoulder. "The first item of importance is to find this alley."

Lance adjusted his collar and hastened toward the elevator. No cane today. Either he forgot or purposely left it behind.

Rushing to catch up, she slipped her arms into the coat sleeves. "Why?"

"A good detective covers every detail of a case, Dana. And I'm a damn good cop. Humor me." Using the side of his fist, he slammed the Down button.

Tim's arrival killed her sense of humor. Then, the flower delivery changed Lance from gentle to brusque in the space of a few seconds. In fact, after reaching the lobby, he urged her onto the street as if the building was on fire. Were the professor's flowers a trigger? Before she left the kitchen, she sniffed the rose scent, but that's what a woman did. She certainly hadn't called the professor to thank him.

With long strides, he limped several paces ahead with his face like granite. She struggled to keep up. "Will you slow down, please? My legs aren't as long as yours."

"You're doing fine. I'm the one with the injury."

And the one in a big hurry. If she kept to his brisk pace, she'd demand some electrodes to monitor her heart rate. *Aw, damn. Forgot my purse.* No way in hell would she ask to return to the condo.

At the precinct, Lance led the way to the garage where he signed for a car.

She hopped in and buckled the seatbelt. "I can't tell you which way."

His stone face cracked a little. "That's okay. You provided some good clues." He started the car. "We'll head for the older section of the city and look for the church." After maneuvering through the garage and toward the exit, he eased the vehicle into traffic. "Can you describe any distinctive pattern to the graffiti?"

She shrugged. "Black paint. Otherwise, nothing."

He sped around cars and drove with an edge of impatience. She didn't understand why the mad dash all of a sudden. If he wanted her out of his life, he could easily pawn her off to another detective. Or, better yet, drive her to Tim's hotel. Releasing a heavy sigh, she rested her head on the seat.

"Are you paying attention?"

Startled at his harsh tone, she straightened. "Sorry."

Snapping his words and acting irritated. *Yup, he wants to get rid of me.* She wasn't helping matters by letting her mind drift. All right, so he wanted her gone. Just like all the men before him. A wave of sadness hit. Somewhere deep down, she hoped he was different. Chest tight, she stared out the windows.

As the neighborhoods changed from middle class to poor and then to destitute, Dana straightened in her seat. This particular area looked familiar. "Slow down,

Lance"

He eased on the gas.

Alert now, she scanned the blocks of houses with boarded windows, cracked sidewalks, and crumbling curbs. Blackened brick homes with no windows and doors showed evidence of long-ago fires while gutted vehicles occupied curbside space, long abandoned by their owners.

A few people milled about, most looking as if they had nothing to do with their time. Some others lounged on worn concrete steps that had to be freezing cold on their butts. A woman with a shopping cart full of her possessions lumbered along, afraid to make eye contact with anyone, and a young man in tattered clothes rooted through a dumpster sitting at curbside. Without question, they occupied a sad area of the city where the forgotten gathered.

Ahead, a tall steeple caught her eye. She shifted in her seat. "There's the church!"

He tapped the brakes. "Are you sure?"

"I'll know as soon as I see the doors."

As the car eased to the curb, she leaned toward the windshield.

Black spray paint covered what were once two beautiful wooden doors. The graffiti was meant to disfigure rather than as a display of art. "Yup, this is the church."

He cut the engine.

"Which alley, Dana?"

She jerked her head to the left. "The one across the street."

With the sun shining, the neighborhood lost its sinister look and appeared downright dilapidated.

Neglect surrounded her, the houses abandoned by the people and city budgets.

"Dana?" With his foot out the door, he nodded toward the alley.

"Right." Sucking in a deep breath, she stepped from the car and followed him across the street.

In daylight, the alley had a crappier look, something akin to walking into a disaster zone. Rats fed on decaying garbage, not in the least concerned about the two intruders wandering toward them. The overhead fire escape looked ready to crash to the concrete with bolts rusted and broken from the brick wall. Loose trash and paper littered the ground and accumulated in every conceivable corner, trapped in the alley forever. She shuddered.

"Where were you dumped?"

"Right under the fire escape."

He shot her a glance which conveyed exactly what she'd been thinking. If the metal staircase had disconnected from the wall, she'd be a corpse in the morgue.

Stepping alongside her, Lance slipped a hand behind her neck and rubbed. "I'll take it from here. Wait in the car."

The damn man confused her. Harsh one minute and tender the next. She wished he'd make up his mind. With no desire to stand among so many rats, she headed for the street. She had nothing to add anyway. Big deal, an alley. She stepped off the curb.

A car engine revved to life. The high-pitched whine echoed and bounced off the brick walls. Tires squealed. Curious, she turned. From nowhere, a black sedan sped toward her. With her heart jumping straight into her throat, she froze in the middle of the street.

"Dana!"

Lance's voice broke her rooted stance. With a flying leap, she flew over the hood of Lance's car and slid to the other side as the sedan missed her by inches. She hit the sidewalk with a thud.

Whirling around the car, Lance clutched her by the shoulders and hoisted her to her feet. He swung his gaze in all directions, but the car had long gone.

His grip tightened. "That was no accident."

Gee whiz. Ya think? Heart racing, she fell against the hood of the car, grateful for the solid feel of the metal. This damn Baltimore trip was one humdinger of an adventure, even more so than some of the archaeology digs in the Middle East where restless natives threatened to chop off a few heads. Maybe she should get the hell home while she could.

"Did you see the driver?"

She brushed the snow and dirt off her overcoat. "All I saw was a car too new for this neighborhood with a strange flapping sound coming from its rear tire, as if it was going flat. And no, I didn't catch a license plate. It was covered by some yellow thingy."

Jerking, he cursed under his breath. "That car followed me home, Dana."

Their gazes locked. The only reason to follow a cop was to discover where he lived, and too many people knew she stayed with him. She swallowed hard.

Lips tight, he stroked her arm. "Are you okay?"

A fine time to ask. After all, he lifted her onto jelly knees. Small wonder she remained on her feet. "Yeah, I'm okay. Luckily, my coat's thick enough to cushion my butt."

"Wait in the car. I want to do one more check in the alley." He ran across the street.

Before her blow to the head, she'd cower in the car like a frightened rabbit but not anymore. She was damn tired of being shoved around—by her parents, Tim, and whoever the hell was after her. Instead, she strolled toward the church steps. Six cracked granite slabs led to the padlocked doors. The lower arched windows—which, at one time, displayed beautiful stained glass—were boarded shut. Toward the roof, a circular window of stained glass had holes large enough to allow birds and bats easy access. *At least, some of God's creatures have a safe haven.*

Lance approached. "I told you to wait in the car."

Ignoring him, she slid her gaze toward the steeple, already leaning precariously to the right. With a good wind, the structure would topple onto the street. She pointed upward. "People who abandon a house of worship abandon the neighborhood. Not only our culture, but around the world. The cross on the steeple, for example—" Jerking, she whirled, eyes wide. "I was in the trunk of a car, Lance. The hood popped open, and the cross caught my eye. The night was dark, but something reflected a spot of light."

He gritted his teeth. "Can you identify who lifted you out?"

She shook her head. "I drifted in and out of consciousness. Lucky for me, I guess. Otherwise, they'd have smashed in my skull to finish the job."

"Well, they know you're alive now. Think about the trunk, Dana. Any smells or objects you pushed aside?"

"Oh, hell, I don't know." She scanned her memory.

Everything was so fuzzy. She rubbed her forehead. "An oily rag. A tool box. I can't recall anything else."

He wrapped an arm around her shoulders and squeezed. "Come on. Let's get out of the cold."

Once inside the car, Lance started the engine and cranked the heater to full blast. Jaw tight, he stared out the windshield. "You were disposed in the worst section of our city, Dana." He met her gaze. "Count your blessings for surviving in this neighborhood." Shifting the gear into Drive, he sped off.

At the precinct, Dana settled on a chair between Lance and Georgette, watching the Q & A video for who knew what. She recalled the lecture easily enough and how so many enthusiastic students joined her around the podium, but how much more could the video contain?

Lance nudged her arm. "Are you concentrating?"

Not again. She shook herself. "Oh, sure." A bold lie. Her mind was so far away she'd need a bus to catch it.

Grabbing the remote, Georgette hit the Pause button. "What's troubling you, honey?"

Lance. Tim. Going home. Staying. Who the hell knew? She forced a smile. "Nothing."

Glancing at her partner, Georgette patted Dana's hand. "Maybe we should take a break."

With his brows pinched together, Lance stood. "Don't be ridiculous. We barely started."

Georgette also stood. "I need another cup of coffee." She stifled a yawn. "At five this morning, I woke the kids for a special, multi-class school trip to Washington D.C. The Lincoln Memorial was all they talked about for a week." She crooked a finger at Dana.

"Come on, honey. You look like you can use a stimulant. Lance, you want a cup?"

Frowning, he shuffled toward the door. "I'll go with you."

"No, you go to your desk and cancel Dana's engagement ring report. I'd like a few moments alone with her—if you don't mind."

With a furtive glance at Dana, he grunted. "Fine. I'll call larceny and no thanks on the coffee." He turned toward his desk.

Puzzled, Dana shifted her gaze between the two detectives. Lack of sleep fogged her brain, and her concentration sucked, but Lance had a few anger issues going on. She followed Georgette across the department floor to a lunch room stocked with all the comforts of anyone's kitchen. A full coffee pot waited.

Georgette poured the hot fluid into two Styrofoam cups and handed one to Dana. "Cream in the fridge and sugar on the table."

"I'm good. Thanks." Dana turned toward the door.

"Hold on, honey. I hauled you from the video room for a reason." She sipped her coffee. "Talk to me."

Facing the woman, Dana met a kind gaze. "I'm okay."

Georgette cocked her head. "I'm a detective. Don't make me pry out the words." She gestured toward a round table and chairs. "Let's sit."

Nodding, Dana pulled a chair from the table and lowered onto the seat. "I've had an adventurous week."

"I'd call your time in Baltimore monumental, what with losing your memory then getting it back. From loving Lance to losing him." Sitting on the chair to Dana's left, Georgette tilted toward her. "Don't act so surprised. I witnessed the change in Lance from the beginning. You can't work alongside a man every day and not see the differences in his gestures or hear the subtle fluctuations in his voice. You affected him, honey, and in a good way. Like any typical male, he's a closed shell. Did he ask you to stay?"

Her chest tightened. "He's been rushing me all day, Georgette. He can't wait to see me go—along with Tim."

"Are you in love with him?"

"Who, Tim?" She rolled her eyes. "Heavens, no."

Shaking her head, Georgette sighed. "I'm talking about Lance, dear."

Was *that* her problem and why she felt so out of sorts? How would she know love when her parents and Tim interfered in her social life and prevented any long-term relationships? After a sip from her cup, she stared into the hot fluid. "I'm not sure what love feels like." She rarely talked about her feelings. Until this moment, no one expressed any interest.

Georgette leaned on the table. "Love is full of great highs and lows. You question your sanity then wonder whether some unknown medical condition has a grip on your heart. You want to be with the person every second of the day and night but can't, and you drive yourself crazy with doubts." She sipped, her gaze never leaving Dana's face. "I'd say you're torn with indecision. You're leaving Lance but don't want to."

Moisture formed in Dana's eyes. Did Georgette have a degree in psychology? Because—damn—she hit the nail on the head. Dana blinked away her tears. "I can't stay where I'm not wanted, Georgette. And really, why would he ask? We've only known each other a few days." Staring into her cup, she sniffed. Every cell in her body felt his rejection. She should let him go and record the experience as a memory to last a lifetime.

"If he asked, would you stay?"

In a heartbeat, but she refused to share the words with Georgette. "He's a man who enjoys being alone. I'm a nuisance. His behavior this morning proves my point." Like every man before him—adios with no explanation. She should have her head examined for getting involved.

Georgette chuckled. "Honey, let me give you a little tip about men. Most of them haven't a clue what they're feeling. They get cranky and pick fights for asinine reasons, always in total denial there's a woman they can't live without."

Meeting Georgette's gaze, Dana cringed. "So, what does a woman do?"

"Not much. Go with the flow until he comes to his senses." She finished the last of her coffee, stood, then tossed the cup into the trash bin. "We don't know for sure how Lance feels. Once you leave, I'll know." With a huff, she stared into the trash. "I may have to shoot him."

Standing, Dana laughed. "Thank you, Georgette."

"Don't mention it." She wrapped a strong arm around Dana's shoulders. "Take him in stride, honey, and you'll survive."

Too bad Georgette wasn't her mother. The detective had a load of common sense. Marta Null had…well, jewelry. Mother-daughter talks were not part of her genetic makeup.

Scowling, Lance studied Dana as she reclaimed her seat before the view screen. "Ready?"

"Yes, ready."

His scowl disappeared, and he rubbed her shoulder. "You need to fight for what you want, Dana. Take a firm stand with Tim and your parents." He dropped his hand.

Interesting. He believed her talk with Georgette related to family. All right, no sense changing his mind. But the brief shoulder rub felt nice.

Georgette re-started the video.

Maybe her little chat with the older woman helped, or maybe she accepted Lance's resistance. She wasn't sure which, but she squared her shoulders and lifted her chin with a let's-do-it-and-get-it-over-with attitude. She couldn't avoid her inevitable departure.

At the part where Babs McNamara entered the lecture hall, Dana grabbed the remote and freeze-framed. Her heart rate kicked up a notch. "Look at Babs' wrist. She's wearing a blue rubber-band bracelet." She clutched Lance's arm. "Do you remember my mention of the two women arguing? That wrist gestured—" Her grip tightened, and she gasped. "Lance, the flash of blue as the two-by-four swung near my head! Babs' bracelet!"

Georgette jumped to her feet and wrapped her arms around Dana. "Finally, a break." Releasing Dana, she twisted her lips into a crooked grin. "I do believe a trip to McNamara's apartment with a search warrant should prove interesting. What do you say, Lance? Want to tag along? I know you're officially on desk duty, but you've been involved with Dana's case from the start. I'll clear your participation with the captain."

Gaze like two blue flames, Lance shot to his feet. "Great. While you obtain the warrant, Dana and I will watch the rest of the video. If nothing else surfaces, I'll walk Dana to my place. You can swing by with the car, and I'll be at the curb, waiting."

And Dana had time to pack her bags and call Tim. She'd be halfway to Pittsburgh before the evening rush.

The video finished, Lance helped Dana with her coat. Grabbing her shoulders, he spun her to face him. "Don't call Tim yet, okay? We might have further questions. Plan on staying one more night." He wagged a finger in her face. "The attempt on your life today confirms my suspicion about your safety. Always be aware of what's around you."

"Yes, sir." *What the hell*? Talk about confusion. "Babs said she doesn't own a car."

"But she can borrow one." His jaw twitched. "Just keep your eyes and ears open."

She might be reading too much into his request. On the positive side, she'd hold off listening to Tim's tirade for another day.

Chapter Twenty-One

Since she neared the end of her stay and felt the need to do something besides succumb to the ache in her heart, Dana searched in the freezer for an appropriate thank-you dinner as a crowning touch to repay Lance's kindness. She loved cooking and rarely had a chance to prepare a full meal for anyone. Since her parents employed a cook, they complained whenever their daughter lowered herself to servant status. Naturally, they refused any invitation to dinner, as if she might prepare a poisonous meal.

On the other hand, Tim jumped at every opportunity to spend time with Dana, even if his taste leaned more toward burgers and fries. For Lance, a nice pot roast and some tasty sides should do the trick. Finding nothing suitable in the freezer, she contemplated where to buy a nice piece of meat. Lance might not approve of her going out alone after this morning's car incident, but too bad. She wasn't about to sit around and cower in a corner. No sooner had she slipped on her glasses and accessed her phone's map app when the front door clicked.

Thelma strolled in. "Oh, I'm sorry." She stopped with a hand on the door knob. "I didn't expect you here."

Lowering her phone, she smiled. "That's okay. Although, I'm curious. Do you and Lance have a special code if he's—er—entertaining a woman?"

Thelma chuckled and closed the door. "See this door chain?" She pointed. "He's supposed to slip the hook in the slot so I can't open the door. But, honey, I've been with him for four years and never once found the links in place. I doubt he even remembers our little signal." She pointed toward the kitchen. "I know you two left in a hurry this morning. So, I popped in here to check on the dishes."

"Thanks, but everything's good." She tossed her eyeglasses on the table. "Can you tell me where to buy a nice pot roast?"

"The best meat shop around is about six blocks from here. Head out the main entrance and turn right. Keep walking straight, and look for The Butcher Shop sign. You can't miss it."

Thelma's timing was perfect. Dana had no key for Lance's condo, and the housekeeper promised to do a little cleaning until Dana returned. Throwing on her coat and slipping her purse onto her shoulder, Dana set out on her mission.

With her memories intact, she could count on one hand the number of times she strolled around Baltimore. Usually, her visits amounted to a single overnight stay. Before the lecture, she and the professor shared an early dinner and, sometimes, a cup of coffee at the cafe across the street from the hotel. All these years, he never hinted at pursuing an intimate relationship. What the hell should she do? Without Anita as a buffer, the professor might push too hard and ruin their friendship. Stopping at a crosswalk, she waited with several others for a green light.

From her travels, one city always resembled

another—concrete and asphalt, with too much traffic and too many people. Baltimore had wider streets than Pittsburgh, and the city blocks appeared shorter, but all cities fought a battle against age by tearing down old structures and then rebuilding. Noise remained constant, too. Car horns, flapping tires, bad mufflers, and overhead airplanes were normal sounds of the city.

Flapping tires. She distinctly heard the sound behind her while she walked and failed to let it register. Coincidence? Craning her neck to see over several tall men, she scanned the area.

As more people gathered at curbside, someone nudged her arm. Stiffening from the unnecessary contact, she shot a quick glance over her shoulder as two hands pushed her into the street. Gasping, Dana flew off the curb straight into oncoming traffic.

A woman screamed.

People shouted.

Car tires screeched to a halt while several hands latched onto her coat and hauled her onto the sidewalk.

The sequence of events happened in the space of seconds, but Dana's heart rate pumped like a runaway locomotive. She gaped at the two men holding her. "Who pushed me?"

An older man released the grip on her coat sleeve. "Some hooded jackass. Reached from behind me to give you a shove. You okay?"

She adjusted her coat. "Yes, thank you." Two attempts in one day. Someone desperately wanted her dead. Her gut clenched with the thought.

The second man bent to retrieve her purse and handed it over. "You should report this to the police."

"I will. Thanks so much to both of you. You saved

my life." Little did they know this was the second attempt today. She lingered behind as the two men crossed the street with the crowd.

Calm down. Slow, deep breaths. She should call Lance…*aw, shit.* She never got Lance's phone number. He was out with Georgette so a call to the precinct to leave a message would be a waste of time. *I'll tell him over dinner.* Sucking in a shuddering breath, she hurried across the street.

The walk settled her nerves, even if paranoia forced her to glance over her shoulder every twenty feet. Once inside the meat shop, she relaxed and let the enticing aromas of smoked meats settle her nerves. She chose a three-pound chuck roast along with several pounds of red potatoes and fresh peas. With a salad on the side and a bottle of wine from Lance's liquor cabinet, she'd make him a feast. *Provided I survive my walk back to the condo.*

Why was someone so determined to kill her? Had the reason been knocked out of her head? Before this trip, she lived a peaceful existence with work and sleep being the two main attractions in her life. Most of the time, traveling for a lecture proved fun, and an outing with a few girlfriends allowed her to let her hair loose—so to speak. Certainly nothing worth killing over. Shaking her head, she left the store and retraced her steps to the condo.

Strolling with purchases clutched to her chest, she contemplated whether this meal was a subconscious desire to make him miss her. Every woman in various cultures used the tactic to snare a man. The old a-way-to-a-man's-heart tactic. Along with sex, of course. Would she stoop so low? Her heart recognized the limitations of their relationship. Despite their chemistry, she and Lance lived in two different cities and had different backgrounds. More importantly, he struggled with the salary issue.

On her part, nothing tied her to Pittsburgh. Her income centered on a computer with Internet connection. The obstacle to any form of union fell strictly onto Lance's lap. His career commitment took precedence. Commendable, but a lonely path. Someday, he might be willing to share his life with a woman—but not today.

At the crosswalk, she glanced over her shoulder to make sure no one followed, but the unmistakable flap of a tire on asphalt sent her nerves into high alert. Whirling in all directions, she scanned the cars. Three black sedans sat at the red light. Two had tinted windshields. The distinct noise couldn't be a coincidence, not after the near-miss by the alley. Someone was following her, and he or she could be in one of those cars. Should she wait to see which car flapped as it drove by?

The opportunity was lost when, through the windows of a corner cafe, Professor Seeley jumped from his seat and waved his hands over his head to catch her attention.

The woman at his table turned to peer out the window then frowned.

Of all people, Kathy Tenemen. What were they doing together? Had the professor accepted the futility of pursuing Dana Null and, instead, settled on Mrs. Tenemen? She wasn't sure if she felt insulted or relieved.

The professor held up a finger in a gesture to wait

then hurried toward the front entrance, leaving Kathy Tenemen with her mouth agape.

Dana scanned for any black sedans, but the light had already changed.

Seeley flew through the door five seconds later, arms outstretched. "Dana, how nice!"

Talk about awkward. Now that she knew he had more than a professional interest, how should she respond? With no time to think, she forced a smile. "Hi, Anthony."

He gaped. "You remember me?"

A small smile toyed on her lips. "Yes, sir. My memories returned. Thank you for the flowers. They are lovely."

"A simple token to show I'm serious about my offer. My house is yours, Dana."

"Anthony, I don't think—"

"Nonsense. Don't think anything. I'm not in a hurry. I shall follow the respectable course and allow an appropriate amount of mourning time."

Her saving grace. Except, why was he having lunch with Kathy Tenemen? Both should be in mourning. "Anthony, I don't want to raise your hopes, but I'm not interested in more than what we have. I love visiting you and giving lectures, but intimacy isn't what we share, and you know I speak the truth."

He twisted his mouth to the side. "We can work on that aspect, my dear." With a finger, he nudged his glasses up his nose. "Strange how events happen. Before Anita's death, I planned to visit my lawyer about initiating divorce proceedings."

Dana simply nodded. What else could she say? Someone killed Anita and saved the professor a ton of money. Too convenient in her book. She shook herself and lifted the bags in her arms. "This food needs refrigeration."

He grabbed onto her elbow. "Will you call me?"

"Oh, sure. As far as I'm concerned, our friendship remains solid. Goodbye, Anthony, and take care of yourself." Solid friendship or not, she cringed at what future visits might entail.

****

"Are you sure your brain is screwed in right?" Georgette maneuvered the car around a double-parked van.

Grumbling, Lance glared at a little old lady walking on the sidewalk. "I expressed my opinion." A little too harshly, unfortunately. For the first time in his career, he lost control.

"You just made my life difficult, you know. I convinced the captain to let you tag along."

He snapped his gaze toward his partner. "McNamara's lackadaisical tone pissed me off. Do you realize she showed no emotion about nearly killing Dana?" He stared out the front window. "I don't buy for a minute her excuse about protecting the professor's reputation." He wanted to wring her thin neck just for the hell of it. A good thing Georgette and several officers stood nearby.

"Relax, will you? We're charging Babs with assault and battery along with grand theft. I'll handle the booking when I return to the station." She braked for a red light and studied him. "She gave a full confession. What's the problem?"

He sneered. "I believe she attacked Dana and stole her equipment, but she denies taking Dana to the alley.

She claims she left Dana in the stairwell."

The traffic light changed to green, and Georgette eased on the gas. "You and I both know Babs is too small for the job."

"Right. So, a second person is involved. Babs knows who that person is." He chewed on his inner lip. "Dana remembers being in the trunk of a car. Since Babs doesn't own a vehicle, someone carried Dana down the stairwell and *that* someone attempted to run Dana over this morning." He shifted on the seat. "I'm convinced Babs and her partner believed Dana to be dead and dumped her body to draw suspicion from the hotel. We should question some fellow students to see who's her frequent companion."

Georgette checked into her rearview mirror. "Not a bad idea. Babs faces a serious felony charge, and unless she gives us a name, she'll serve some substantial jail time."

After rubbing a kink in his neck, Lance stared out the side window. "I wouldn't be a bit surprised to hear Babs has a mean jealous streak."

"Of what?"

"The professor's interest in Dana."

George braked for another red light and glanced his way. "Are you saying Seeley wants more than a professional relationship with Dana?" She stared into her rearview mirror.

"Definitely more."

Snapping her gaze toward him, she gaped. "Are you shitting me?"

A horn blew behind them.

"Green light." Lance pointed toward the traffic signal.

George hit the gas. "Explain, oh, partner of mine."

Lance detailed the professor's visit and then the arrival of the flowers. He also included Tim's unannounced intrusion during breakfast.

After releasing a long breath, Georgette shook her head. "The woman has men falling at her feet and not the best choices either. From a grandfather figure to a bully." She turned right at the next corner. "I knew something bothered you the second you trudged in this afternoon. You and Dana probably had a wonderful night only to have the mood squelched with interruptions." She maneuvered around a double-parked car. "So, why'd you call Tim?"

He winced. "To save Dana from his verbal abuse by explaining her need to stay in town another day. He was not happy." The man couldn't get Dana's lack of interest through his thick skull, and his obsessiveness bordered on the psychotic. A dangerous precedent. And to think Dana's father encouraged the man. Lance squirmed on the seat. "I'm not comfortable with Dana driving to Pittsburgh with such an SOB."

"You can drive her."

He snorted. "The ride would be awkward."

"You've already made things awkward by asking her to stay another night." Slowing the car, she glided to the curb in front of his building and stopped. She touched his arm. "Try not to break her heart, okay? I like her. She has a good head on her shoulders."

Yeah, asking Dana to stay another night wasn't a bright idea, but something pushed the words from his mouth. Ever since he met the beautiful doctor, he changed from a cautious man into an impulsive idiot. Had he an inherent desire to protect her from her abusive family? But for how long? She had to return home sometime and resume her life. To ask her to remain in Baltimore would be wrong. Sure, she captured his heart. As yet, she hadn't cornered his soul, and for that, he patted himself on the back. He would never be right for her.

With a slight nod to Georgette, he exited the car and entered the condo lobby.

Needing to dispense of some restless energy, he skipped the elevator and ascended the stairs. Four floors might cramp his leg, but he had to work the muscle outside of physical therapy. Now was as good a time as any.

Chapter Twenty-Two

As Lance stepped from the stairwell, he gave himself a fist-pump for not cramping his leg. He was on the mend, and every day proved it. Nearing his front door, he sniffed. The delicious aroma of roast beef and onions hit his nose, and his stomach growled. Visions of peas and mashed potatoes smothered in heart-clogging butter floated into his mind. To hell with cholesterol and fat. He'd die a happy man.

Yo, whoa. Wait a minute. Was she playing the way-to-a-man's-heart trap? Every mother taught her daughter the age-old con. Add a little sweet talk, a flowing negligee followed by plenty of sex, and a man found a dog collar around his neck. *Not me, sister.* The ploy might work with a weaker man, but not him. No, sirree. Only one more night with Dana. For her sake, he'd make it a short night. Slipping his key into the lock, he straightened his shoulders and opened the door.

Eyeglasses perched on her nose, Dana sat on the sofa while staring at his open laptop on the coffee table. She still wore her jeans and sweatshirt. So, no sexy negligee. A wave of something passed over him. Whether disappointment or relief, he couldn't tell. He wasn't a man willing to analyze his feelings, but damn, if she didn't look brainy and beautiful at the same time.

Tearing her gaze from the view screen, she smiled. "Hi."

All right, so maybe he had the scenario pegged all wrong. She wasn't stretched out on the sofa to entice him as he strolled through the door. No soft music or lighted candles, either. Too bad. He could envision her greeting him after a day of chasing bad guys. Shaking away the thought, he cleared his throat. "Hi, yourself." He hung his coat and sniffed. "Smells good in here. Did Thelma cook?"

"No, my doing. You deserve a payback dinner for taking care of me." She flicked her gaze to the computer screen. "Thelma directed me to the butcher shop a couple of blocks from here. Nice place, too. I bought a roast big enough for leftovers." She tapped a few buttons on the keyboard then leaned back, her gaze scanning him. "Was I right about Babs?"

"What—wait." He narrowed his gaze. "You went out?"

She cringed. "Yeah, sorry. I—eh…well—" She cleared her throat. "Look, someone pushed me off the curb, okay? I would have called you but didn't have your phone number."

Holy hell. She would give him a heart attack yet. He flopped onto the sofa and sighed. "You are to tell me when you leave the condo. You're not safe alone." *What a friggin' moron.* He left her unguarded, knowing full well two people were involved. She wasn't safe to go anywhere without an escort. Jaw tight, he gritted his teeth. "What time was this?"

She bit her lower lip. "I'd say around three."

"We had McNamara in custody then so she's eliminated." Gut twisting, he gripped his knees. No ignoring the fact now. Someone wanted Dana dead. Two attempts in the same day. Why? They destroyed her equipment. What else did she know? More than ever, he must get the name of the second culprit from McNamara. Dana wouldn't be safe until both were locked behind bars.

"I didn't get hurt. Two men caught me."

Well, thank the Lord. At least, someone took care of her. He clenched his teeth. "Babs confessed to the assault and the theft of your equipment but went mum on a partner's name. She claims she hadn't meant to hit you so hard."

"And you don't believe her."

A statement, not a question. He scowled. "In my experience, an assailant doesn't go after someone with a two-by-four for a gentle tap on the noggin."

"And her excuse for stealing my equipment?"

Frowning, he rubbed his stubbled chin. "To spare the professor the embarrassment of his wife sitting with Tenemen. She was afraid you would post the shot on your website."

Dana shook her head. "I post the questions, not the video. She should know my habit by now. What about her argument with Anita?"

"She admitted arguing but not to the murder. She also denies the attempt to run over you this morning." Dana just provided proof of a partner in Babs' scheme. That partner had to be strong enough to carry Dana down a flight of stairs. A man? And someone with a car. That thought narrowed the suspect list to maybe a couple hundred university students. *Hmm.* He pointed to the laptop. "What's up?"

"I'm checking my email. I hope you don't mind." She typed a few keystrokes then stopped. Puckering her lips, she rotated toward him. "On my way back from the butcher shop, I ran into Professor Seeley having coffee with Kathy Tenemen. You think it means anything?"

An interesting twist and a possible angle to consider. Dead husband, dead wife. Co-conspirators. "Worth checking out. Tomorrow, I'll mention it to George and…" He tapped a finger on her knee. "I'll also tell her about your push from the curb and the fact that you'll give me a stroke before all this is over."

Her cellphone rang. Reaching around the laptop, she grabbed the phone for a quick glance at the caller ID. Groaning, she dropped her chin to her chest. "Tim again. He's called three times already. Plus, two from my mother, and one from my father." Lifting her head, she sighed. "From here on, all calls go to voicemail." The ring stopped. Removing her eyeglasses, she met his gaze. "Everyone's upset because you asked me to stay another night. Why did you?"

Because fools do stupid things. He forced a smile. "To wrap up loose ends." What a dumb excuse. Hell, a phone call served the same purpose. He clenched his jaw. "I hope you didn't get the wrong idea."

"What, another night of freewheeling sex?" Smile brief, she faced forward. "Yeah, but that's okay. I'm a big girl." She tossed her glasses onto the coffee table.

The sparkle disappeared from her green eyes. He should use his brain a little better. What else would she think, especially after their wonderful night together?

Feeling like a heel, he placed his elbows on his knees while avoiding any glance in her direction. "We recovered your equipment from the dumpster two blocks from McNamara's apartment building. She smashed everything to oblivion." He looked her way.

"Once our forensics team dusts for prints, I'll ship the equipment to your home address. An expert can download the contents onto another hard drive."

"No, don't bother. The important stuff is on my desk computer, and everything else is on the cloud. Besides—" She closed his laptop. "The damaged equipment will remind me of you." She met his gaze. "I'd rather not."

He held her gaze for a long time. Uncertainty registered in her eyes. She had a right to her doubts. Hell, he was loaded with so many conflicting feelings, he might as well flash a neon sign over his head with the words *Totally Befuddled*.

Slapping her thighs, Dana stood. "Let's eat." She turned toward the kitchen.

"I need to wash my hands." Grateful for a chance to collect his thoughts, he headed for his bedroom to remove his ankle gun and splash cold water on his face.

She took the two attempts on her life with a grain of salt. How could she act so calm? Another woman would be in hysterics. If he had his way, he'd have her in his arms and—

No, don't go that route. Dana had the potential to do so much with her life. How could she be interested in a cop, a guy who earned less money and had only a BS in criminology? Not to mention he came from a middle-class family with two parents who worked off their asses to provide for their three children. He was doing Dana a big favor. After tossing the towel onto the sink, he joined her in the kitchen.

Dinner was everything he imagined. The beef was melt-in-his-mouth tender. Butter and chives smothered tiny red potatoes. Peas, salad, and gravy along with a perfect red wine rounded out the meal. Delicious. To make his supper even better, he had a gorgeous woman across the table. No denying the obvious. The woman could cook. He served himself more meat. While cutting, he studied her. "I want you to call me on your next trip to town."

Something flickered in her gaze.

Hesitation? He deserved every ounce of reluctance.

A sad smile curved one corner of her mouth. "I won't call, Lance. We're done after tonight. It's what you want."

Even so, the words cut into his heart like a knife. He wasn't sure what he wanted. How could he make any relationship work, especially with a woman too damn smart and financially independent to be with a guy like him? The breadwinner called the shots, right? Or was that thought too old fashioned? She made a hell of a lot more money, and in no time, he'd face a submissive existence, one where the woman cracked the whip and dictated all the rules. He wasn't that kind of man.

The meal became tasteless.

After dinner, he relaxed on the sofa with his stockinged feet resting on the foot stool, TV remote in hand. The evening news began the broadcast with a four-car pileup on the Beltway. Then came the murders, rapes, and political posturing. The same old bullshit of which nothing registered.

Dana squatted on the floor by his DVD shelves and rummaged.

While staring at her back, he felt the strangest wave of something. Peace? No, more like contentment. She belonged here—three words he never thought he'd use. Not once had she said a condescending word about his self-assembled furniture or mismatched china. Yet, he'd bet his meager bank account she lived in a much better condo, or even a house in a swanky neighborhood. What if he asked her to stay? Would she? *Why do I beat myself up over her*? They lived in two different worlds, and nothing would change those glaring facts.

She released a cry. "*Star Wars*!" Face beaming, she whirled while waving the disc. "Want to? I haven't seen this movie in ages."

Smiling at her enthusiasm, he motioned toward the DVD player. "Put it in."

After popping the movie into the player, she kicked off her shoes and curled onto the opposite end of the sofa.

Away from him, of course. Hell, she should be cuddled under his arm. They'd spent a beautiful night and morning in each other's embrace, and here, they behaved like two friends again. He raked his fingers through his hair before catching her gaze. "I had selfish reasons to delay your departure, Dana, and it didn't have anything to do with the attempt on your life this morning or the case."

She gave him a long, searching look but said nothing.

Dropping his feet to the floor, he leaned toward her, never breaking his gaze. "I wanted one last night together."

A slow smile appeared. "Before we say goodbye?"

"Yes…that."

The searching look continued. After what felt like an eternity, he sucked in a huge breath and lowered his gaze. She had every right to refuse him—asshole that he was.

"Lance."

He slid his gaze to her face.

Her lips quirked to the side, and she nodded. "I wondered if you'd let me go without a move."

Unable to hold off another second, he stretched across the sofa to pull her onto his lap. To hell with Luke Skywalker and the Death Star. This woman agreed to one last night, and he intended to relish every second.

He clamped a hand behind her neck and captured her mouth. Their tongues danced. She tasted of beef and potatoes and smelled like flowers. Damn, what an aphrodisiac!

Her hand drifted to his crotch where an erection strained against his blue jeans. As she deepened the kiss, she massaged with a slow motion. The heat of her hand plus the furnace under his jeans threatened to end their liaison before it began.

He moaned into her mouth.

Lifting her head, she smiled. "We might as well make this a memorable night."

Swinging over her leg, she straddled his lap and unfastened his belt. She worked the zipper next with a pause after every inch.

The seductive unfastening nearly did him in.

Slipping onto the floor and dropping to her knees, she patted both his thighs. "Lift your hips."

She already had him hard and ready, but her command caused an ache to pulse. He obeyed—which surprised him. This was the submissiveness he detested…or so he believed. Deep down, he longed for her to do whatever she damned well pleased.

Gripping his belt with two hands, she tugged his pants and underwear down his legs.

He kicked the garments free and sat exposed, rigid with need. "Dana—"

"Shhh."

She lifted her sweatshirt over her head.

At the sight of her nipples screaming to be suckled, he reached.

Swatting his hands, she again straddled his lap. "I'm doing the titillation here, detective."

She unbuttoned his shirt to expose his chest. Her green eyes darkened as she ran her fingers along the contours of his muscles.

Goosebumps surfaced and sent a shiver straight to his core.

Smiling, she leaned close and licked his nipples, her tongue toying with the tit.

His cock twitched, and he growled. "You better lower those jeans, woman."

"In a bit."

Oh, my God. She purposely went out of her way to torture him.

Her soft fingers gripped his shaft.

Dear Lord Almighty. He wouldn't last much longer. Heat rushed from every pore on his body as her hand worked its magic. Heart pounding, he swore he'd go into cardiac arrest and die on the spot, and what a wonderful way to go. Climax beckoned…without her. "Dana?"

She pulled away.

The glint in her gaze floored him. She enjoyed his agony, and the mischievous imp winked as she hopped from his lap and ran to his bedroom. Seconds later, she returned with a condom packet between her teeth as she unsnapped her jeans and kicked them loose. His breath hitched at the sight of her beautiful, naked body, and his gaze followed the contours of her small shape, from the delicate curves of her breasts to the slight flare of her hips. Like a prized sculpture, only better.

She tossed him the packet.

Catching it, he smirked. "Obviously, you saw where I stored them."

"Yep, right next to your thirty-eight." Gaze twinkling, she cocked her head. "Symbolic, wouldn't you say?"

He frowned. "I don't consider my penis a smoking gun, if that's what you mean." He gestured with his head. "Bedroom first?"

"Oh, no. We're christening the sofa."

Under her watchful gaze, he rolled on the condom. His hands shook so badly, he doubted if he'd seat the latex before exploding. Finished, he clamped onto her hips.

She straddled his lap and placed her moist heat against his shaft. Rocking gently, she slipped his shirt from his shoulders in one smooth move.

"I don't often allow a woman the upper hand." He rolled his eyes closed. She felt so damn good.

"Oh? And why not? Seems to me you're enjoying my machinations."

She could machinate all she wanted. He wouldn't dare complain. He lunged at her mouth, and she responded by jabbing her tongue in deep while her vagina took him in one deep thrust.

Fireworks exploded behind his eyeballs. His

thoughts shattered as pure pleasure took over. He turned into her slave now and forever. "Dana, I can't hold back."

"Then, let loose, Lance—please!"

He clamped onto her hips and drove to her core, shuddering against her chest as his release hit.

Still locked together, she rocked until a moan escaped from her throat.

He grabbed her butt and humped, giving her the ride she deserved.

Within minutes, she threw back her head, closed her eyes, and released a cry.

Every part of her skin flushed pink, and her muscles tightened around him. Her incredible responsiveness shot a bolt of manly pride straight to his heart.

Once the pulsing of her muscles eased, she collapsed onto his chest, her breaths heavy.

He wrapped her in a tight embrace, unwilling to let her go. After a lapse of time that felt like heaven on earth, she shifted to release their connection.

Her gaze dark, she pecked his lips. "That was nice."

"Nice? You're wonderful, Dana. I mean it."

Sadness replaced the smile in her eyes, and she traced a finger along his chin. "I'll miss you, Lance."

He took her head in his hands. "We've had a memorable week. I'll never forget you." Not the best way to tell a woman goodbye, but he couldn't ask her to stay any longer.

She slipped off his lap and gathered her clothes.

This was it, then, the end of a brief affair. He should be happy, maybe even overjoyed, but only emptiness filled his chest. Fighting emotions so incredibly foreign, he coughed to clear his throat. "I'll be out the door before you wake, Dana. Don't let Tim bully you." Damn, he sounded as if marbles replaced his tongue.

"How will I lock the door?"

"I'll leave Thelma's phone number on the table. Call her when you leave."

Clutching her clothes to her chest, she nodded. "Thank you, Lance, for everything."

He loved every minute of her being here but, for some reason, couldn't verbalize the words. Sighing, he followed her naked body as she moseyed toward the hall and disappeared.

Chapter Twenty-Three

Georgette slammed a fist on her desk. "What the hell are you so grumpy about?"

The damn woman had the nerve to smile after causing everyone in the department to jump from their seat. So what if his attention centered on a woman at his condo? Officially, he wasn't on duty and only escaped into the hustle of the department to avoid another heart-wrenching goodbye. Lance glared at his partner. "I am not grumpy." Just irritated as hell and mad at the universe. He should be happy being in familiar surroundings and not dwelling on what could never be.

"You aren't expected here until Monday, you know." George leaned across her desk. "Why don't you go home and be with Dana?"

Lance kicked shut his desk drawer. "She's leaving this morning." He checked his watch. "I'm sure Tim's swept her away by now."

The image of Tim near Dana boiled his blood. The damn man didn't deserve such a wonderful woman, and no way in hell would Lance Barnes stick around to see his smug expression. With luck, Dana would show her newfound backbone and fight for her right to choose her own mate. He grumbled a few obscenities.

"What was that?"

Lance glared at his partner. "I wasn't talking to you."

"Then, maybe I should tell the captain you're having conversations with yourself." She tapped a pen on the desk, lips pursed. "I know what you're thinking, Lance. A doctor of anthropology can't be interested in a cop."

He clenched his jaw. "You read my mind, sister. She makes way too much money. I don't want to wind up divorced like everyone else in this place."

She snorted. "I suppose my twelve-year marriage has no bearing on this valued opinion of yours?"

"You're the exception." More than an exception. Georgette and her husband, Mark, were the envy of the entire department. He straightened a stack of file folders.

While shaking her head, Georgette reclined in her chair. "If you're sticking around, then I'll discuss the case."

"Please do." Anything to divert his mind from Dana. Of course, he could go through his desk drawers and clean out the accumulated junk.

Georgette knocked on her desk. "Hey, concentrate, will you? I don't want to repeat this stuff."

Jerking to attention, he swiveled his chair to face her. "Yes, I'm ready. Go ahead." He couldn't fool her. He was about as ready as a sloth in a foot race.

She waved her pen at the case board. "First, we need to put the facts into proper perspective. We've very little in the way of concrete evidence. No witnesses, no fingerprints, and no DNA." She faced him. "Not even a murder weapon. So, let's talk about circumstances."

Lance loved how Georgette broke down a case. She analyzed every minute detail, no matter how insignificant. Each single shred of evidence had to fit. Five years ago, she took a young detective named Lance Barnes under her wing and taught him the finer aspects of investigative work. Her skill with body language was legendary. Nothing slipped past her sharp eye, not even her partner's funky moods.

Hell, he couldn't hide his anger, even though he accepted Dana's leaving as for the best. Early this morning, before sunrise, he slipped into her bedroom to watch her sleep. In her hand, she clutched a tissue, and a tear puddled at the bridge of her nose. She cried herself to sleep. He never meant to hurt her, but in time, she'd understand the importance of going their separate ways—she in her world of science and fine wine, and he in his world of criminals and beer.

Georgette's chair squeaked.

The harsh sound broke into his thoughts, and he shook himself. "Start from the beginning, George."

"Of course." With her elbows on her armrests, she steepled her fingers and stared at the board. "Anita Seeley attends a lecture for reasons unknown, has never bothered to step foot into any lecture hall before that night, and only shows on campus for a new boy toy." She swiveled toward Lance. "What enticed her to the lecture?"

He leaned back in his chair. "To meet a new squeeze, or perhaps curiosity about her husband's work." He shrugged. "An infinite number of possibilities. How about her cellphone records?"

"The list shows calls to and from her sister, the professor, a boyfriend who's in Indiana until next Sunday, and several others, none of which panned out. The most recent call came from a disposable phone at six-thirty on the night of the lecture."

With one eyebrow cocked, Lance leaned on his desk. "The call lured her to the lecture."

"My thoughts exactly—although I'm curious about the excuse the caller used. How do you entice a woman to a place she's never been?"

"Maybe a monetary reward."

She shook her head. "She had enough money. What else?"

He pursed his lips. "How about a frat party where she's the main attraction?"

Chuckling, Georgette tucked a loose hair strand behind her ear. "She's known for visiting a few fraternity houses."

"Then, whoever lured her to the hall knew what to say. I'm banking on a sexual angle of some sort."

"Me, too. As part of the professor's rules, Anita must return home before ten. His curfew was a well-known joke around campus and made it convenient for whoever waited outside the house." She relaxed her arms onto the chair's armrests. "So, halfway through the lecture, Anita walks in and sits next to a handsome man seemingly by chance. The seats are random, not assigned. I can't find any proof they knew each other. Everyone I've talked to labeled Michael Tenemen as a good family man, always with his wife and kids, and active in the community. Whenever he went somewhere, he told his wife. Since he spoke three languages, he had a genuine interest in Doctor Null's work, read the notice for her being in town, and attended the lecture. Excuse me."

She yanked a tissue from the box on her desk and blew her nose. After lobbing the rolled ball into the trash, she sniffed. "Last week, my cousin, Alice, came over and gave me her cold. I hope I don't pass it along to the kids." She swiveled. "Where was I? Okay, so Anita strikes up a conversation with Tenemen and discovers he's a real estate broker. He shows her a few houses on his tablet then hands her a business card." She scratched her nose. "I found the card in the trash bin by the outside doors. Maybe Tenemen wasn't her type."

A young man in handcuffs shuffled by with a pant's belt cutting into his crotch. The detective escorting him glanced at Lance and rolled his eyes. Cops loved a young man's show-the-underwear phase. No man, no matter how athletic, ran fast with a pants crotch at his knees.

Georgette stared at the young man's ass. "I sure hope this fashion statement passes before my boys reach puberty." She returned her gaze to the board. "Tenemen's cell records confirm he called his wife prior to leaving the lecture hall. No records show he called Anita or vice versa. One hour after leaving campus and as she steps from her car, Anita is stabbed to death. The neighborhood is upper-middle class with single homes and average crime. The following morning, Tenemen is bludgeoned to death on his daily jog at the high school track." A frown forming, she plunked her elbows onto the desk and met his gaze. "At first, I considered Tenemen's murder as the wrong place at the wrong time."

"Until Dana's video."

"Right, and this brings us to our suspects and their alibis." Standing, she strolled to her case board. "Let's start with the professor." She tapped his photo. "I confirmed his presence at a faculty meeting. Afterward, at nine-twenty, he and several other teachers walked to the parking lot. Before heading home, he stopped at a convenience store for a newspaper and a bottle of juice. Security cameras clocked his time at nine-thirty-five. He arrives home at eleven to see cops all over the place."

Lance narrowed his gaze. "Quite a commute. Where's he live?"

She smiled and rested a hip on the corner of her desk. "I drove from the store to his house—in the daytime with more traffic on the road. I only took twenty minutes. When confronted with the discrepancy in time, he admitted parking outside Dana's hotel. Street cameras confirmed he sat and sipped his juice. When questioned why, he said the hour was too late to call on her."

Meanwhile, Dana was upstairs and becoming a victim herself. *Damn the man.* Leaning forward, Lance bristled. "He had the perfect opportunity to prevent her assault."

"Or be attacked along with her. So, the question is did he hire someone to kill his wife while he conveniently placed himself in front of cameras? He expressed genuine surprise when I told him of Anita's attendance at the lecture. Truthfully, Seeley's prenup gave Anita more of a reason to kill her husband than the other way around."

Standing and turning to the board, she tapped another photo. "Babs McNamara is next. She's on her way to receive a doctorate in anthropology and been the professor's assistant for two years. She arrives at the hall, sees Anita with another man, and assumes the worst. To save the professor from the embarrassment, she assaults Dana and steals her equipment, thereby assuring no one sees the video, unaware of Dana's habit of transferring 'the lectures onto a flash drive. Babs' apartment is four blocks from the hotel, an easy distance to carry the equipment. She does not own a car but has a driver's license. Time-wise, her assault on Dana coincides with the time of Anita's murder."

He frowned. "So, Babs is not Anita's killer." He drummed his fingers on the desk. "Strong motive. No opportunity." He shot a quick glance at his partner. "What about Tenemen's murder? Any possibility Babs performed the dirty deed?"

A sad smile lifted one corner of her mouth. "Tenemen's murder took place somewhere between seven and seven-twenty. That same morning, Babs arrived fifteen minutes late for her seven-thirty class. She said she received a call from the Dean's office about a package for the professor. No one in the office admits to making the call nor was a package waiting. Cell records show the call came from a disposable phone." Scowling, she sat on the corner of her desk and stared at the board.

Crossing his arms over his chest, Lance rocked his chair. "Who knew Tenemen well enough to know where and when he jogged?"

She glanced over her shoulder. "Besides his wife?" Gaze twinkling, she again tapped on a photo.

He raised a brow. "Anita's sister?"

"Yes, Margaret Horton. She jogs the same track every morning." She huffed. "Except that morning, of course. She claims she slept late and barely arrived at work on time." Moving away from the board, she flopped into her chair with a grunt. "Too much circumstantial evidence."

"Here's more." Lance related Dana's news about Seeley and Kathy Tenemen at the cafe.

Pursing her lips, Georgette rocked her chair, creating a series of faint squeaks. "The professor has a history of marrying women in their mid-to-late twenties. At forty, Mrs. Tenemen is a bit old." She stopped rocking. "I'll question them to see their reaction."

"Wouldn't hurt." Lance advised Georgette of Dana's push from the curb. Jaw twitching, he pounded a fist on his desk. "I was damn stupid for leaving her unguarded. She could have been killed."

"You're human, Lance, not super cop." She bit her lower lip.

Still, he should kick himself in the ass for leaving her alone.

Once again, resting her elbows on the armrests, Georgette steepled her fingers. "Let's do a little speculation. Why was Anita killed?"

The woman had a knack for analytical banter. He loved it. Leaning back, he intertwined his fingers behind his neck. "I'd say our strongest motive is embarrassment for the professor. Flaunting his money comes second."

"Who stood to gain by her death?"

"I see only Babs. Same age. Adores the professor. Maybe she wants to take Anita's place."

"But Babs is the one suspect who has a good alibi."

"All right then, she whacks Dana on the head while her partner kills Anita. Where does Tenemen fit in?

Who gains?"

"His wife, who has an alibi." She sighed. "At the time of the murder, Mrs. Tenemen arrived at the daycare center to deliver her kids."

Dropping his hands to the armrests, Lance stared at the board and at all the faces in the photos. "This case stinks."

"Agreed. We've holes big enough for an elephant." She stood and stretched. "I'm taking a walk to clear my head. Want some coffee?"

"I'll take a cup. If there's a carton of French vanilla cream in the fridge, pour in a hefty amount. Otherwise, I'll sit here and mull things over."

When she left, he let his gaze wander over the case board. What were they missing? Could the deaths of these two people be random, or was something more sinister going on?

Lance locked his gaze onto Dana's photo in the bottom center of the board. She photographed well, and when her smile reached her eyes, she had the power to knock any man off his feet. For some reason, the thought jabbed a corkscrew right into his heart.

Georgette returned with two covered cups of coffee. "No French vanilla. Your black as usual." She handed him one. "Any light bulbs going off?"

Tossing the plastic lid in the trash, Lance sipped. Someone made the coffee from tap water. Ugh. The brew tasted like a metal pipe. He slipped the cup onto the desk. "What if we're looking at this all wrong?"

Grimacing while staring into her cup, Georgette replaced the lid and shuddered. "I knew I should have gone down the street for coffee." Placing her cup to the side, she cocked a brow. "You were saying?" She flopped into her chair.

He drummed his fingers on his desk pad then glanced her way. "Is McNamara still in lockup?"

"Not anymore. The professor posted her bail. If she has a cohort, she'd rather go down alone than give me a name." Folding her arms on the desk, she leaned forward. "What's on your mind?"

Georgette scrutinized him with an intensity all too familiar. She was the teacher waiting for the student to respond. She had tremendous patience during their early years together, and a rumor circulating pegged her as the next captain of homicide. He wagged a finger at the board. "This case is an elaborate plan to thwart us, one carefully plotted and executed." He met her gaze. "You mentioned earlier about Dana being the key to your case. I agree. I've the strangest feeling everything hinges on Dana's attack."

Her gaze twinkled. "All right, let's work that angle." Reaching across her desk toward a pile of case folders, she took the top one, opened it, and flipped through the pages. "The coroner places Anita's time of death between ten-ten and ten-forty. Dana's attack occurred at roughly ten-fifteen." She looked up. "What else?"

"The hotel manager, Gary Cary, bothered me."

She grinned. "You might be experiencing a male reaction to his close proximity to Dana, but let me see." She flipped more pages. "On that night, he was the sole employee on the front desk until his relief arrived at midnight. More than likely, Mr. Cary sat in his office and away from the camera view screens when Dana's assault took place. The main entrance automatically locks at eleven every night. Anyone needing to enter must use their hotel key or be buzzed in by the front desk." George tapped a fingernail on the case folder before sliding her gaze toward his. "I walked down the stairwell and headed out a side door opening directly into the alley. No one at the front desk saw me. So, Dana could have been carried down and placed into the trunk of a waiting car." Slipping a pen between two fingers, she drummed the tip on the pages. Stopping, she pointed the pen at Lance. "Did Dana see anything else besides Babs' blue band?"

He shifted on his seat. "Diamonds."

Mouth agape, George stared. "A ring?"

"She said no."

His cellphone rang. The caller ID caused a little pitter-patter within his chest. *Dana*. The thought of hearing her voice lifted his spirits. He missed her, damnit, and he hadn't realized how much until this very second. He turned away from his desk. "Hi."

"Hi, yourself. Thanks for inputting your cell number into my phone. Listen, something occurred to me. Do you remember I mentioned diamonds?"

He swiveled to face his partner. "George and I were just discussing them."

"Well, I think they were white with an aura of red."

"The image can be from the blow to your head, Dana." He chewed on his inner lip. "The hotel hall had an awful lot of red but no red in the alcove." Hell, more confusion. He stole a quick glance at Georgette and shrugged. *Whoa, hold on a minute!* His gut tightened. A mental picture flashed into his mind, and damn, his blood boiled. "Dana, do you think the diamonds were Argyle socks?"

A loud gasp. "Yes!"

Grinning, he fist-pumped. "Honey, I could kiss you."

"Well, you've already done that."

Multiple times, and the thought broadened his grin. Catching Georgette's lifted brow, he coughed and again turned from his desk. "Where are you?"

"Waiting for Tim. He'll be here any minute." She paused. "I didn't call him right away."

"Good girl. Make him suffer. Will you let me know when you're home safe?"

A long pause. "If you want."

"Yes, I want."

He disconnected and stared point-blank at Georgette. "I know who McNamara's partner is."

Chapter Twenty-Four

Sighing, Dana dropped her suitcase by the front door and stared down, as if waiting for her luggage to walk on its own. The time had come to go home and face her life before this Baltimore trip. Not that she existed in a mundane world. Her career took off years ago because of her multi-lingual talents. She had a load of friends and money in the bank, but she had yet to achieve a satisfying love life.

For as long as she could remember, her parents pestered her to marry Tim. "He'll take care of you. He's the man you can trust." The more she resisted, the more they instilled her with this overwhelming fear of never finding the right man. As history proved, they might be right. No man stepping across her threshold had yet to squelch this deep-seated fear. Not even Lance. He, like so many others, rejected her.

Despite experiencing his gut-wrenching brush-off, she'd treasure every moment of her stay and the memory of his strong arms around her. If she sniffed spicy aftershave or watched a man hobble on a cane, she'd think of Lance. If she ever spotted a muscle mag again, she'd remember his broad chest and thick thighs. In just a few short days, Lance filled her with a new and wonderful world—one full of love and a sense of belonging. A short-lived world, for sure. Shaking her head, she turned toward the closet.

How many times in life must she experience the heartbreak of a failed relationship? Men expressed their attraction and, after a few days, disappeared into oblivion. Why? She enjoyed sex as much as the next woman. She certainly had a great time with Lance, but like all the men before him, he made his feelings clear by leaving this morning without so much as a goodbye. He said he'd be gone before she woke, and he kept his word. She wouldn't be surprised to hear he ran down the stairwell like his heels were on fire.

All right, admit the truth. For the first time ever, she fell in love with a wonderful man. Lance took care of her, soothed her fears, and cleared the confusion clouding her mind. Pride prevented her from telling him. He didn't feel the same, and she wasn't about to open her heart so he could stomp it flat. Reaching inside the closet, she yanked her overcoat from the hanger and closed the door.

Maybe she needed a good book on the mysteries of manhood. Men passed in and out of her life like Houdini. Poof, gone. She never understood why. She wasn't needy-greedy, and every time she looked in a mirror, a decent image stared back. No ugly scars or face full of zits. After meeting and loving Lance, she liked the idea of a man with some muscle, one who literally swept her off her feet. She hadn't met too many anthropologists with a drool-worthy build. Most were skinny as a rail—like her. Ignoring the emptiness in her chest, she draped her overcoat across the back of the sofa.

Because of Lance, she had the courage to face her demanding parents and their asinine marriage plans. As soon as possible, she'd cut off their *Tim this, Tim that* speech. Like Tim existed for the sole purpose of becoming Dana's mate. *Bloody hell.* What a thought. Their generous offer to raise Tim as their own turned into little Dana's curse, destined to follow wherever she roamed. Well, enough was enough. She felt love for the first time and yearned to experience the feeling again. *And damnit, I will.*

Like so many times in the past, she accepted defeat. Years of men disappearing taught her life moved on. Her first plan of action—aside from telling her parents and Tim to take a hike—was to send out feelers for a condo in State College, Pennsylvania. After that, she'd sell her Pittsburgh place and maybe check out an archaeology dig for some fun. She'd have a fight on her hands with her parents' constant meddling, but Lance instilled a strong sense of self-worth. She would fight them…she had to.

The doorbell rang. Squaring her shoulders, she took one last look around at a home permanently embedded into her memory, with its assembled furniture and the sofa christened with their lovemaking. The latter flooded her heart with irony. *Never again.* She opened the door.

She expected Tim to be on the other side, but a sudden coldness hit her core.

Babs McNamara stood on the threshold.

Resisting the urge to slam the door in her face, Dana glared at the woman who nearly ended her life. "What?"

Cringing, Babs shifted on her feet. "I'm sorry to bother you, Dr. Null, but I'm here to apologize."

Was she joking? How the hell could she respond after having her world turned upside down? With her hand gripping the doorknob, Dana narrowed her gaze. "How did you know I was here?"

Diverting her gaze, Babs kicked the doorsill. "In the lecture hall, you mentioned you were staying with Detective Barnes." She shot Dana a quick glance. "Professor Seeley looked up the address. He had me send the flowers. Did you get them?"

"Yes, they were nice." She tossed them into the trash. She couldn't take them with her, and they'd wither and die in Lance's care.

Babs peeked around Dana. "Is the detective here? I'd like to apologize to him, too."

What the hell for? She wasn't in the mood for niceties, but she kept her tone civil. "He's at the precinct."

"Oh." She pointed toward Dana's suitcase. "You're leaving?"

Pretty damn obvious with a suitcase by the door. "Yes, my ride's on the way. Forgive me for not asking you in."

"I understand." She tugged on her shoulder strap. "I hadn't meant to hit you so hard, but I wanted that video before the professor faced another of Anita's embarrassments." She rotated her shoulders and threw her chin high. "Professor Seeley told me my coming here is the right thing to do…apologize to you, I mean."

Oh, yeah, and you sound so sincere. The woman raised the hairs on the back of Dana's neck. Without any experience in such matters, how did one react to a face-to-face encounter with one's attacker? Her instincts warned her to pull back, be polite but cautious. Something felt all wrong. For one, Babs showed no emotion, not even the flick of an eyebrow. Her hazel eyes appeared like two bottomless pits. Big deal, she shifted on her feet like a nervous Nelly and clutched the purse strap with a death grip, but other than that, nothing showed on her face. Dana crossed her arms over her chest. "You dumped me in an alley."

"We thought you were dead."

We? She inwardly jerked. Squinting, she shot a quick glance behind Babs. "Who are 'we', Babs?"

"Me, of course," said a male voice.

Gary, from the Red Wolf Hotel, slipped around Babs and used a two-finger push on Dana's shoulder to nudge her into the living room.

Gary? The man who acted more like a friend than a hotel manager? Stunned, she backed away from his nudge.

Babs followed and closed the door.

Oh, shit. Chills ran straight up her spine and tingled her hair follicles. She didn't need a PhD to understand their intentions. While Babs had a blank look and acted like an automaton, Gary flashed a wild gaze which cut through to Dana's soul. But something familiar… She started at the similarities about the two. They stood at different heights with Gary being two to three inches taller, but the same prominence to the jaw and arched eyebrows made her throat constrict. With her stomach rolling, Dana gaped. "You're brother and sister!"

Babs' mouth twisted to the side. "Leave it to an anthropologist to see our resemblance."

Sneering, Gary took a quick look around the living room. "Same mother, different fathers, and different last names. Funny that." His colorless eyes turned into slits. "Who's your ride?"

"Brother. He'll be here any second." And for the

first time ever, Tim was late. Did they meet him downstairs? If Tim got hurt, she'd never forgive herself.

Gary plucked a pair of leather gloves from his coat pocket and shrugged into them.

Apology, hell. They came to finish the job. The revelation shot bile up her esophagus, and her heart rate skyrocketed. They wanted her dead. Plain and simple. She had to act fast. But how? Two against one. *Fight or die*. Fists clenched, she took another step back. "What do you want?" Obvious to her but she asked anyway. Buying time. Praying for a miracle, like maybe Lance returning to say goodbye. *Yeah, dream on.*

With a wicked grin, Gary tugged a lead pipe from the waistband of his trousers. "What better way to confuse the cops than to kill another person connected to the Seeley case and in a cop's home? Babs was brilliant when she concocted the plan."

These two were on a killing spree. How the hell could she fight insanity? She swallowed the acid in her throat. "But why me?"

Babs' emotionless face flared into a fireball.

My God, the woman twitched her jaw and bared her teeth, like an animal ready to charge. Pure hatred emanated from her stiff stance as she locked gazes with Dana. *What did I ever do to the girl?* Dana opened her mouth to speak, but words wouldn't come.

Throwing her purse to the floor, Babs approached with a finger pointing in Dana's face. "The professor wants *you* as his next wife. I didn't plan Anita's murder to let you waltz in."

Dana gasped. "But I'm not interested in the professor."

"Doesn't matter. He won't look my way until

you're six feet in the ground."

Gary waved the pipe. "I'll take care of her this time, Babs. Guard the door."

Desperate to stretch her remaining time on earth, Dana kept an eye on Gary but pointed at Babs. "But your sister already confessed to my assault. She'll become their number one suspect."

"Ha!" Babs stuck out her chin. "This scheme is all about confusion, Doctor. After Gary kills you, he'll leave me to call the cops. I'll be so upset to find the door open and you dead." She tapped the side of her head. "I've a brain inside my skull." With a crooked grin, she squared her shoulders. "I can make the professor happy."

"And his money will make us both happy." Gary pounded the pipe against his opposite palm.

Another couple of feet and he'd be within striking distance. What the hell should she do? With a bone-dry mouth, Dana took another step back and swallowed hard. "Was my assault premeditated?"

Babs took a position by the front door. "Not in the beginning. Anita sitting next to Tenemen and being on your camera changed our plans. I couldn't have the cops connect them, and I figured I should get rid of you while I had the chance."

Gee, how thoughtful. She walked into Babs and Gary's elaborate plan for an easy life with the professor's money. And poor Anita's fate was sealed before the lecture. *Oh, God, I'm going to be sick.* She sucked in a shuddering breath. "But why Tenemen?"

Gary's gaze shot fire. "That SOB sold me a house destined for the city's imminent domain project. All hush-hush. He denied any knowledge. I'm suing his firm. Then, Babs saw him sitting right next to Anita, and we couldn't pass on such an opportunity."

"And confuse the cops even more." Babs narrowed her gaze. "Then, wouldn't you know? The professor groaned about the faculty meeting keeping him from your usual dinner. He told me he married the wrong woman. He meant you, Doc. So yeah, you had to go."

Stepping forward, Gary lowered the pipe to his side. "Everything went well except you're still alive. I'm here to correct the problem. Then, I'll finish off your brother." Noting Dana's step backward, he wagged a finger. "You can't go anywhere, Doc."

Yeah, no shit. Why didn't they build condos with a secondary door? Who the hell designed these places anyway? She bumped into the end table. "I can scream, Gary."

He laughed. "I happen to know this building has firewalls thicker than normal. I almost bought the condo on the second floor, but Tenemen convinced me a house was a better investment." He sneered. "For him, anyway."

Something snapped inside her, and every muscle tightened. Was he right about the thick walls? Was anyone even home to hear her scream? Heart slamming against her rib cage, Dana scanned her surroundings for a weapon. Anything would do, but Lance had no knickknacks to throw, no large books, nor any sign of sports equipment. She hadn't a damn thing to grab.

Fear gripped her throat in a way she never experienced. A scream lodged in her mouth. Damnit, she had two arms and two legs. She might lose, but she'd give them one hell of a fight.

Whirling, Dana grabbed the lamp by the sofa and

threw base and shade at Gary only to have the plugged-in power cord stop its forward motion. The lamp crashed to the floor. *Shit*!

Lance's gun in the nightstand.

Somehow, she had to reach Lance's bedroom.

The easy-to-assemble end table consisted of lightweight particle board. Grasping the edges, she lifted the piece to her chest and charged toward Gary, using the legs as a battering ram.

Mouth gaping, he swung the pipe and cracked the table into pieces.

Dana's push was enough to knock him off balance and fall backward into Babs. They crashed against the front door and slid to the floor. As an afterthought, Dana grabbed her overcoat and threw it over Gary's and Babs' heads then bolted to the bedroom, slammed the door, and jammed a chair under the doorknob. Leaping to the night table, she yanked one drawer after another and searched. The gun was gone! *Damn.*

Now, what?

Cussing, Gary pounded the pipe into the door, sending splintered pieces of wood in every direction. "I'll kill you for this, bitch!"

Somebody had to hear all the noise, right? The building couldn't be totally empty.

Running to Lance's closet, she threw open the door with a bang and scanned the contents, tossing aside stuff in search of a weapon. Something…anything, damnit. What sport jock didn't own a baseball bat?

Eureka! She found a bat tucked into the corner. Rushing to the door, she held the weapon ready as Gary stuck his hand through the opening to grab the chair. Dana swung and connected. The bat hit with a solid shot to his forearm, and bone snapped.

Gary released a blood-curdling scream.

A commotion followed. Shouts. Scuffling. Loud crashes along with the smack of fists striking flesh.

"Dana!"

Lance! Shaking uncontrollably, she threw the bat to the floor.

"Move the chair, sweetheart."

Oh, God. His voice sounded wonderful. Forcing herself to move, she dragged the chair from the knob, and the door flew open, nearly falling off its hinges.

Breathing heavy, Lance rushed in, face pale but tight. Their gazes locked. He spread his arms.

She ran into them, relief and tears flooding her.

"You're okay." He wrapped his arms tight. "We got them."

Unwilling to look out the door, she buried her face against his chest and shuddered.

He stroked her hair. "Thelma heard all the racket and called me. If I'm not mistaken, I broke my high school sprinting record getting here."

"And on a bad leg, too." Georgette strolled through the door and slapped Lance on the back. "You can burn the cane, Lance. You'll do our five-mile run easy." She touched Dana's arm, her eyebrows furrowed. "You okay, honey?"

Trembling, she nodded since her vocal cords refused to cooperate.

Georgette dropped her hand. "I called an ambulance for Gary. His arm's broke." She lifted Lance's hand from Dana's back. "Looks like you can use an X-ray."

X-ray? Dana broke away and grabbed Lance's right

hand. Blood covered the knuckles.

Grinning, he flexed his fingers. "I rearranged Gary's face."

His voice held a hint of pride, and she almost broke into hysterics. Time and again, the man charged to her rescue. Gad, she would miss him.

Another commotion snapped their gazes toward the open door. Tim burst in followed by cops reaching to grab him.

Red-faced, he locked his gaze onto Dana. "What the hell is going on? Honey, are you—"

Georgette grasped Tim's arm and guided him toward the door. "Come with me, Mr. Gardner. I'll explain the situation."

Drawing Dana into his arms, Lance buried his face in her hair.

As before, his strong calming effect took hold. The pounding eased within her chest, and she released a long, shuddering breath. She clung but not out of fear. She wanted to embed his touch and smell into her memory forever.

"You're safe now."

Reluctantly, she lifted her head. "I rushed in here for your gun."

He smirked. "I wear the thirty-eight on my ankle, Dana. I won't leave a weapon around when I'm not home." With a finger touch, he lifted her chin and smiled. "Can you shoot?"

"Oh, sure. Some years ago, I learned on an archaeology dig. A soldier guarding the site taught me." She replaced her head onto his chest. "Gary and Babs are behind the murders of Anita and Tenemen." She took a long sniff of his aftershave. "It's over."

Slipping a hand into her hair, he massaged her scalp. "You can go home with a clear mind."

And a broken heart. Blinking away the moisture in her eyes, she left the comfort of his arms and forced a smile. "You have a wonderful habit of showing when I need you the most, Lance. For that, I thank you. But I want to say what's on my mind before I leave, and they are three words you won't want to hear." Tilting her chin upward, she squared her shoulders and met his gaze. "I love you, Lance. You don't have to love me back, but I had to tell you. We might never meet again, and over time, my love will fade and shift to another man, but you will always hold a special place in my heart."

He peered through eye slits, silent.

She swallowed hard. "I'm telling you this because Gary and Babs made me realize I was about to leave this earth without once telling you how I feel."

"Dana, I—"

Reaching, she pressed a finger against his lips. "Relax. I'm asking nothing of you. I'll start a new phase in my life all because of you." Standing on tiptoe, she brushed her lips against his cheek. "I'll never forget everything you've done for me."

"Dana, let's go!" Tim's angry voice bellowed from the living room.

Lance caught her arm. "We'll need a statement on this incident before you leave."

Nodding, she turned toward the door.

"Dana—"

She stopped. Without facing him, she held her head high. "Don't say anything you don't mean, Lance." Meeting only silence, she walked out the door.

Chapter Twenty-Five

Lance couldn't say the "L" word to Dana. And why should he? He had no idea what love felt like. Big deal, he took care of her, and she misidentified gratitude for love—plain and simple hero worship. Lance slammed his desk drawer, which rattled the computer screen and shifted his cellular phone three inches to the left.

Every cop in the department snapped their head in his direction and stared.

He growled in return.

With a cup of coffee in hand, Georgette strolled to her desk and reclaimed her seat. "I hope you realize a few cops clamped onto their guns after that last slam. I heard you all the way in the lunch room." She nudged her chair closer to her desk. Leaning on her elbows and with her cup close to her nose, she squinted. "You're acting like an orangutan on drugs. You better buckle in your emotions before the captain ships you to the mail room."

Lance grunted in answer. Three weeks had passed, and he struggled to climb out of the abyss. He repaired the damage to the condo, but the image of Dana shaking in his arms stayed locked in his memory. She'd turned so pale, and he, like a jerk, acted with his professional air. Hell, he practically patted her on the head for all the comfort he offered. She needed someone to hold her until the shaking subsided, but no, not Lance Barnes.

Tim received the privilege to hold her all the way to Pittsburgh. *Stupid, stupid shithead.*

Resting her cup on the desk, George shifted through the pile of manila folders in her inbox. "Why don't you admit you fell in love? You're human like the rest of us."

Women and their damn preconceived notions. Couldn't a man be moody without them romanticizing about love? Narrowing his gaze, he snarled. "Don't you have something better to do?"

"Not really. My partner fell in love, and he's in total denial."

"That's ridiculous." Jamming his elbows onto the desk, he pointed an accusing finger in her direction. "A woman is too big of a commitment. She'll want a nice house and family, big parties, and weekend barbecues. What the hell am I made of, gold?" His outburst raised a few eyebrows from nearby detectives. Lance cleared his throat. "Dana's better off with someone else." Flipping the pages on a case file, he pretended to read, hoping George would change the subject.

Never gonna happen.

She released a long sigh. "I suppose Timmy is that someone else." Tapping her keyboard, she activated her computer. "He strikes me as a slap-'em-around kind of guy."

"No, he doesn't." He glared at his partner. "Dana won't take any shit."

While staring at her computer screen, she smiled. "You seem sure."

These days, he wasn't sure about anything. After

Dana left, he had a hard time sitting in the living room without thinking of her curled in the opposite corner of the sofa. Or how attractive she looked staring at his laptop with her glasses perched on her nose. *God, I miss her.* If the knot in his belly was any indicator, he missed her damn bad.

"Don't you think it odd her parents are pushing a marriage she doesn't want?"

Frowning, he watched Georgette's fingers fly across her keyboard. She always had a knack for typing. "The Nulls have money. They dictate to others."

Georgette shook her head. "Wealth intimidates a lot of people...even you. I thought you were more secure than most. Aw, drat. Wrong line." She pounded the backspace key. "So Dana earns more than you. The difference in your salaries probably never entered her mind." She shot him a sideways glance. "Just think. She can say money in sixteen different languages."

"Ha, ha." He slammed shut the file folder and grabbed another. Not like he had an ounce of concentration. If anything, he'd look busy should the captain stroll across the department.

Flipping through the pages in the next folder, he stopped with a sigh. "By including Dana in their plan, Babs and Gary pretty much sealed their fate."

Pausing with her fingers over the keyboard, Georgette met his gaze. "You read Babs' statement? The professor was hell-bent on making Dana wife number four. Babs had other plans." With her gaze focused over his shoulders, she gaped and fell back in her chair. "Wow! Am I seeing double?"

Following her gaze, Lance pivoted his chair and rolled away from the desk as Robert Barnes sauntered toward them wearing a big smile. His eyes and face glowed as he said hello to everyone he passed. Lance stood to greet him with the typical male hug. He introduced Georgette.

While fanning her face with a hand, Georgette extended her other toward Robert. "Oh, my, your handsome genes are strong."

Laughing, Robert grasped her hand with both of his. "Nice to finally meet you."

Lance smirked. "What the hell hit you, brother? A bottle of happy pills?"

"I'm on a detour from Atlanta to give that little lady of yours a big hug." He released George's hand and scanned the department. "Where is she? She wasn't at your place."

"She went home to Pittsburgh. Why?"

Robert unbuttoned his overcoat. "She talked to Mary about a top-notch speech pathologist who practices in North Jersey. In two short weeks, the man has done miracles with Johnny's stutter." He slapped Lance's shoulder. "You should hear Johnny. His confidence is back, and he's studying hard to elevate his grades." Smiling, he clapped his hands together and rubbed. "Mary wants to meet her. When's Dana coming back?"

Lifting her coffee cup, Georgette cleared her throat and arched an eyebrow. "Your brother let her go."

Eyes wide, Robert snapped his gaze to Lance. "What do you mean 'let her go'? Oh, wait, you said she's engaged."

Georgette coughed. "Turns out she isn't. Lance let her go anyway."

Scowling, Lance glared at his partner. "Look, she

regained her memory and left. End of story." Resting his butt on the corner of his desk, he faced Robert. "She wasn't right for me."

Brows furrowed, Robert shifted his gaze from Georgette to Lance. "Mary and Dana talked a few times already, but I wanted to thank her in person." He tugged on his ear. "Mary has her phone number, but I don't." His gaze locked onto Lance. "Do you?"

Of course, he knew her number. He stopped himself from calling a half dozen times over the past three weeks. Frowning, he held out his hand. "Give me your phone."

Robert slipped his phone from his shirt pocket and slapped it into his brother's palm.

While inputting Dana's number, Lance again wondered if he was being an ass. He never really sat down and talked to Dana. Would she move to Baltimore, or did she expect him to move to Pittsburgh? How did she feel about their salary difference? A thousand questions, none of which he asked. *Too late now.* He returned Robert's phone.

After slipping his phone to his coat pocket, Robert tugged on his coat collar. "I'm sorry to hear she's gone, but I'll give her a call while I'm waiting for my flight." He smiled at Georgette. "Lance talks about you all the time. I'm surprised how he surrounds himself with beautiful women and yet stays single." Turning to his brother, he slapped Lance on the shoulder. "Anything you want me to tell Dana?"

Dear Lord, no. She was out of his life. Period. Ignoring the question, he hugged his brother then accompanied him to the elevator. When the elevator doors closed, he returned to his desk and flopped into his chair. With a heart feeling like lead, he stared at the floor.

"Dana did a nice thing for Robert." Georgette tossed her empty cup into the trash and returned to her keyboard.

Robert's news surprised the hell out of him. Dana remembered Robert's son. She *hadn't* remembered to call Lance as he requested. When he queried her with a brief text reminder, he received a return message with one word—*Home.* After his cold send-off, he got what he deserved.

So, why all the heaviness in his chest? Sure, he missed her, but how could any woman crawl under a man's skin in one short week? Hell, she spent four nights in his condo, and he should be glad she's gone. But he wasn't. Not by a long shot. He sighed. "I've learned a valuable lesson. Never take a stray home— animal or human. Both toy with a man's sanity."

In between clacking on the keyboard, George snorted. "I agree, because at this precise moment, I think you're bonkers."

He swiveled to face her. "How do you do it?"

Fingers pausing, she glanced from her computer, a brow cocked. "Do what?"

"Have a happy marriage with this job?"

Biting her lower lip, she turned and leaned on her desk. "It's not the job, Lance. It's what you make of the marriage. You can't let the job consume you and expect a happy-go-lucky home life. You have to allow some give and take." With a smile touching her lips, she reclined in her chair. "Career-wise, Mark and I are total opposites. I'm a cop. He's an accountant. He never demanded I quit because of the danger. He married me for who and what I was and has been a godsend when a case ties me to my desk. The woman who shares your life needs to do the same and not make demands impossible for you to keep. Sure, Mark worries, as will any spouse, but he entered our marriage with his eyes wide open."

Frowning, he drummed his fingers on the desk. "You got lucky."

"No, Lance, I *love* my husband. I *like* my job. That's the big difference." She wagged a finger. "Deep love, Lance, the kind where both spouses show a mutual respect. Neither of us bosses the other around."

"But the man in your family makes more money than you, the way it should be."

"True a few decades ago but not now. We bank my salary and live off his. This way, we're building a great college fund for the kids. You can't let ego override common sense." She locked onto his gaze. "When two people love each other, they find a way to jump over the hurdles. Remember that." She returned to the keyboard.

Hell, he had a big *mental* hurdle called caution. Why? His brother and sister enjoyed successful marriages. Even his parents stared at each other all lovey-dovey. Had too many murders committed in the name of love tainted his opinion?

"Dana said she loves me." He shot George a quick glance. "I couldn't say it back."

"Well, then, you know how she feels."

With one hand, he rubbed his forehead. "A long-distance relationship will never work." He dropped his hand. "You should know that."

"What long-distance, Lance?" Without looking his

way, she paused her typing and stared into space. "The woman has the perfect at-home business when children enter the picture." She shifted her gaze toward him. "I hope she's strong enough to resist a marriage destined for hell."

Her cellphone rang. Checking caller ID, she turned away and answered. Her familiar posture indicated a personal call, usually her husband or one of the kids. Since he had no desire to eavesdrop, he busied himself with a new folder.

Disconnecting the call, Georgette slid the phone onto the desk. "That was Mark. How about you come over for dinner tonight? Mark researched something for me, and he has a load of info to relay."

"About what?"

"Howard Null."

Brows arched, he straightened in the chair. "And?"

She waved a hand. "I don't have all the details. Stop by around six." She returned to her computer. "Remember how you expressed curiosity about why Howard pushed his daughter to marry Tim? You never followed through, but I got curious. So, I asked Mark to help me out."

What about Howard Null? Mark worked as an accountant with a large law firm and had resources as vast as law enforcement. Lance checked his watch. "Six o'clock is a long way off. Maybe I should call Mark."

"Don't you dare!" She shot him a glare. "He's making his famous beef stroganoff, and he'll explain while we eat." She repositioned her fingers over the keyboard. "And, no, I won't let him tell you anything until you put some food in your body. These days, you're hardly casting a shadow."

Jane Drager

His appetite disappeared the second Dana stepped out the door. Nothing appealed to his taste buds, not even his favorite roast beef sandwich from the deli shop.

Oh, hell. He missed Dana so much his insides hurt. Every night, he wandered into the spare bedroom and pictured her snuggled under the covers. In such a short time, he'd gotten used to having her around, how her green eyes sparkled with a smile, and how the sight of her mouth tempted his self-control. During their sexual romps, passion poured from her soul, and he had yet to compare her with any woman from his past.

Georgette paused to read the lines of text on the view screen. She stole a quick glance in his direction. "She said she loves you, eh?"

Snorting, he flipped through the folder's sheets. "Simple infatuation. People don't fall in love at the drop of a hat."

"Ha! I met Mark on a fender-bender call." Gaze dreamy, she rocked in her chair. "While on street patrol, I responded to the 911 dispatch. As soon as I walked up to him, I damned near stuttered the entire time." Her lips twisted into a smile. "Something about him got my heart racing."

His heart beat like a jackhammer every time he looked at Dana. She caused reactions in his body so incredibly foreign yet, at the same time, truly wonderful, almost like a king-of-the-world feeling. Was that love? Did love cause a man not to eat or sleep? Every night, he circled the living room, thinking about her small hands massaging his calf or how lost she looked in his oversized pajamas. Not an hour passed without his thoughts drifting in her direction.

Oh, God, he loved her.

Lance Barnes loved Dana Null.

The revelation released a flood of emotions. Fear. Joy. Terror. Exhilaration. Like prison walls crumbling all around him to set him free. He jumped to his feet and grabbed his overcoat from the rack.

Brows high, George cocked her head. "Going somewhere?"

"Pittsburgh."

She swiveled. "Not until you talk to Mark."

After slipping an arm into one coat sleeve, he stopped and peered. "His information is that important?"

"He thinks so. You've waited three weeks. You can wait one more night."

Shoulders slumping, Lance rehung his coat. "All right."

A commotion by the elevators forced him to turn.

Thelma hurried across the department floor, waving an envelope. After loosening the scarf protecting her face, she thrust the envelope at Lance. "This packet arrived special delivery. I had to sign away my life. Must be important."

He stared at a registered letter from Null Industries, Pittsburgh. Using a letter opener, he slit the envelope and removed the contents. One sheet was a typed letter from Howard Null. The second slip of paper floored him, and his heart caught in his throat. Dumbstruck, he handed the two pieces to George. "Here's proof why all Dana's boyfriends disappeared without a word."

Chapter Twenty-Six

Frustrated beyond the scope of tolerance, Dana resisted the urge to pull out every strand of hair, regardless of pain. This afternoon, Marta and Howard Null, along with Tim, barged into her condo and demanded her participation in their all-consuming wedding plans. Once again, they interrupted her work, as if she lounged around all day polishing her nails. Why were her parents so insistent she marry Tim? They'd been relentless over the past three weeks, and nothing she said persuaded them to leave her alone. For spite, she should allow them to proceed and then, on the eventful day, hop on a plane for Europe, leaving all three standing at the altar.

Throwing her hands in the air and pushing past her intruders, Dana left the kitchen and hurried into the spacious living room where she'd find more room to breathe. The three followed like puppies on a leash. Since they burst through the front door, they took turns badgering. "No, no, no! A thousand times no. I refuse to listen anymore." She placed her hands over her ears— for what good it did. Now, she heard the pounding of her heart along with their jabbering.

Well, she wasn't about to hide in her own condo. Her work centered on the computer in the den, and right now, the transcript requests amounted to four case studies and twenty-eight abstracts—a worthwhile workload…*if I get a chance to sit at my damn computer*. She needed a miracle. Or divine intervention to rid her home of three unwanted pests. Hell, what would it take? Certainly not marriage to another man. The way her men disappeared, she'd never recite any holy matrimony vows. Maybe she should move to Canada. Or better yet, Italy. With luck, a handsome, dark-haired Italian would sweep her off her feet.

Who am I kidding? The only dark-haired, blue-eyed hunk on her mind didn't want her.

Dana drew the drapery cords in the living room to allow the bright afternoon sun into her condo. Hopefully, the glare blinded her family and reduced their bodies into puddles of goo, like the infamous wicked witch. Oh—wait. Water killed the bitch, melting her like butter.

At ten stories high, her condo had a bird's-eye-view of the University of Pittsburgh campus—her alma mater. She'd hate like hell to leave the place, but she had some good prospects in State College. If these three persisted…

Her mother grabbed the drape cords from Dana's hand and readjusted the opening. "Tim found the nicest brownstone in D.C., honey. The house is perfect for the president's interpreter. We sent in a deposit last week."

Yeah, they even bought a house without her approval. *What am I, thirteen*? Sight unseen, Dana knew the home contained too many bedrooms, perfect for her mother and father to visit and stay forever. She ambled from the window. "I'm not taking the job."

"They accepted you, dear. You can't refuse. Only a fool dismissed such a prestigious position."

"Then, I guess I'm a fool." Fool to open the front

door and let them in.

"Dana, honey, it's a great job." Tim hopped into her path. "You've already cleared security. And just think, the job will be a great stepping-stone for your career."

She pushed Tim out of her way. "Yes, *my* career." She tapped a finger against her chest. "I support myself very well with my translation business, work that is being delayed because of your constant interruptions."

Her mother fussed with the bracelet on her wrist. "My darling daughter. Think of the galas at the White House, and you know how good Tim looks in a tux."

Like Tim's wardrobe was a criterion. She crossed her arms over her chest and huffed. "I hate dressing up." Well, she did. She loved jeans and sweatshirts and saved her dresses for her lectures. If she wanted, she could work in her pajamas.

Oh, God. The thought of a certain pair of pj's gripped her throat.

Her mother wagged a finger up and down Dana's torso. "Blue jeans and sweatshirt are not appropriate anymore, dear. You should toss them."

Dana rolled her eyes. Her mother's idea of proper attire was sequined gowns.

"I don't have time for all this constant debate." Stepping forward, her father pointed a finger in her face. "You'll take the D.C. job, and I don't want to hear another word. For once in your life, you'll do as you're told."

She bristled. "I'm old enough to make my own decisions."

Walking to a mirror by the front door, her mother used a pinkie finger to smooth her eyebrows. "If your business decisions are anything like your choice in men, then you're incapable of running your own life. Listen to your father. He's a smart man."

Tim stepped to Howard's side. "Maybe D.C. is too close to her Baltimore memories. The detective, right, Dana?" He snorted. "You were nothing more than another notch on his belt."

That's right. Rub it in. Tim's comment shot an arrow right into her heart. Lance never called. Every morning, she ached to hear from him. That kind, wonderful man took her into his home and eased her fears. In the process, he captured her heart. *Oh, God, I miss him so much.*

All right, like a fool, she fell for the guy. Something about him hit from the start, and she couldn't help herself. He had strength, even with a limp. And the way his pupils dilated whenever their gazes met caught her breath like some stranglehold. Even his subtle smile—the one that was sexy as hell— weakened her knees. No man created such wonderful sensations. *And I'll probably never feel them again.* With the hope the gesture would keep her heart intact, she crossed her arms over her chest and meandered to the center of her spacious living room.

Turning from the mirror, her mother clucked her tongue. "Your gown fitting is tomorrow, dear. Don't cancel this one." Bending, she rearranged the knickknacks on the coffee table.

Dana tightened her arms around her chest. "I'm not marrying Tim." *Antarctica is looking pretty good right about now.*

"Of course, you are, darling. He's perfect for you, and you're simply going through bridal jitters." She straightened.

Jitters, my ass.

Coming alongside, Tim patted Dana's shoulder. "Relax, sweetheart. I'm not like your other guys who disappeared and broke your heart. I'm here to stay." He tugged on his belt.

If this bullshit continued, she might puke all over her clean rug. *Enough.* Gathering their overcoats from the sofa, Dana threw each their coat before marching to the front door. With a defiant lift to her head, she placed her hand on the knob. "I've work to do. Time to leave." She threw open the door...and froze. Her heart somersaulted.

Lance stood in the hall.

Holy hell, the man looked positively delicious in suit and tie. With dark hair slightly windblown and cheeks flushed, he could light any woman's furnace. She gripped the doorknob to prevent a collapse to the floor.

She never expected to see him again...ever. Over the past few weeks, she convinced herself their brief affair was done. Yet, his being here, outside her door, forced an avalanche of emotions to surface. Her eyes watered and chest constricted, but damn, once more, her knight-in-shining-armor came to the rescue.

Face tight, Tim rushed forward. "What are you doing here?" He shoved his body in front of Dana. "She wants to forget Baltimore, pal, and your being here reminds her of her broken vows."

"What?" Gaze narrowed, her father approached. "What broken vows?"

Tim pointed a finger at Lance. "Dana and I were saving ourselves for marriage, but this jerk seduced her.

Why the hell do you think I wanted her out of his condo?"

Well, well. Tim played a trump card. Too bad he shut his ears about her losing her virginity in college. Dana almost laughed.

Marta clutched Dana's arm. "You had sex with this man?"

"Yes." She smiled at Lance and met the warm glow of his gaze. "I enjoyed every second we spent together."

Lance gave his sexy little smile and winked.

Her father shoved his way between Lance and Tim while directing a fiery gaze at the big man in the hall. "Why are you here?"

"I'd say for obvious reasons."

With his overcoat draped over his arm, Lance entered, his size forcing Howard Null to move out of the way.

"They were just leaving." Dana waved toward the door, but three stunned bodies stood frozen to the rug. Of course, Lance blocked the doorway, and no one dared push him aside, not with the man wearing a silly smirk on his face.

Lance closed the door. "I'm glad I caught everyone here." He tossed his overcoat onto a chair. "Dana, do you know why your parents are pushing you and Tim to marry?"

Howard grunted. "She knows very well why."

Chuckling, Lance used a hand to smooth his mussed hair. "I'm talking the *real* reason." After scanning the area, he shot Dana a quick glance. "Nice place."

Tim snorted. "She buys *quality* furniture."

Shooting Tim a glare, Dana stiffened her back. "Thank you, Lance. I want to know why my family is pushing me and Tim together." Except maybe to drive her to drink. She already knew she hated beer, and a smile quirked on her lips.

Lance positioned himself before her father and crossed both arms over his chest. "You made one serious mistake, Mr. Null. You aroused the curiosity of a detective."

Aw, damn. With his tone so business-like, he arrived in an official capacity, nothing more. Her heart sank. She stared at the floor.

"Dana?"

Jerking her gaze to Lance, she squared her shoulders. "Yes, go on. I imagine my parents want to keep us under their thumbs."

"And for good reason. Did you know Tim's deceased father owned quite a vested interest in Null Industries?" Dropping his arms, he strolled toward the center of the living room.

Gut tight, Dana snapped her gaze between her father and Lance. *What the hell is he talking about?* Her mother slapped a ringed hand over her mouth, but her father stood rigid, like a pillar of salt. Dana swallowed. "Continue, Lance."

His lips twisted to the side. "If you two marry, by law, half of the vested interest becomes yours, Dana, thereby keeping control of the company within the family. I imagine no prenup has been discussed?" Eyebrow cocked, he slid a glance to Tim.

Mouth agape, Tim moved alongside Dana and shook his head, his gaze riveted on Lance.

All their constant badgering was about money?

With a flush rising from her neck, she whirled to face her father. "Is what he said true?"

Tim touched her arm. "I didn't know either, Dana." Squaring his shoulders, he glared at Howard. "Does this mean I'm due an inheritance?"

Her parents stood mute.

Coming alongside, Lance slapped Tim on the shoulder. "You're getting quite an inheritance, Timmy. I'm not surprised they kept quiet."

Wide-eyed, Tim glanced from Howard to Marta than back to Lance. "All these years, they handed me an allowance like they were doing me a favor."

"Then I suggest you sit with Howard and ask some straight questions, preferably in a lawyer's office. Don't you agree, Mr. Null?"

Face flushed, the older man narrowed his gaze. "I did nothing wrong. The inheritance takes effect at the age of thirty-five."

Staggering, Dana fought to control her quivering muscles. "Nothing wrong? You're pushing me into a marriage I don't want."

Her mother coughed. "He's still perfect for you, dear, and with your history of men…"

"Ah, yes." Lance cleared his throat. "Let's discuss that topic."

Lance placed himself between her and Tim, forcing Tim to step to the side. Not that Tim protested. Her childhood friend and brother stared with a gaping mouth.

Rotating, Lance faced her. "The men in your life left without so much as an *adios*, correct?"

One brow raised, Dana nodded. She wasn't sure where this speech was going, but something in his voice told her she wouldn't like any part of his news.

Slipping a hand inside his suit jacket, Lance extracted two pieces of paper. One, a letter, he flipped open.

The second looked suspiciously like a Null Industries check. Dana snatched both from his hand and read. The fire simmering in her gut boiled into full lava. With jaw tight, she faced her father. "A fifty-thousand dollar check? You paid off Lance?"

With a casual wave, her father faced her. "Your marriage to Tim is important for the company, Dana. Now that you know the stakes, you'll agree to the nuptials without a fight."

Oh, what she wouldn't do to take a swing at her father. She gritted her teeth. "Are you crazy? You paid off all my boyfriends, didn't you? And that's so no one is left but Timmy. Dad, how could you?"

The humiliation of her own father's actions hit like a brick. *Now* she understood why all her men disappeared. Scanning through the paper in her hand, she bit back the urge to scream. The letter spelled out the conditions for accepting the check with the most glaring stipulation for Lance never to contact Dana Null again.

How embarrassing! If she could strangle her own father, she would, but Howard Null's neck was too thick for her small hands. And with a cop standing nearby...

Cringing, her mother positioned herself alongside her husband. "Your father acted in the best interest to save the company, dear. At the age of thirty-five, Tim will control half of the business, and we can't afford to buy him out."

"I'm wealthy?" Tim asked.

Lance grinned. "Not until thirty-five, Timmy. You need to grow up and be a real man first, take command of your life, and stop playing puppet to Howard and Marta. Above all, you must stop chasing a woman who doesn't want to be your wife."

"I'm wealthy."

The poor guy looked just about comatose. Dana almost felt sorry for him—almost.

Grabbing both his shoulders, Lance guided Tim to the front door. "Put on your jacket, Timmy. Mr. and Mrs. Null, time to leave." He snapped his fingers.

Dana smiled at their stunned silence as her three visitors slipped into their outerwear and shuffled into the hall. Lance wore a triumphant glow on his face while Tim meandered in a daze. Her mother fussed with her coat's buttons, and her father looked practically apoplectic.

Placing a hand against the older man's chest, Lance blocked Howard's exit. "Your check, sir." Stretching, he snatched the slip from Dana's hand and stuffed it into the older man's suit jacket pocket. "For the record, I couldn't stop thinking about your daughter." Stepping aside, he pointed to the outside hall. "Go, all of you!"

Dana blinked at the man she assumed she'd never see again. "How did you uncover Tim's inheritance?"

After closing the door, he shot her a sly, little grin. "Credit Georgette. Her instincts said you and Tim were being pushed together for a reason."

And what a reason. *Damn them.* She swallowed hard. "Fifty grand is a lot of money, Lance."

He shook his head. "*You* are what I want, Dana. After you left, the condo felt empty."

Her heart lurched, and every bit of anger at her parents flew out the window. "Then, you meant what you said, you know, about thinking of me?"

"Oh, yes. Every single minute of the day." Closing the distance between them, he ran his hands down her arms.

Goose bumps surfaced, and if she wasn't careful, her knees might give out. "Lance—"

After pressing an index finger against her lips, he slipped his hand into his trouser pocket and extracted a small, black box. "We found your ring."

Mouth agape, she stared at the box. "You know it wasn't stolen."

"Well, it matched the description." He placed the box in her hand.

Shaking, she opened the lid. A beautifully cut, diamond engagement ring sparkled from the sunlight glowing through her open drapes. Nothing about the ring matched the description in the theft report, and she looked at him with an arched brow.

Using one finger, he pulled the shirt collar away from his neck and shrugged. "The diamond isn't worth fourteen grand, but I'm hoping you'll wear it and be mine."

She couldn't breathe. A sob stuck in her throat, and tears clouded her vision.

Leaning close, he gazed into her eyes. "Marry me, Dana. I've been through hell without you. I'm not sure how great a husband I'll be, but I know I love you. I'll work hard to make the marriage work." He cringed. "That is, if you still love me."

The ring was even more beautiful than the one she returned to Tim. But her hands shook so badly she dared not touch it. She closed the lid to the box.

His gaze followed her movements, and a pained expression crossed his face.

With her heart beating wildly within her chest, she stroked his cheek. "I love you very much, Lance. You're all I thought about since I left."

"But?" He cocked his head.

"No buts. I'm so happy I can barely hold onto the box."

Eyes growing wide, he clamped onto her arms. "You'll marry me? A cop?"

Oh, God, how she loved him. She smiled at his tone. "Hell, yeah, I'll marry you if you put the ring on my finger. I can't do it."

Taking the box and flipping open the lid, he removed the ring and, with a gentle touch, slipped the ring onto her left ring finger.

Holding up her hand to the light, she stared at the sparkling angles to the diamond, but she'd wear a plastic curtain ring if it came from Lance. In her entire life, she never experienced such a strong wave of love, and she had a lifetime to enjoy it. Smiling, she placed both her hands on his cheeks. "You just made me the happiest woman in the world."

He wrapped her in his arms and captured her mouth.

The sensations of their short time together surfaced like a volcano rising from the sea. She loved this man with all her heart and would never get enough of him. After she lifted her head for air, she pulled away to gaze into his beautiful eyes. "The bump on the head was the best thing to happen to me."

"Me, too." He kissed her nose. "I hate to admit it,

sweetheart, but I listened at the door. You had no chance in hell of winning the argument. Your father had too much to lose." Dropping his arms, he took out his cellphone and typed.

She leaned over to see the screen. "What are you doing?"

"I'm sending George a message. I know she's waiting on pins and needles." He showed her the text.

—*She said yes!*—

He hit the Send button then slipped the phone into his pocket. Pulling her into a tight embrace, he recaptured her mouth.

All thoughts dissipated—all except one. She took a chance that day by swinging at a cop, but she liked what she saw then and sure as hell liked what she held now.

A word about the author…

With a growing backlist of books, Jane Drager continues to write mysteries with a strong romantic element, always with a happily-ever-after theme.

An avid reader as well as writer, Jane has lived her life as diverse as her stories. She was a journalist, sports editor, office manager, firefighter, ambulance captain, caterer's assistant, but retired from her long career as a respiratory therapist and instructor.

She's married to a wonderful organic farmer who keeps her busy with canning and freezing.

~

Other Titles by this Author

Ask Nothing in Return
Infinite Choices
Secrets and Assumptions
The Riddle Key
Until We Say Goodbye

Thank you for purchasing
this publication of The Wild Rose Press, Inc.

For questions or more information
contact us at
info@thewildrosepress.com.

The Wild Rose Press, Inc.
www.thewildrosepress.com